PLAY NICE

NOVELS BY RACHEL HARRISON

The Return
Cackle
Such Sharp Teeth
Black Sheep
So Thirsty
Play Nice

SHORT STORY COLLECTION BY RACHEL HARRISON

Bad Dolls

PLAY NICE

RACHEL HARRISON

Berkley
New York

BERKLEY
An imprint of Penguin Random House LLC
1745 Broadway, New York, NY 10019

Copyright © 2025 by Rachel Harrison
Penguin Random House values and supports copyright. Copyright fuels creativity, encourages diverse voices, promotes free speech, and creates a vibrant culture. Thank you for buying an authorized edition of this book and for complying with copyright laws by not reproducing, scanning, or distributing any part of it in any form without permission. You are supporting writers and allowing Penguin Random House to continue to publish books for every reader. Please note that no part of this book may be used or reproduced in any manner for the purpose of training artificial intelligence technologies or systems.

BERKLEY and the BERKLEY & B colophon are registered trademarks of Penguin Random House LLC.

Book design by Kristin del Rosario
Title page art: tail © backUp / Shutterstock; background © Dmitrıch / Shutterstock

ISBN 9780593642573

Printed in the United States of America

*For the crazy girls.
This one is for us.*

Yes.
Yes.
I accept you, demon.
I will not cover your mouth.

—ANNE SEXTON, "DEMON"

It needs, it seeks affection
Hungry, it fiends
Look at me, look at me, you lookin'?

—DOJA CAT, "ATTENTION"

Behind every crazy woman is a man sitting very quietly, saying, "What? I'm not doing anything."

—JADE SHARMA, *PROBLEMS*

Play Nice

1

WE'RE coming up on midnight. The room is loud, everyone champagne drunk, ignorant of volume, and, wow, the air in here is *intense*, all hot breath and designer perfume. Everyone wants to smell good because this is the hour it happens, when it's determined who goes home alone, and judging by the pungency, a lot of people in here don't want to end up in an empty bed tonight. They want to attract. They want to be chosen. So they sneak off to the bathroom to fix their hair, stare at their smudged reflections, primp, powder, perfume—spritzing excessively, with reckless abandon. I inhale.

It's hope, is what it is. It's sweet but also pretty desperate. Pretty boring.

I turn to the guy next to me. He's deliberately underdressed in a white T-shirt and jeans. He's drinking a beer. I thought this party was too chic for beer.

"Where did you get that?" I ask him.

"The bar," he says in a tone I don't care for. I stick my tongue out at him, and he cracks a smile.

"Clio Louise Barnes," I say, holding out a hand.

He stares at my hand for a moment before shaking it. "Ethan."

"What do you do, Ethan?"

"Really?"

"What?"

"Small talk?"

"We can exchange childhood traumas if you like," I say, helping myself to a sip of his beer. He allows it to happen, and I decide I'm into him. He reeks of cologne, so I know I can leave with him tonight if I want to.

"We've already met. Several times, at brand parties just like this one," he says. "I was waiting for you to remember."

I do remember. But the easiest way to tell who a man really is, is to injure his ego and see how he reacts.

"I'm bad with names. And faces," I say. "And I meet a lot of people. I'm sorry. Please don't take it personally."

He rubs his jaw, considering. "You really don't remember?"

"Do you forgive me?" I give him puppy eyes, bat my lashes.

He sighs, then lifts his chin and points to a thin scar, about three inches long. "Car accident when I was five. Blood everywhere. Mom was driving. She was in a coma for a week."

"Is she okay?"

"Yeah. She's got scars, too. But that's it."

I sip my champagne. I like it better than the beer. I wish I had simpler tastes, but I don't. "Lucky to live with scars."

"Better to live without," he says. "What about you, Clio Louise Barnes? Childhood trauma?"

I debate making something up, but I'm intoxicated. From the alcohol, yeah, but also from the balmy heat, the formidable amalgam of smells, the city outside alive with that magnificent Saturday night energy. So I tell him something true. "I grew up in a haunted house."

"Bullshit."

"Sorry, not haunted. Possessed," I say, bringing the coupe to my lips and taking a delicate sip, letting the effervescence dance across my tongue. I'll need a refill soon.

"Possessed by what?"

I shrug. "That's all I've got for you. If you get me another drink, maybe I'll tell you more."

"We've been down this road before," he says. "You flirt with me, so I buy you a drink. Then you disappear at midnight like some kind of Lower East Side Cinderella."

"Oh, was I flirting?" I say with a grin. "My bad."

He doesn't react.

"The drinks here are free."

"And?" he asks.

"So, what do you have to lose?"

He downs the rest of his beer. "All right. Another champagne?"

"Yes, please."

He takes my near-empty coupe. "You better be here when I get back."

I cross my heart.

WE step onto the sidewalk, the click of my heels echoing, harmonizing with the rest of the city sounds—traffic and drunken gossip and subway squeals and club bass. Ethan is warm, which is convenient, because it's early April, and the night air carries a tenacious chill, winter dragging its feet.

"What time is it?" I ask him. He's the CEO of a cool, successful watch company. He used to date my friend Veronica's friend Laurie before the cursed launch of her lipstick line. She named the shades stupid things like "Get Him Back" and "Divorcée" and the supremely controversial "Jailbait." Then customers found hair and a mysterious gritty substance in the product, and just like that, her career was over. She moved to Florida, and now she does makeup for Disney weddings.

I'm not sure if Ethan broke up with her before or after the fiasco. Not sure it matters.

"Clio?"

"Sorry," I say. "What time?"

"One twelve," he huffs, annoyed at having to repeat himself.

"Amazing," I say, spinning. "I didn't turn into a pumpkin."

"Do you want to get an Uber?" he asks. "We can't walk to Brooklyn."

He thinks he's coming home with me. I suppose it's a fair assumption since we left the party together, but I still haven't made up my mind.

I like that he's warm. I like that he's good-looking.

I don't like that he's got on so much cologne. I don't like how he thinks he's so successful that he's above a dress code. And I don't like that I'll forever associate him with poor Lipstick Laurie. Maybe it isn't his cologne that I'm smelling but the persistent stink of someone else's failure.

"Your phone's ringing," he says. "It's been ringing."

"Mm." I hear it—my phone—I'm just keen to ignore it. I watch a group of girls in short dresses stumble out of Scorpio, a nightmare of a club no one goes to if they know better.

"Are you going to answer it?" he asks.

"Nah," I say, swinging my gift bag from the party. "Nobody calling this late has anything good to say."

"What if it's important?" he asks.

"Relax, Daddy."

"I don't get you," he says, shaking his head. He's not mad, just disappointed.

"All right, all right," I say, unclasping my clutch to get to my phone. My hand shimmers, covered in glitter from the party, which is to be expected since the theme was "All That Glitters." A jewelry-line launch, Veronica's partnership with Shine Inc. Gold charms. Cute but nothing special. I take out my phone to discover I have seventeen missed calls, all from my sisters. "Uh-oh."

"What is it?" Ethan asks. "Everything okay?"

"I'm about to find out," I say as my phone rings again. It's Leda. I hit ignore and call Daphne instead. Whatever the reason they're calling, I'd rather hear it from Daphne.

She picks up immediately. "Hey, baby Cli."

It's bad news, I can tell by her voice. Daphne's like a shape-shifter, a side effect of being the middle child. She adapts to the circumstances, fits into whatever space she's allotted; the queen of appeasing.

"What's up, Daffy?" I ask, walking away from Ethan. I turn the corner, lean against a boarded-up, graffitied storefront.

"Did you talk to Leda?" she asks.

"No. Why?"

She takes a breath. "Where are you right now?"

"Out," I say. "On the town."

"Are you with someone?"

"Considering," I say. "What's going on? Is it Dad?"

"No," she says. "No. Dad's fine. Amy's fine. Leda's fine."

"Don't tell me it's Tommy," I say, picking at my gel manicure like you're not supposed to.

"No, it's not Tommy," she says. "Thank God."

"Thank God," I repeat, crossing myself. Tommy is Leda's push-over husband, who wears sweater vests in earnest. He's too pure for this world and we love him.

"It's Alexandra," she says.

She doesn't call our mother "Mom" because she hasn't been that to us since we were kids. It's cruel, I think, but it's Daphne's prerogative. Leda's, too.

"Is she okay?" I ask.

"She's . . . she had a massive heart attack. She called nine-one-one, but . . . she was gone before the paramedics arrived."

"Oh." I bring my glittery hand to my face, press into my cheek. "Gone as in . . ."

"I'm sorry, Cli," she says. "Hold on. Leda's texting me asking if she can talk to you. Can you call her?"

"Is she upset?" I ask.

"I think she's worried about you."

"Why?"

"Come on," she says.

"Are you upset?"

"I'm processing," she says. "I'm actually driving right now. I'm on my way to Dad's. I think you should plan on making the trip tomorrow."

"All right," I say. My phone beeps. Leda's on the other line because of course she is. "I'll see you tomorrow, then?"

"Yep," she says. "Love you, Cli."

"Love you." I switch over to Leda. "Hey. Daphne just told me."

"We all had our own thoughts and feelings about Alexandra. But I know just because she wasn't an active presence in our lives doesn't necessarily make it easier to know she's no longer with us," Leda says. She for sure has been rehearsing this line since the moment she found out. Maybe even before then.

"Thanks, Leeds."

"I wanted to be the one to tell you," she says, stating the obvious. "I wanted you to hear it from me."

"Daphne did a fine job," I say. I notice a shadow creeping into my peripheral vision. It's Ethan, standing at an awkward distance, watching me, a concerned look on his face.

"She was our biological mother," Leda says through what sounds like a clenched jaw. Someday Leda will discover Xanax, and her quality of life will improve drastically. Until then, she needs to wear a night guard so she doesn't grind her teeth to powder.

"Are you going to Dad's?" I ask.

"Yes, I'm packing now."

"'Kay," I say. "I'll catch a train in the morning."

"If Aunt Helen calls, ignore it. I will handle," she says.

"All right," I say, aware that Ethan's hovering ever closer. "I'm about to get a car back to my apartment. I'll call you in a bit, yeah?"

"Text me when you get home," she says.

"Will do. Love you with a cherry on top."

"I love you, too," she says.

I hang up and immediately open the Uber app, request a car.

"What service! Mitt is only two minutes away," I tell Ethan. "Silver Toyota Corolla. Plate ends in X3."

"Uh, is everything okay?" he asks me.

I drop my phone back into my clutch and pinch it shut. "My mom died."

Seconds pass. A siren sounds somewhere in the distance. Someone else's misfortune temporarily louder than mine.

"Wait, for real?" he asks.

I nod. "For real."

"Holy shit. I'm so sorry."

Mitt pulls up in his Toyota. I open the door, look back at Ethan, who stands stiff on the sidewalk, his eyes watery and wide, as if he were the one who'd just gotten the gloomy news.

"You want to come home with me or not?" I ask before sliding into the back seat.

He climbs in beside me, undeterred by my tragedy. Or perhaps motivated by it. If he wants to be my knight in shining armor, so be it. I snuggle into him, steal his warmth.

That's all he is to me, body heat.

If there is an afterlife, if any of the wild things my mother believed are true, she's somewhere watching me, proud.

I'd rather you girls open your legs before you ever open your hearts, she said once, half a bottle deep. I was too young to understand then. So many things.

"Actually," I tell Ethan. "I changed my mind. Get out."

2

RAIN taps at my window, a polite alarm. My eyes are slow to open, yesterday's mascara gluing my lashes together. I got back to my apartment and fell into bed without undressing, brushing my teeth, or performing any of the many steps of my p.m. skincare routine.

"I have forsaken my serums," I groan to no one.

There's makeup smeared across my pillow, glitter all over my sheets. I roll onto my back and hear a soft crunch, reach underneath me to find my gift bag from last night's party. I finger the heart-shaped tag with my name on it, then dump out the bag's contents. Metallic tissue paper, clumps of glitter that will linger for eternity, and, finally, a small gold jewelry box with *Veronica X Shine Inc.* written in loopy script across the top. Inside the box is a pink velvet pouch, and inside that is a charm. A white gold snake with tiny diamond eyes.

I hook a nail through the jump ring and hold up the charm. There are a few ways I could take this. Veronica chose this charm for me because it's the edgiest and most expensive in her collection and suits my style better than a heart or key or flower or whatever. Or I could be offended that she would gift me the snake, read too far into it. Thinking back, I don't think I've ever done anything to her that would earn me the title of snake, but who knows.

My feet find the floor and I shuffle over to my dresser, to my jewelry tree, pick out a suitable chain, slide the charm on, and clasp it around my neck. I lift my eyes to the mirror, to my reflection, to study how the charm looks resting against my skin, but instead I see my mother, the traces of her face in my own, and I remember she's gone. She's dead, and I'm supposed to go to Dad's today. Which means I need to take New Jersey Transit. As if the one tragedy wasn't enough.

I find my phone still in my clutch, battery at ten percent. I plug it in and call Dad on speaker.

He answers right away. "Hey, sweetie. How you holding up?"

"Oh, fine, fine," I say, yawning. "Are Daffy and Leda there yet?"

"They're here. Amy's making them pancakes," he says.

"Dang. I love Amy's pancakes." My stepmom's lone success in the kitchen.

"What time do you think you'll be here?"

"Not sure yet," I say, staring at my unmade bed, at the mountain of unwashed clothes in the hall. A wicked idea pops into my head. "I have to do laundry. I have to pack. How long am I coming for? Will there be a funeral?" I force my voice to break. "I'm sorry, Dad. I just, I wasn't ready for this."

"I know, Cli," he says. "Why don't I come pick you up?"

Too easy. "Really? Are you sure?"

"I don't want you taking the train if you're this upset. Let me go tell Amy and I'll be on my way."

My father. Steady and reliable, the captain of the ship, the benevolent king of our lives, his love as sure and powerful as gravity.

"Thank you, Dad. I love you."

"Love you, too."

I'd feel bad, but it's not so far. An hour and a half, two with traffic. And, yeah, I may be a twenty-five-year-old woman calling her daddy to come pick her up, but the train is *such* a nightmare. I'd do worse things to avoid it.

I leave my phone plugged in, shove the laundry pile into the washing machine, and take a quick, cold shower. Towel off, then brush my teeth. Start my morning skincare routine. Consider what to wear.

Dad didn't answer my question about a funeral, but I'm assuming there will be some kind of service. I own so many black dresses, yet none of them seem appropriate for mourning my mother. Which maybe *is* appropriate since I don't know how to mourn her.

Would she even want to be mourned? She didn't believe in death.

Once my makeup is done, I climb back into bed, unplug my phone, clip on my selfie light, and take a photo of myself in my bra and my necklace, my shiny new charm on display. It's good enough to post to the grid. I tag Veronica, tag Shine Inc. Caption it with a snake emoji, a diamond emoji, some stars.

I stare at the picture. It's obvious to me that my smile is fake. But it won't be obvious to anyone else.

Another lesson from my mother, one she taught by unfortunate example. By showing us what not to do. By showing us how important it is to be in complete control of your emotions. It's too dangerous the other way around.

SEVERAL hours later Dad is cleaning out my fridge and I'm still packing.

"It's all takeout in here, Cli," he says scoldingly.

"What can I say, cooking isn't a priority for me. And before you lecture, remember feminism."

"I know, I know," he says. "You sound like Daphne."

Daphne thinks she's the most progressive in the family, but she got awfully judgmental when I told her I was considering starting an OnlyFans.

"All right. I'm going to take out this trash, and then we should be getting on the road," he says. "I'm sure your sisters are anxious to see you."

"I'm sure," I repeat. We all love each other, but Daphne and Leda don't always get along. I'm the family's social lubricant, the special sauce.

I kneel before my open suitcase, contemplating its contents. Working in fashion has ruined my ability to be spontaneous, to be nimble even under these circumstances. What I wear matters, how I'm perceived matters. Sometimes I think it's all that matters. Sometimes I know it is.

Dad comes back and waits impatiently as I finish packing, as I check and double-check that I have everything I could possibly anticipate needing or wanting. He carries my suitcase out to the car, griping about its heft as I lock up. When I get to the car, I throw my duffle in the trunk and slide into the passenger seat, putting my purse between my feet and shifting the seat back. There's an unopened bottle of water in the cup holder, and I help myself, assuming it's for me.

"Probably warm now," Dad says. "It was cold when I got here."

The plastic is wet with condensation, the label soggy. "That's okay. Thank you for bringing it. And for driving me. And for waiting. And carrying my suitcase."

He massages his shoulder before starting the car—perhaps an attempt to guilt me. He's a six-foot-four Viking, and his hair has been salt-and-pepper for as long as I can remember, so it's easy to forget that he's creeping toward his mid-sixties, that he's not indestructible. "What do you do when you go on all your trips? If this is what you bring for a few days."

Maybe a few days. I don't have enough information," I say, adjusting the vents so the heat isn't blowing directly into my face. There's still glitter on my hands. There will always be glitter on my hands. Glitter is permanent.

"I don't either," he says. "Helen didn't call me. She called Leda."

Not surprising. Aunt Helen, Mom's older and only sibling, hates my father. *Hates.* Amy is a close second on her hit list. To say my parents did not have an amicable divorce would be like saying the *Challenger* did not have a pleasant flight.

"They have lunch sometimes," he says, turning onto Flatbush Avenue. "Helen and Leda."

"Are you asking me or telling me?"

He doesn't respond, so I don't respond. I know Leda has met with Helen, they both live in Boston, and Helen has been trying to get back in touch with us for years, and while Leda, a chronic overachiever with an iron will, could probably stop the earth on its axis if she put her mind to it, Tommy is a soft kitten who grew up in a normal family. He's her well-adjusted Achilles' heel and never approved of her steadfast disavowal of our mother. And while he couldn't get her to budge on the issue of Alexandra, he could talk her into a lunch with Helen, which turned into several lunches, because Leda and Helen are cut from the same glorious rigid bitch cloth.

I know all of this, but I don't know if our father does. It could be a trap, so I don't confirm or deny.

"Can I put on some music?" I ask, already reaching for his phone.

"Sure, Cli," he says. "Not too loud."

I put on some Quiet Riot because Mr. James Arthur Barnes can't resist some glam metal. Their cover of Slade's "Cum on Feel the Noize."

"Hell yeah," he says, head bobbing. "Turn this up."

"Sir, yes, sir."

I continue to DJ for the rest of the car ride. We get stuck in traffic, so it takes longer than it should to make it to New Jersey, to my father's house. Leda's Mercedes is parked on the street, perfectly parallel to the curb. Daphne's Subaru is parked haphazardly in the driveway—the beat-up hatchback she's had since high school. She can afford a new one, but since Leda and I are materialistic, she decided not to be. Dad is careful as he pulls around her car into the garage, which is unnecessary. What's another dent?

A simultaneous feeling of relief and unease rushes through me. It happens every time I step foot in this garage, in this house. Considering it's the childhood home of mine that wasn't haunted or cursed or whatever, I shouldn't feel so haunted coming here. The feeling is fleeting, it never lasts, but it *always* happens. A swell of memories, the ghosts of past me, the precocious kid who was glad to be out of Mom's house, where the atmosphere was tense, and there were no snacks, and everything stank of cigarettes and Chardonnay. But then also the guilt, confusion, missing her, unsure which parent I loved more, which parent I trusted more.

It's child-of-divorce syndrome. It's so annoying.

Dad lugs my suitcase out of the trunk, I gather all my bags, and Amy opens the door into the mudroom for us. She wears a face of pity, though I know she's probably happy my mother is dead. Maybe not *happy*, but something in the vicinity.

"Oh, come here," she says, pulling me in for a hug. Her signature smell is comforting, too sweet and too much and yet somehow just right. It's like inhaling caramel, snorting straight sugar. When she was our dance teacher, everyone wanted to smell like her, to look like her, be like her. Whenever I conjure up her image in my mind, it's the box blond twentysomething in leg warmers and a leotard, not the stepmother who stands before me, with dark roots and skin specked from gratuitous time unprotected in the sun, wearing kohl eyeliner that's sunken into her crow's-feet, and an unflattering sweater tucked into low-rise jeans. Her style never evolved past 2010. I find it equally tragic and endearing.

"Hey, Amy," I say.

"Let me take your bags," she says. "Your sisters are in the sunroom."

"Then that's where I'm headed."

She leans in for another hug and says, "I made them some sangria. They might be a little tipsy."

"Good. They're more fun that way," I say, hoping they left some for me.

3

LEDA and Daphne are indeed in the sunroom, each holding a near-empty glass with shriveled pink fruit settled at the bottom. There's a pitcher on the coffee table between them resting atop a cluster of coasters. Leda stands in the corner, a hand on her hip, looking like a mannequin at an Ann Taylor. Her back is to me, her platinum hair in a sleek low bun. She started dyeing it blond in high school to look more like Amy and to spite our actual mother.

Daphne kept her hair dark but chopped it all off into a short wolf cut—close cousin of the mullet. She lies across the couch, her legs draped over the side. She gnaws on an orange rind.

"Heard you were getting wasted," I say.

They both turn to me, startled, as if awoken from a deep sleep. Daphne jumps up to hug me.

"We're not drunk," Leda says, defensive.

"Relax. I won't tattle," I say, crossing my heart. "But just so you know, God knows."

Leda scoffs. She's not religious; none of us are—we had our fill of "the power of Christ compels you" nonsense in adolescence. She just can't stand the idea of doing something wrong.

"Don't tease her," Daphne whispers in my ear. "She's fragile."

"I heard that! I am not *fragile*. I just don't think this is a very funny time."

"You're right," I say, wriggling free of Daphne to go hug Leda. It's unpleasant, like embracing a flagpole.

"You smell good. What is that?" she asks.

"Me," I say, flipping my hair. I left mine alone. Dark, long, thick, curly. One of the few things our mother gave to us that's never come up in therapy. When you inherit mostly complexes, why not appreciate the rare gifts? "And Tom Ford. And Oribe. A mix."

"Mm," she says, taking a step back to examine me. I return the favor. She's always had sharp features, but now, in her thirties, her cheeks have hollowed, the angles of her face gone harsh. She has Mom's epic brows but Dad's round green eyes. She has Mom's prominent nose and wide mouth, but Dad's slight lips and cleft chin. A perfect mix. She doesn't think she's pretty because Mom used to tell her she wasn't, but I love looking at Leda's face. It's art.

She clears her throat and takes the daintiest sip of her sangria. "I talked to Helen. There is going to be a funeral."

"Okay," I say, pausing in anticipation of details that don't follow. Instead, there's a prickly silence.

"We're not going," Daphne says. She's returned to the couch, this time with her feet up on the coffee table, perilously close to the pitcher.

"We, as in you and Leda?" I ask. "And Dad and Amy, I'm assuming?"

"Dad and Amy are not welcome," Daphne says. "Aunt Helen made that clear."

"Well, yeah," I say, circling the coffee table and sitting on the chaise. The afternoon sun streams through the big windows, so bright it's verging on belligerence. I shield my eyes. "But I want to go."

Leda sighs a heavy, dramatic sigh. Daphne clicks her tongue.

"It's gonna be a fucking circus," Daphne says. "A freak show. You know that, right?"

"I love freaks. I am one."

"Wearing old Salvation Army wedding dresses on the subway doesn't make you a freak," Daphne says, studying the contents of her glass.

"It makes me one of New York's most stylish people, according to the *Times*," I say. They both roll their eyes. "I'm not trying to convince you two to go."

"Good. Because I've already been through this with Tom," Leda says. "This is my decision."

"Where is Tommy boy?"

"Upstairs on a work call."

"Tommy!" I shout. "Maybe he'll go with me."

Leda gives me a death glare.

"Fine. I'll go by myself."

Daphne shakes her head. She continues shaking her head. Just watching her makes me dizzy.

"Clio . . ." Leda starts.

"Leda. Leeds. Lee-Lee. Leda-ba-dee-da."

She purses her lips, sighs again. "I really don't like the idea of you there. With all of Alexandra's . . . strange associates."

"I'm a big girl," I say.

It's Daphne's turn to scoff.

"What?" I ask, kicking her legs off the coffee table.

Leda interjects before Daphne can answer. "You can't play the 'I'm an adult' card when you still have Dad do everything for you."

"I appreciate your candor, but you're wrong. Dad doesn't do *everything* for me," I say. "Just my—"

"Not just your taxes," Leda says. "Setting up your internet.

Mounting your TV. You don't even have your Social Security number memorized."

"So?" I ask, and her eyes go wide. I grin. "I'm kidding. I do too have it memorized. Sometimes I just reverse the last two numbers. Whatever."

"My point stands. You call him for everything. Every little thing."

"On a phone he pays for," Daphne says. Traitor.

"You're still on the family plan, same as me," I say, tossing a decorative pillow at her.

She catches it. "Yeah, but I pay him. I pay for my phone."

"Really?" I ask.

"Is this productive?" Daphne says, closing her eyes and hugging the pillow to her chest.

"I don't know. Is it?" Leda asks, again with the hand on the hip. "You talk her out of it, then."

"There's no talking me out of it. It's our mother's funeral. I get not wanting her in our lives, not chasing a relationship after everything, but . . ." I trail off. "Why do I have to justify it to you? I respect your decision. I think it's a bad one and don't agree with it at all, but I respect it. Can't you respect mine?"

"It's not about respect, Clio. It's about safety," Leda says. "You don't remember what it was like."

That's their trump card. I was too young to remember what they remember, too young to comprehend the damage being inflicted. The chaos of Mom fully losing her mind after Dad had enough of her drama and filed for divorce.

"I'm sorry, but I'm with Leeds here," Daphne says.

"I'm sorry, but I don't really . . . care?" I say, standing. "I don't need your permission."

They exchange a look of worry and frustration and maybe

something else. Heartbreak. I blow them kisses, pick up the sangria pitcher, turn on my heel, and walk out of the room, escaping upstairs, where I can be alone.

MY bedroom is still very much *my* bedroom, even though I moved out a decade ago, the week after I graduated high school, wasting no time. My bedding is the same old bedding, the art on the candy pink walls all pieces I picked out when I was a kid. Photographs of carousel horses and Paris in the rain. I was a baby romantic who fantasized about a beautiful future filled with beautiful things. A future that is now my present, my reality, mine.

Not this second, though. This second, I get to lie on top of the squeaky double mattress staring at the chandelier on the ceiling, watching the crystals reflect fading daylight, sipping sangria straight from the pitcher, being salty about my sisters.

Bored, I set the remaining sangria on my nightstand and slide off the bed, allowing gravity to deliver me to the floor. I lift the area rug to find the constellation of nail polish stains on the carpet. Proof of a childhood memory, an incident of reckless behavior, the momentary panic of retribution, the realization I could use tears to circumvent punishment, a promise to not do it again, sweet relief.

I'm grateful for it—the proof. The hard evidence. I wish I had more of it with Alexandra. There's little to validate the memories of my mother. Despite what Dad and Leda and Daphne may think, I do have them—memories—but they're hazy. Brief and confused, like waking from a vivid dream, one you can't articulate anything that happened in, only that it happened, and it made you feel intensely.

No stains from my mother. Only scars.

I push up my sleeve and find the remnants of a small burn on my right forearm, the delicate skin above my inner wrist, where my veins are blue and faint and busy. It's barely noticeable. A little pale, a little rough, the shape of an eye—round but coming to sharp, defined points on both ends. I could never bring myself to blame Mom for the injury, even though everyone else was convinced she was responsible. I don't remember getting it, only having it. No one was ever keen to discuss the specifics, not Dad, not Amy, not my sisters, and I've now forever lost the opportunity to ask my mother.

Though, there is a good chance she mentions it in the book.

Ominous music plays in my head whenever I dare think about *the book*. Mom's memoir of our time in the house, *Demon of Edgewood Drive: The True Story of a Suburban Haunting*. It was moderately successful for all of two minutes, popular among paranormal conspiracy junkies and the like, before they moved on to their next spooky misfortune. The book was optioned for film, and Dad and Leda and Daphne and I all held our breath, fearing an adaptation that, luckily, never came. It's now long out of print and mostly forgotten. Mostly.

Stricken by a sudden, devious curiosity, I crawl over to my bag and dig out my laptop. I open my browser and Google my mother's name to see if her death has made headlines or if her brief fame was too niche to merit remembrance. I immediately think better of it and snap my laptop shut, slide it under my bed with my foot like its contaminated.

Promise me you girls will never read it. I'm at the kitchen table. It's 2009, Leda and Daphne to my left, Amy to my right, Dad standing above us, the look on his face terrifying because he was clearly terrified. I'd never seen him like that, so when I promised, it wasn't with my fingers crossed behind my back, like usual. I meant it. I've kept my promise. I thought it was out of virtue, but maybe it was because I'd never really wanted to read Mom's book. The idea of it always sincerely freaked me out, having to stare at the ugliest part of our lives in print. Holding our domestic horror story in my hands, in paperback.

Part of me figured we'd all come to terms someday, that Mom would get sober and reach out, apologize, and we'd be in each other's lives again. I'd get any answers I wanted from the source, and so I had little motivation to ever hunt down a copy, though every once in a while I'd find myself in a bookstore or library checking if they had it on hand. They never did, so I never got the opportunity to run my fingers along the spine and see if it would make me feel anything other than sick.

The urge returns. To Google. To seek an answer for this pesky question. Does anyone else care about her death as much as me?

Does anyone care at all?

I resist the pull of the internet, busy my hands by painting my already manicured nails on the patch of already stained carpet. It's clear polish, so whatever.

It's a subpar distraction, and the unanswered questions multiply fast, like rabbits, until they fuse, until there's just one big ugly bunny. Why do I care?

She abused us, abandoned us, so the story goes. But the details are elusive; the ending is unsatisfying. I resent it.

Eventually, Amy knocks on my door and tells me it's dinner.

"Be down in a minute," I say, blowing on my nails so they dry faster. Futile, but I appreciate the guise of power. Of control.

4

EVERYONE'S already seated at the table by the time I arrive, nail polish dry. Only Tommy appears happy to see me, in his wool sweater with elbow patches, in his round tortoiseshell glasses, the lenses cartoonishly thick. He's not good-looking, not attractive by any measure—Daphne once described him as having the sex appeal of a raisin—but Tommy is beautiful, radiating this sweet and pure innocence, like a golden retriever or adolescent nerd.

"Tommy!" I say as Dad rises to pull out my chair for me. I catch Leda and Daphne exchanging a look.

"How you doing there, Clio?" Tommy asks, reaching across the table for my hand. He gives it a squeeze, which is a comforting gesture in theory but unpleasant in practice since his hand is so clammy.

"Oh, I'm fine," I say, smiling.

"And I'm hungry," Dad says. "Let's eat."

"Help yourselves. There's more of everything," Amy says. She serves herself some salad and passes the bowl to Leda. Leda will have a small portion of salad and nothing else and no one will say anything about it.

Daphne serves me some chicken without asking. It looks dry, and I'm reacquainted with the frustration of sitting next to my sister, an exceptionally talented chef who has worked at Michelin-star restaurants, who doesn't cook unless she's getting paid to do it. Not even for her beloved family.

Both of my sisters' lives revolve around food, in different ways. This is my mother's fault, according to them, to my father, to Amy, and I've taken their word for it. But now that our mother is dead, I wonder . . . how? How can she be to blame? She's not here. She hasn't been here.

Our family scapegoat is gone. Whose fault will everything be now?

Still Mom's? A dead woman's?

The table is quiet, even after everyone's served and eating. It's not exactly a comfortable silence. It's itchy.

"So," Daphne says, compelled to oust the awkwardness. "Anyone have any vacations planned this year?"

Tommy and Leda are going to Florida to visit his parents, Dad and Amy are going to Big Sur, and I'm going to Paris, London, LA, and Ibiza.

"Paris for fashion week, London for a shoot I'm styling, LA and Ibiza for brand sponsorships," I say. "For work."

"Work," Leda scoffs. She doesn't take what I do seriously because it's glamorous. Same with Dad and Amy. Daphne gets it. Tommy doesn't, but he respects it anyway because that's who he is. He's a social worker.

"But before that I'm going to Mom's funeral," I say to shake things up.

Dad spits out his sip of water. Amy drops her silverware. Daphne laughs a little, a good sport.

"Where is it, Leeds? Here or in Connecticut?" Mom stuck

around for about a year after losing joint custody. She was still permitted visitation, but she'd show up drunk to see us if she showed up at all, and then there was what is known in our family as the infamous "recital incident." That was the last time I saw her. She put her haunted house on the market and started a new life without us, making no effort to regain any custodial rights, no effort at all, no phone calls or birthday cards, forgoing her mom duties for good. She moved to Connecticut with her demonologist boyfriend, Roy. As far as I know, they're still together. Or were still together, until yesterday.

Dad clears his throat and says, "Leda."

"She won't listen to us," Leda says. "You have to tell her."

"You can't tell me not to go, Dad," I say. "None of you can. Besides, you're overreacting. I can handle weirdos. I live in New York City. I work in fashion."

"We should just let it go. Let her go," Daphne says, sawing into her chicken. "The more we try to talk her out of it, the more she's gonna want to do it."

"What can I say? I'm a rebel."

"We just worry about you being there by yourself," Amy says so Dad doesn't have to. "The people. The narratives . . ."

"Then I'll bring someone. A chaperone," I say, turning my head slowly, until I face directly across from me. "Tommy."

Tension drops in like an anvil, hard and swift and graceless. Sir Thomas Robert Kowalski turns about as red as a stop sign.

"What do you say? How would you like to finally meet our mother?"

EVERYONE comes around on the idea except for Leda, who pouts through the rest of dinner until Dad announces that he's taking us to Dreamies, a soda shop on Main Street that's been a family staple for years. It's impossible to be upset at Dreamies, with all its old-world charm—black-and-white tile floors, tin ceilings, sepia-toned photos on the walls, chrome-and-red-vinyl chairs, banana splits the size of an infant.

Leda, Daphne, and I get a banana split, three spoons. We each take a cherry, holding them up by the stems to cheers. It's the only time Leda ever indulges, so Daphne and I allow her to eat all the strawberry without complaint, though it's our collective favorite flavor. Chocolate and vanilla just aren't as special.

Dad and Amy share a float, and Tommy is lactose intolerant, so he just gets a Coke. They sit at another table, speak in hushed tones, likely discussing the funeral.

"He doesn't know what he's in for," Daphne says. "Poor guy."

"It's cruel, Clio," Leda says. "You shouldn't subject him to it."

"He's seen worse at his job. Real-life horrors. He can deal with a bunch of fake psychics and self-proclaimed witches," I say, mining for hot fudge.

Leda doesn't argue because she knows I'm right.

"The banana is the least desirable part of the banana split. Don't you think?" I ask, attempting to change the subject.

"It's necessary," Daphne says. "You'd miss it if it were gone."

"I would never miss a banana," I say. "Ever."

"I think you would," Daphne says. "I think you absolutely would."

"What are you two even talking about?" Leda asks, scooping up some whipped cream and offering it to Daphne, who eats it off her spoon.

"Why do we keep getting banana splits if you don't like the banana?" Daffy asks. "Why not just get a strawberry sundae?"

I gasp.

"We *always* split a banana split," Leda says.

"Always," I say.

"It's tradition," Leda says.

"Sister tradition."

"Okay, all right," Daphne says, holding her hands up in surrender. "Point taken."

There's a lull, a moment of silence. Space for me to start a fire in.

"Have you ever read Mom's book?" I ask.

"Clio!" Leda says, scandalized.

"What?"

"No, I've never read that book. I've never wanted to read that book. I don't even think about it," Leda says.

"I think about it," Daphne says. "Sometimes. I looked it up on Amazon once. It's got a few reviews. Not good ones. Just, you know, wackos who believe in all that. I've never read it. I don't want to either."

"Don't tell me you have," Leda says, pointing her spoon at me. "We promised."

"I kept my promise. I haven't read it."

"Good," Leda says. "It's a bunch of lies. Lies making bad memories even worse. I know it's hard to accept."

"Accept what?" I ask.

"Who she really was," Daphne says. "And when you go to her funeral, you're going to hear stories about her that aren't true. Not for us, anyway. None of those people were there when we were kids. When we were alone in that house with her."

I nod, swirling the melty remains of the split. "Do you think she really believed? About the demon?"

Leda says "No" at the precise time Daphne says "Yes."

"It doesn't matter," Daphne says, shaking her head, "if she believed her delusions or not."

"She was an alcoholic and a narcissist and a terrible mother," Leda says, setting her spoon down and sitting up straight, lifting her chin. "And I have to be honest—I'm not sad she's gone."

After a moment, Daphne says, "Me either."

"Wow." I reach up to my neck and fiddle with my new charm, my diamond-eyed snake.

"It's good we have each other," Daphne says, eating some banana mush.

"Yes," Leda says, revealing a small tube of hand sanitizer that she spritzes into her palm.

Daphne and I both turn our hands over, and Leda sprays us, too. She puts the tube away and for her next trick, materializes some lip balm that she passes around the table. We've always been good at sharing, never the types to fight over toys or clothes or the spotlight.

Daphne gathers our napkins and carries them over to the trash.

"I'm sorry I volunteered Tommy without getting your approval first," I tell Leda. "I'm sorry you don't want me to go."

She waves a hand. "It's fine. Might be for the best. You'll come back understanding what I tried to save you from."

I blow a raspberry.

"How many times do I have to prove that I'm right about everything?" she says, standing.

"You're lucky you found Tommy," I say, leaning back in my chair.

"Ha-ha. Let's go home. I want to walk off that ice cream before bed."

We leave Dreamies, Dad chauffeuring us back to the house. Tommy and Leda go for a walk around the neighborhood, Dad and Amy go to bed, and Daphne and I smoke a joint out on the old playset.

We sit on parallel swings passing it back and forth, kicking dirt, pointing out constellations.

"I can't see shit anymore," Daphne says, squinting at the sky. "Not without my glasses."

"Didn't we used to have a telescope?"

"Yeah. Might be in the basement. I bet Amy sold it, though."

"Facebook Marketplace?"

"She's *obsessed* with Facebook Marketplace."

"Loves it."

"I worry she's gonna get murdered. She'll tell me about how she went to some random person's house in the middle of nowhere to pick up, like, junk. Like an old end table or some shit like that."

"Yeah," I say. I take a hit and pass the joint back, then start pumping my legs, start to swing.

"Hey, are you serious about going to the funeral, or are you just being . . ."

"Being what?"

"Difficult."

"Me?" I ask, feigning shock and indignation.

"Dude."

"Okay," I say. "No. I'm serious. I'm going."

She blows smoke rings, showing off. "Yeah. I was afraid of that."

"You all need to relax." I hop off the swing, landing hard on my feet. I raise my arms like a gymnast. "Ta-da!"

"Very good," she says, unimpressed.

"I'm going in," I say. "It's too chilly out here."

"All right. I'm gonna finish this."

"Go for it," I say, turning to head inside. "Night. Love you."

"Love you."

I take two steps before she says, "Wait."

"Mm?"

"Can you just . . ."

I look over my shoulder at her. It's dark, and she's just a shape, a shadow beyond a floating ember.

"They're gonna talk about how much she loved us. How much she loved you. But she didn't. What she did to us, it wasn't out of love. *We* love you. This, what's here, this is love. Just remember that, okay? When you're there?"

"I will. I do," I say. "I know."

I keep walking, and as I march up the slight hill toward the house, I wonder what right Daphne has, what right anyone has, to say what is and isn't love. I wonder if love can be ugly. If it can do the wrong thing. Bad things.

I wonder if it can ever really die.

5

TOMMY asked what I wanted to listen to on the ride up, but I could tell he was nervous, so I let him pick the music. It was a lot of nu metal, which I found kind of funny and kind of tragic.

Did u know Tommy listens to Slipknot? I texted Daphne.

Woof, she responded. **Maybe he just wants you to think he's cool.**

I replied with a broken heart emoji.

The drive from Jersey to Connecticut was about two and a half hours. Tommy insisted we leave early in case of traffic, which we didn't encounter, probably because we left so early. We arrived forty-five minutes before the start of the service, so we found a spot in town to get coffee and muffins. Now we sit at a small corner table, eavesdropping on the locals and waiting for our too-hot coffee to cool enough that it won't burn our tongues.

"How are you feeling?" he asks me as I decapitate my cinnamon muffin, streusel crumbling everywhere.

"I'm not going to cry, if that's what you're worried about," I say.

"I'm not worried about that. It's okay to show emotion," he says. "To be sad."

"I know. I don't cry when I'm sad. I only cry when I want something." I wink at him as I take a bite of my muffin. It's a little stale.

"Leda doesn't cry either," he says, frowning.

"She did when we were kids, but only in private. She's too proud."

His frown deepens, the corners of his mouth practically dripping off his face. He pushes his glasses up his nose. "I'm glad we're doing this. I wish Leda were here. And Daphne. I think it's the right thing."

"Thank you, Tommy. I appreciate you saying that. And for coming with me." I wipe my muffin fingers on a napkin and raise my coffee cup to him. I take a cautious sip. "Ooh. Good coffee. Thank God."

"Leda got me a Nespresso for my birthday," he says, then proceeds to tell me all about it with such enthusiasm that I'm tempted to record him so I can watch this whenever I want to experience joy again. After he finishes waxing poetic about the process of frothing milk, I excuse myself to go to the bathroom.

I stare at myself in the mirror, brush muffin crumbs off my prized thrifted black Prada minidress. Of everything I packed, it seemed the most appropriate for the occasion, with a modest neckline and flared hem. It wasn't worth the fuss to badger Leda to ask Aunt Helen about the dress code for the funeral, or to reach out to Helen myself, and while I'm skeptical it'll be a traditional black attire affair, I figured better safe than sorry. Black Prada dress, black Prada loafers, sheer black stockings, my black cashmere cardigan with the mismatched gold buttons that I got at the Brooklyn Flea for ten bucks, sewed on myself. Black velvet headband. Small, chunky gold hoops, my lucky dice studs, my white gold snake charm necklace that I've become inexplicably, incredibly attached to sometime in the last few days.

My reflection betrays what I'm feeling—nothing. No nerves, no sadness. Maybe that will change once we get there, to the place where the service is being held, or maybe it never will. Maybe there's no right way to mourn someone who hasn't been in my life for eighteen years.

PLAY NICE

Of my sisters, I look the most like her. The olive complexion, big dark eyes. The same bone structure, the high cheekbones. The thick arched brows. The long curly hair, inky black. My nose and lips aren't hers, but they come from her side. That's why she loved me most, I think. I bear no resemblance to Dad. She could look at me and see none of him. Not have to be reminded of the man who hurt her.

I turn away from the mirror, turn on the faucet, examine my hands as I lather and rinse them clean. I tear off a paper towel and use it to touch the knob, open the door.

When I return to the table, Tommy isn't there. He's by the door, waiting.

"Ready?" he asks.

"As I'll ever be."

"IS this a funeral home or does someone live here?" I ask as we pull up to a stunning gray-and-white Victorian, the grandest on the street. It looks like a giant dollhouse. The kind of house someone would assume is haunted. Though, according to my mother, any house can be haunted, not just the old pretty ones. A demon will move into a split-level on a cul-de-sac. I mean, in this market, mortgage rates being what they are, I'm sure they take what they can get.

"Don't park on the driveway, we'll get boxed in," I tell Tommy. "Park on the street."

Thus begins the ordeal of finding a spot, of Tommy attempting to parallel park.

"How'd I do?" he asks, craning his neck.

"You're good," I say, even though he's crooked. I unbuckle my seat belt. "Good enough, Tommy."

"Let me straighten out," he insists.

It's another fifteen minutes before we're finally out of the car and walking up the pathway toward the house. There's a sign that hangs from the porch, and I expect it to say, "Insert Name Here Family Funeral Home," or whatever, but it reads, **Welcome Spirits**.

My chest tightens, heart pounds, and I regret the coffee, the caffeine an enemy inside my body, inducing a jitteriness that I wish I could be rid of. I shake out my limbs, pull my hair to one side, and hold it up off my neck.

"Cashmere was the wrong call," I say. "Why is it this hot in Connecticut?"

"It's normal to be a little nervous, Clio," Tommy says, offering a hand to help me up the front steps.

I wave him off. "I don't get nervous."

"I do," he says. "Did I lock the car?"

The door opens before we can get to it. A woman wearing a long red satin dressing gown and a black mourning veil stretches out her arms to me, wailing.

"Darling," she says, drawing me into her. I'm too shocked to resist. I allow her to hug me. She smells like vinegar. "Oh, you angel. She's so happy you're here."

The woman steps back to look at me. I don't recognize her, her features obscured by the veil. She has on costume jewelry, magnificently gaudy. Sheer black opera gloves. Her long white hair falls in glamorous waves. I admire the look she was going for. She's just shy of pulling it off.

There are stains on her gown, all along the collar. She's crying now, but she's cried in this gown before. There's clear evidence. Phantom slicks of saline and black mascara. So even with the veil, I can see her well enough. This woman isn't sad about my mother. This woman is just sad.

"You look just like her, Clio," she howls, clutching her chest.

I may not know who she is, but she knows who I am. I take a

step back and introduce Tommy before she makes any awkward assumptions. "This is my brother-in-law, Leda's husband, Tom."

Tommy offers his hand. "I'm so sorry for your loss."

The woman ignores his hand and hugs him, too. He embraces the stranger with genuine empathy because that's who he is. I doubt he notices the tear stains or her balsamic fragrance.

"Come in, come in," the woman says, retreating into the house and beckoning us forward with a gloved hand.

We step into the foyer. The whole place reeks of incense, with subtle notes of vinegar. It's crowded with antiques, multiple grandfather clocks, dusty knickknacks like teacups and porcelain figurines. Crowded with people. More people than I anticipated. My eyes ping-pong around. There's a lot to look at. Framed Ouija boards hung on the walls, sepia-toned photos of cemeteries and séances.

"My grandmother was at the forefront of the spiritualist movement," the woman says. "She knew the Fox sisters."

She leans into me and whispers in my ear. "They were drunks."

"No," I say, pretending to be scandalized. I have no idea who the Fox sisters are. "This is your house?"

"Yes, of course," she says. Her brow furrows. "I'm Mariella, darling."

She expects me to know her, so I continue to play along. "The one and only. I love your jewelry. You're so beautiful."

I mean it. She is. I want to get champagne drunk with her and have her tell me all her wild bullshit stories and give me compliment after compliment and let me rummage through her closet. I just know she must have the most incredible collection of silk scarves. And a stash of good pills in a vintage hatbox.

"An angel, you are. Truly," she says. "I suppose it's been quite some time since you've seen my nephew. Roy is just devastated. He loved your mother very much. Roy? Roy!"

Mariella puts her hands on my shoulders and guides me into the parlor. I look behind me to make sure Tommy is following. He's not, he's distracted by the artwork in the foyer, studying it with his hands on his hips.

Mariella delivers me to Roy, who stands in the corner of the room holding a glass of red wine. He's handsome for someone who is so obviously a demonologist. His silver hair is tied back in a low ponytail. He wears a billowy black blouse tucked into leather pants, a belt with a big buckle that has some kind of symbol on it. The same symbol hangs from a chain around his neck. His ears are pierced. I understand why my mother was attracted to him. He's the polar opposite of my father.

I know I've met him before, when I was a kid, but that memory is hazy. He came to the house at some point. A lot of paranormal experts came through Edgewood Drive; their faces blur together. And my exposure to them was limited. Sometimes I was at dance class or doing homework or at Dad's house or camping out on the deck in protest of having strangers in my room, sticking their heads in my closet to confirm that a monster lived there.

I don't spend a whole lot of time pawing around my memory. A childhood like mine doesn't exactly invite reminiscing. But sometimes it eats at me. Wondering what memories are beyond retrieval, are totally lost. Wondering what hides in the haze.

Roy takes one look at me and sets his wine down on the nearest coaster, which happens to be on top of a truly spectacular antique organ. He takes my hands in his and gazes deep into my eyes. His are disarmingly blue.

"Clio," he says, his eye contact too intense.

"Roy," I say, wanting to look away but refusing to yield.

"She was so proud of you. And of your sisters . . ." He has a very pretty speaking voice. I bet he can sing. I bet he plays guitar. I bet if he were more talented, he'd be doing that instead of chasing demons. Demonologist is a strange fallback career, but I suppose it'd be an even stranger first choice. And there are worse plan Bs. Charlie Manson was a failed musician, too.

Wow. He's still talking. "She sacrificed so much for your happiness. For your safety."

I don't know what to say to that. To agree would be a betrayal of my sisters, of the truth.

"I'm glad she found you," I say finally, diplomatically. Honestly. A good-looking freak she could cuddle up to at night, who would believe her, who she could talk demons with. I'm grateful she wasn't alone.

"I have things for you," he says. "If you'll excuse me a moment."

He releases my hands, holds up a finger, and then disappears through the doorway into the dining room, past clusters of people eating cold cuts and potato salad. There are trays on the table, along with stacks of paper plates and plastic cutlery. It's not an impressive spread, and it bums me out a little.

"He'll be back with a vial of holy water for you to wear around your neck. Regrettably, I don't believe it's in vogue."

I turn around to a tall, statuesque woman with gray-streaked curly black hair, a cigarette tucked behind her ear, impeccably dressed in Eileen Fisher. Aunt Helen. She raises an eyebrow at me.

I crack a smile. "Anything is in if I say it's in."

It's been so long since I've seen her. My high school graduation, maybe?

"Quick. Let's steal away before someone tries to read your palm or tarot or aura."

"I don't mind a reading."

"You say that now. One thing leads to another, they're receiving a message for you from the dead. Your mother says she knew you'd come."

6

HELEN leads me upstairs, down a hallway, then through a bedroom, and finally out onto a balcony with a wicker love seat, cushions stiff and dirty.

"Mind if I smoke?" she asks, slipping the cigarette out from behind her ear and into her mouth.

"Not at all," I say.

"I'd offer you one, but your mother would kill me," she says.

"Not sure she's capable of that anymore."

"Not if you were to ask any of these people," Helen says, lighting her cigarette with a match. She closes her eyes as she takes a drag.

"You don't believe in ghosts and demons and vampires and werewolves?" I ask her. "Ghouls and goblins?"

"No," she says. "But I believed my sister. I believed in her belief. I never held it against her. Some people believe in God, a bearded man who lives in the sky. We don't call them crazy, do we?"

"Depends," I say, sliding off my loafers and tucking my feet underneath me on the sofa, getting comfortable for what I expect to be a weighty conversation.

"Alex had a hard life. Things she went through that you don't know about, that your sisters don't know about. Our childhood. Our father . . ." she trails off, takes another drag as she stares into space.

"Was abusive. And an alcoholic. Like Mom," I say. Dad told us all about Mom's hard life. Sat us down on multiple occasions attempting to explain her behavior so that we wouldn't think it was our fault. "We knew. We know."

Helen shakes her head. "You don't. You may think you do, but . . . She was always on the defensive after your father . . ."

The disdain on her face flips my stomach, sends a legitimate chill up my spine. The temperature of the entire planet drops. The ice caps experience fleeting relief.

"Doesn't matter," Helen says, standing. She ashes her cigarette over the side of the balcony, looks out at the view of this quiet, picturesque Connecticut street. "She found some semblance of happiness. Acceptance. With Roy, with these people downstairs. That's what I choose to focus on. That's what brings me comfort now that she's gone."

I sense the "but" coming.

"I just wish you and your sisters could have . . ." She stops herself. "It's a shame. She loved you three so fiercely. Everything she did was for you. She knew she couldn't protect you, so she tried to prepare you for the world. I hope you can appreciate that."

"She didn't try. She left us," I say, catching myself off guard. I sound bratty and resentful, which is weird, because I swear I'm only one of those things.

"It's not that simple."

This is what my sisters meant about the twisting of narratives. Of the truth.

"I'm here, aren't I?" I say, putting my shoes back on. It's fine if Helen wants to lecture me—I figured she would—but I need to signal to her that I can up and leave whenever. That listening is my choice. The power in this moment belongs to me.

"You are. It's disappointing that they're not, though not surprising. Leda is firm in her thinking, and Daphne wants to keep the peace. You were always more open, even as a child. Very perceptive."

"Thank you," I say, relaxing back onto the cushions. "You've seen Leda, though."

"I have," she says, putting her cigarette out on the banister. She takes another out of a pack in her pocket. "She's willing to see me, but we don't speak about your mother. A condition."

"Always a condition with Leda."

Helen smirks. I recognize myself in her face, her expression, and it's exhilarating. This is the magic of family. The sense that you're not alone in the universe, in your body, because there's someone else out there who shares your DNA, who's made up of the same stuff you're made of. I haven't seen Helen in years, but I saw her earlier in the mirror. We don't know each other, but we do.

And suddenly I miss my mother. Suddenly, I understand that she's dead. That what I'm sharing right now with Helen, I'll never have with Mom. She's half of me, and she's dust downstairs.

The sound of my sob shocks me. I try to choke it down.

"Sorry," I say, clearing my throat, but now my eyes are leaking.

Helen stands where she is, watching me, lighting her second cigarette. I appreciate that she doesn't say anything, that she doesn't try to comfort me. That she doesn't show any pity. Doesn't react at all, which is just further confirmation of an understanding we share because of our genetic code or whatever, and it makes me even sadder. Makes me wish Mom were still alive. Would she know me the way Helen does? Know what to do, what to say?

She would. She did.

A memory surfaces. Falling and skinning my knee in the Shop Rite parking lot. She picked me up, brushed me off.

It hurts right now, but by the time we get home, you won't feel it.

But then there's Leda and Daphne, my sisters somehow policing my thoughts. Reminding me that our mother didn't love us. That she hurt us. My fingers find my scar, rub the rippled, silky skin.

And now here's Dad, reminding me that winners look to the future instead of the past.

I take a deep breath, reach up and wipe the tears from my eyes. "I'm good."

Helen nods. She opens her mouth to speak, but then changes her mind, pinches her lips.

I get up and walk over to her, carefully pluck the cigarette from her hand, and take a drag. Cigarettes are repulsive, but I'm making a point. Showing her that I'm an adult. That I can handle whatever it is she's holding back.

She clicks her tongue, the way Daphne does. The way Mom did. "I assumed Leda would handle the logistics, but in the spirit of honesty, I don't entirely trust her with your mother's estate."

"What estate?" I ask, passing her the cigarette. She takes it. "I didn't think *Demon of Edgewood Drive* was a real moneymaker."

Helen's only response is an aggressive exhale into the silence between us.

"Not that I care about money. I don't. I'd take her clothes. Her jewelry. You're right not to trust Leda. She'd donate all that. Probably without telling me first."

"If you want her clothes and her jewelry, you can have them. Alex didn't have much money. She spent most of the last twenty years climbing out of the debt your father left her with."

Again her wrath turns the air bitter. I pull my cardigan closed.

"It's essentially just the house," she says.

My eyebrows knock into each other. "What house? Her house here?"

Helen turns to me, equally confused. "No. Edgewood Drive."

"What . . . what do you mean? She sold that house."

My aunt scoffs. "Did your father tell you that?"

"No . . ." Though I'm not sure. I can't remember who told me. If anyone told me. Maybe I assumed.

I've looked up the house before on various real estate sites, because of course I have. There's a single super pixelated photo taken from the road. No other information, no sales history or whatever, which I figured was to protect the current owner. It's not a normal property.

"But . . . she didn't live there," I say. "Right? How has this never come up?"

"Why would it? That house is quite the sensitive subject for everyone, is it not?"

"That's a polite way to phrase it. Very diplomatic. Still . . ."

"Would I board a plane and turn to the person next to me to chat about Nine-Eleven? Walk into a burn unit and ask if anyone needs a light?"

"Okay. Wow. You've made your point."

"To answer your question, Alex moved out about a year after she lost you girls. She moved in with Roy here in Connecticut. But she didn't sell the house. She believed it was possessed and that she had a moral responsibility to rid it of evil before passing it on to some other family to suffer there as you all did. She hung on to it. She and Roy spent time there over the years trying to exorcise it—to some success from what I understand. I did my best to talk her into selling, but she couldn't bring herself to put it on the market. I think it was hard for her to let it go, for as much pain as it caused, it's the last place she had you girls. Where you were all together."

She puts out her cigarette, flicks the butt over the side of the banister. All the world's an ashtray. "In a way, I'm glad to know she was there in the end. In a place where she felt close to you and your sisters."

My hands find my snake charm. I rub it between my fingers as my brain somersaults inside my skull, trying to work out something I already know but just don't want to believe. "She was . . . wait. She was where in the end?"

"In the house. At Edgewood. Leda didn't tell you?"

"Tell me what?"

"She was there when it happened. The heart attack. She died there."

Of all the places to go. I can accept her dying, but I can't accept her dying *there*.

"Must have slipped Leda's mind," I say.

"Mm. Must have," Helen says.

"I don't get it. What was she doing there?"

"She'd visit sometimes. When she missed you and your sisters. And to make sure . . ."

"Make sure what?"

"That the demonic activity remained dormant."

"Ah."

"Your judgment is wasted on me, I'm merely the messenger," Helen says. "I didn't approve. Didn't think it was good for her mental or physical health to be there. Turns out, I was right. But so often, being right means nothing but winning a round of a losing game. What an empty victory. My sister is gone. The house is still there. And it's yours now. And Leda's and Daphne's."

The thought of the three of us going back, pulling up to the end of that sleepy suburban street, up the long, cracked driveway. Seeing the house waiting there, shaded among the trees. That clunky

1970s shed-style split-level with such uninviting sharp angles. Narrow windows that didn't let in enough light or air. The uneven stone pathway that led to the splintered stairs, wooden railings always wet, stinking of rot. The front door painted black, heavy and thick, but like all the other doors at 6 Edgewood Drive, it would allegedly open on its own and slam itself shut. How many mornings did I wake to find that front door wide open, a dead animal on the welcome mat? Offerings from the stray cats we would feed, which Mom took as proof. She thought that the cats were making sacrifices to the beast within the walls. That they could sense the sinister supernatural presence.

"Well then. I should probably go see Roy about that vial of holy water."

Helen laughs, then offers me her arm. "Shall we?"

7

I FIND Tommy downstairs getting his tarot read by a gaggle of fabulous hags.

"The Fool," one of the women says.

"The Fool *reversed*," says another.

"No, you're looking at it upside down. It's not reversed to him."

"What does this one mean?" Tommy asks, wide-eyed. "The Fool?"

"Don't be offended."

"I'm not," Tommy says. "Just curious."

Such a fool, I think. I stand against the wall and observe for a few minutes before getting bored. It's not as fun to hear other people's fortunes.

Aunt Helen went to the bathroom, and now with Tommy preoccupied, I've been left alone to navigate the funeral, or "remembrance celebration" as they're calling it. Left alone with the knowledge that I am now—or soon to be, officially, legally—a homeowner. I'd be the envy of everyone under thirty-five if only the house didn't come with such a reputation.

I put my head down and slink out of the parlor, find my way to the kitchen, where there's a little bar area set up on the counter.

Liters of store-brand soda and bottles of cheap liquor. I pour myself a whiskey and cola in a clear plastic cup. There's no ice anywhere, so it's warm, and flat, and pretty disgusting, yet somehow exactly what I need. I down it and pour myself another.

The kitchen is miraculously empty, so I linger while I drink, skimming the printed-out flyers on the fridge for paranormal conventions and psychic fairs. One of them is in Milwaukee, and it reminds me of my friend Sarah, who was on my dance team in high school. An angsty bulimic who wrote poetry and had a Maine coon the size of a German shepherd named Frankie.

Sarah and I fell out of touch after she moved to Chicago to go to Northwestern, but we follow each other on Instagram. She got married a few years back and moved to Milwaukee. She bought a fixer-upper there and renovated the whole thing herself, documented it on her page, got herself thirty-five thousand followers in the process. Not anywhere near as many as I have, but nothing to sneeze at.

"There you are." It's Roy. "We're going to have the circle of remembrance now. Will you join us?"

"I didn't come all the way here to miss the main event."

He smiles at me, then holds out a small satin pouch. "You can open it later."

I accept it, whatever it is. Slip it into my bag. "Thanks, Roy."

"I'm here for you, Clio. You and your sisters. If you ever need anything. I hope we can all sit down someday."

I kiss his cheek in lieu of a response. I doubt I'll ever see or speak to this man again. In six months, he'll move on with a psychic medium, probably one with a bad dye job and a name like Misty or Rainbow, and his beloved Alexandra, his partner of the last fifteen-plus years, will become an afterthought. *Men are all the same,* Mom once told us, *but it's the ones who try the hardest to convince you that they're good that you really have to watch out for.* My mother was wrong about a lot, but not this. How many times have I witnessed a man declare he was outraged over some indiscretion that he himself was later found guilty of? How many proud gentlemen revealed to be wolves?

I top up my drink, and then Roy leads me into another room where there's a broad circle of chairs set up around a small end table with an urn on top. It's a pretty urn, white marble with gray veins. I pretend it's empty.

People filter in and take seats. Roy pulls out a chair for me. I save the one next to me for Tommy, who finds his way over a few minutes later.

"So, what's your fate?" I whisper to him.

"I should be more open to the unexpected," he whispers back. "I got a something-of-Cups, a Fool, and the Hanged Man, which didn't look great, but they said it's more about perspective."

"Isn't everything?"

Mariella sweeps into the room and starts lighting candles as she monologues about death. Maybe it's the whiskey or the weird vinegar smell or how many people are here or how many of them are wearing hats or just general overstimulation. I can't pay attention.

I think about Sarah and her massive cat and her before-and-after Reels. I think about the shaggy beige carpet at the house. The horrible linoleum in the kitchen. The sunken tub in the downstairs bathroom. My tiny bedroom with the window up high on the wall, my view of dead grass. Leda and Daphne in the big room upstairs, directly above mine. Sometimes I could hear them, up late, whispering secrets to each other. I would hold perfectly still, hold my breath as I listened, trying to make out what they were saying, if they were talking about me, but it's like they were speaking another language, one I couldn't translate, in voices not theirs. No one sounds like themselves through the floorboards.

I haven't thought about their late-night gossip sessions in years.

I'm hot in my sweater again. I sit up and gather my hair, yearn for a butterfly clip.

A woman wearing a birdcage fascinator like a courthouse bride shares a memory of Mom bringing over lemon bars on a random Tuesday.

The mother I remember was a terrible baker. One year she botched Daphne's out-of-a-box birthday cake so badly we ended up going to McDonald's for apple pies and McFlurries instead. On the drive home, sugar high, I declared my love for McDonald's in song and dance, kicking the back of the passenger seat. Leda complained. Daphne asked me to sit still, so I leaned over and licked her. She screamed. Mom slammed on the brakes after nearly running a red light.

"I shouldn't have taken you there," she said, pounding a fist on the steering wheel. "You're going to be chubby. Do you know how hard it is to be a chubby girl in school? Do you want that for yourselves? To get bullied? You know what? Go ask your dad how he feels about chubby girls."

The light turned green, but she didn't go. She wasn't paying attention; she was too busy yelling at us.

The driver in the car behind us laid on their horn, and so Mom hit the gas. The tires squealed.

Thinking back on it now, I suspect she was drunk.

Haven't had a McFlurry since.

I become aware that the room is quiet and that there are eyes on me. I like to be looked at, but not like this. Like I'm Godzilla rising out of the sea.

It takes me a minute to realize that I just made it my turn to share a memory, that I just relayed the McDonald's story aloud, and that it has not gone over particularly well.

The cup in my hand is empty, the whiskey gone, but I lift it anyway.

"To my mom," I say, smiling sunnily, attempting to recover the crowd. "And the tough lessons delivered imperfectly. And her great hair. Okay, that's it for me. Who's next?"

TOMMY and I stick around until the end of the remembrance circle. It goes on for far too long. All the stories are about someone I don't know. That I never knew and never will. This version of Mom is theirs, not mine.

Ideally, I'd just quietly up and leave, but Tommy has a conscience, so we say goodbye to Aunt Helen.

"I'm sorry I talked about McDonald's," I tell her, going in for a hug.

"Grief is strange animal," she says, rubbing my back.

"You have my number, yeah?"

"I do. If it's all right with you, I'll be in touch," she says, pulling away. "I'll be taking her ashes, unless you want them."

I shake my head. "I wouldn't know what to do with them."

"Thank Mariella for us," Tommy says.

On the walk out to the car, I have Tommy take a few pictures of me on the sidewalk. The outfit is too good to go to waste, and no one outside my family will know where I wore it or for what occasion. Aside from maybe Ethan, and if I cared about his judgment, I wouldn't have kicked him out of the Uber the other night. He's already texted me twice since. Men love when you're callous.

Tommy hands me back my phone and I scroll through the photos. "These are good. I should hire you."

"It was nice to hear all those stories. About your mom," he says, sniffling. He wept during the sharing circle.

I shrug. "That's all they are. Stories."

He opens the car door for me, and I slide into the passenger's seat. I notice him admiring his parking job. He comes around to the driver's side, gets in, buckles his seat belt. I wait for him to start the car, but he doesn't. He turns to look at me.

"I'm married to your sister, you know."

"I'm aware," I say. "I have a hideous bridesmaid dress still hanging in my closet to commemorate your wedding."

"I have years of practice reading a hard-to-read Barnes woman. It's okay not to be okay, Clio."

"That's very after-school-special of you, Tommy. But I'm fine," I say, crossing my heart.

He nods and starts the car.

"I'm not Leda," I say. "I'm not repressed; I'm genuinely unemotional."

"I think you do have emotions, Cli. You choose not to feel them," he says. A little sassy, for him. A little bold, for Mr. Kowalski.

"All right. I did almost cry in there," I say. "Okay, I did cry. Upstairs with Aunt Helen. Are you happy? Does my transient display of vulnerability excuse me from whatever heart-to-heart you're teeing up?"

He pulls out onto the street. "Tears can be cathartic."

"I find they mostly just ruin my makeup," I say, cracking my window. "Did you know about the house? About Edgewood?"

He doesn't respond. He pretends he's watching the road.

"Pleading the Fifth?"

"This is a conversation for you and Leda."

We've got two-plus hours back to Jersey; he'll cave eventually. "Was she planning on telling me?"

"Telling you what?"

"About the house," I say.

"I love you, Clio," he says, "but Leda is my wife."

"Fine." I lean against the window, and he turns up the music, the same playlist as this morning. It's "Freak on a Leash" by Korn. I don't object. What's the point? It's been such a weird day already. Why not?

About an hour into the drive, he pulls off to get gas and we stop at a Burger King. Notably not a McDonald's. We go around the drive-through and eat in the car.

"Cheers, Tommy," I say, lifting my giant cup of Diet Dr Pepper to him.

"Cheers," he says. He bites into his burger, and ketchup oozes out the sides.

I savor a fry. All I ate today was that muffin, which is probably how I ended up drunk at my mother's funeral.

"So, how bad was it?" I ask.

He's got ketchup on his glasses, now. He doesn't ask me to clarify, which is an answer in and of itself. "I knew that story. Leda told me."

The sun sets over the parking lot, bathing the grim capitalist landscape in divine light. At this hour, the parking lot is holy ground, the distant Target Valhalla.

"I'm proud of you for showing up," he says. "I'm proud of you for speaking your truth."

I pop another fry into my mouth. "Woof. This is worse than you just telling me that I fucked up. Do you want a nugget?"

He takes one. "Worse than me telling you that I think you should give therapy another try?"

"No, not worse than that," I say, passing him the barbecue sauce.

He dips his nugget. "Leda didn't know about Edgewood."

"She didn't?"

"Not until Aunt Helen called and told her about your mother's passing."

"So she did know? She knew Mom died there."

"She knew Alexandra passed there, yes. But before she got that call, she had no idea your mom kept the house all these years," he says. "She's upset about it."

"I bet." I fold over my bag of food and drop it at my feet.

"It's going to be a pain to sell," he says. "Real estate is a headache."

"*That's* the reason she's upset?"

"She doesn't want anything to do with the house. Doesn't want to go there. Doesn't want to see pictures. Doesn't want to transfer the deed, that whole rigmarole. She doesn't want to think about it. And now she has to think about it." He wipes the ketchup and grease from his face with a napkin.

"What if she didn't?" I hand him another napkin because he needs it.

"Hmm?"

"Leda's assuming that she's going to be the one to take care of house stuff because she's the oldest and most responsible and fancies herself the most intelligent and competent. But she doesn't *have* to," I say, with visions of before-and-after photos, of me in overalls holding a paint roller, of selling the house in a few months for a pretty profit and investing that money in a property somewhere in the Hudson Valley that I can put up on Airbnb for passive income whenever I'm not spending time there creating bucolic content. "I can handle the house."

8

WE hit traffic and don't get back to Dad's until after nine. Leda and Daphne sit at the kitchen table drinking tea. They pretend like they weren't anxiously awaiting our return.

Tommy kisses Leda on the top of her head.

"Hey, honey," he says. "Awful traffic. There was an accident. Hope everyone's okay. We saw an ambulance."

The TV is on in the family room, Dad and Amy watching an episode of a sitcom they've probably already seen a thousand times before.

I sit down and steal Leda's tea. Daphne drinks hers black—same with coffee—to be cool and low-maintenance, and to never have to put anyone else out by asking for sugar or cream. Leda takes hers with a splash of milk and a packet of stevia, the same way I like mine.

"Excuse you," she says as I take a sip. The tea is cold. They've been sitting here awhile.

My sisters are both dying to know what it was like, but they don't want to admit it, to have to ask. I could be mean and let them squirm in their curiosity, but that would be a strategic misstep, considering where this conversation is headed.

"It was fine, since you're wondering. I saw Roy. He's good-looking for an old warlock. Everyone there had lovely things to say about Mom. No one tried to cleanse my aura or anything. No one tried to convince me of the supernatural. No one brought up the demon. Tommy did get a reading, though."

Leda and Daphne's heads swivel to Tommy.

"I need to be open to new experiences," he says, pulling out the chair next to me and sitting down. "That's what my reading said. Though I suppose I was open to the new experience of getting my cards read . . ."

"Why would you subject yourself to that?" Leda says.

"What? Like you've never looked up your horoscope or whatever?" Daphne asks, spinning her mug around for something to do with her hands. "It's harmless. Not like the shit Alexandra put us through."

"It's a gateway drug," Leda says.

"Chairman of the D.A.R.E. program over here," I say.

"Oh, fuck off, Clio."

It's harsh, out of character for Leda to curse at me like that. I turn to Daphne, her jaw hitting the table. This is why I like having two sisters. There's always a witness.

"I'm sorry," Leda says. Even more shocking than the curse, an apology!

"It's okay." It's easy to forgive her because she's obviously not in her right mind. Not guilty by reason of temporary insanity. "I can admit it was harder than I thought it'd be. Seeing Aunt Helen again. Seeing Mom in an urn. But it wasn't a circus. No one offered me Kool-Aid."

"Must not have been too traumatizing since you posted a picture," Daphne says.

"Don't shame me for doing my job," I say.

"I wasn't."

I give her my meanest look. Tommy shudders. He can't handle it. Neither can Daphne.

"I wasn't!" she says, hands up.

"Good," I say, smiling. I take another sip of Leda's cold Earl Grey and slide the mug back across the table, then stand up, push my chair in. "Only development post-funeral is that I will be taking the lead on the house we now own."

Daphne closes her eyes, which is proof that she already knew about Edgewood and that she's not prepared to fight over it. She doesn't have the energy. Plus, she sucks at fighting. She prefers peace.

"Clio," Leda says.

"You knew I'd find out from Helen at the funeral. Is that why you didn't want me to go?"

"Why can't you see that I'm trying to help you? Both of you," she says, gesturing to Daphne, whose eyes are still shut, who's probably wishing she'd stayed up in Hudson, where she spends her evenings cooking in the state-of-the-art kitchen of a beautiful restaurant, or eating braised rabbit and truffle risotto and turnips that she plucked from the earth with her own two hands, or eating box, her true favorite dish. "And what do you mean by 'taking the lead'?"

"I feel like it's pretty self-explanatory. I'm going to take care of all house-related stuff and whatever. You and Daphne don't have to worry about it. You're always telling me that I don't remember the worst of it, that I was too young. It's not going to affect me to be there. Not like it would with you."

Daphne finally opens her eyes, looks at Leda.

"We're selling the house," Leda says. "I've bought and sold property before. You don't know what you're doing."

"Let me figure it out. You disparage me for being the baby and then you baby me."

"She has a point," Tommy says. I appreciate him standing up for me, especially because I know there will be hell to pay.

"Tom," Leda says, jaw clenched even more tightly than usual, an angry vein appearing on her forehead. She's going to break something.

"I'll go by and check it out. See what work needs to be done. What potential there is. I could spend time there over the summer. Paint, rip up carpet," I say. "I'll throw in some sweat equity, and then we can put it on the market in the fall. List it for way more. No one's going to want to buy it as is, especially with its history."

There's a lull, and I notice the volume on the TV has been lowered and realize Dad and Amy are eavesdropping from the other room.

"You're assuming it's still in rough shape. Alexandra might have . . ." Daphne trails off.

"Might have what? You know she didn't take care of that place," I say. "She didn't have the money, and she didn't live there, and that wasn't her thing."

"You're underestimating the amount of work it takes," Leda says. "It's not just about the cosmetic. It probably needs a new furnace. A new roof."

"I'll hire people to do that stuff," I say, walking over to the fridge to get a seltzer.

Leda follows me. "It's expensive."

"I have money. I made five K off a single post last month. And besides, I'll make it all back when the house sells," I say, offering her the last can of lemon. She accepts it, and I take a cherry. "Daph, you want a fizzy?"

PLAY NICE

"No, thanks," she says. "I mean, I agree you're underestimating what it takes to flip a house."

"See?" Leda asks, self-satisfied.

"But . . ." Daphne says, and Leda's smugness suddenly disappears. "If you really want to do it, if you think you can, that's your call. I have no objection to you trying."

"Great," Leda says, slamming her seltzer down on the table. "Thanks, Daffy."

"What? She's going to find one spider or spot of mold and immediately give up," Daphne says.

"Hey!"

"Prove me wrong, then."

Leda taps her nails on her can. "It's so Alexandra to do something like this."

"What? Die?" I ask, opening my seltzer and taking a sip. They all stare at me.

"No. Leave us with that house," Leda says.

"That *fucking* house," Daphne says.

"It'll be money in the bank soon enough. Out of our lives for good. Forever." I wave my hands like a magician after disappearing something into his sleeve.

My sisters exchange a look. Leda relents. "Okay."

"Cool," I say. "I'm going to go change into comfy cozies. You want to watch a movie?"

I don't wait for them to answer because I know it's a yes. I know they can't say no to me.

EVERYONE sleeps in the next morning except for me. I set my alarm early, put on a pair of jeans and a vintage Rolling Stones T-shirt, find some old Adidas in my closet with the soles worn smooth. I also discover a hoodie that once belonged to some guy I hooked up with in high school, a band geek with good hair whose name I can't remember. Sean? Scott? Sam?

The hoodie is big in just the right way and still smells like Axe. Makes me want to go to second base.

Last night, after a viewing of *Thelma & Louise*, I opened the little pouch from Roy to find one of my mother's rings—chunky silver with a white stone. It's beautiful, and I think it would fit, but I'm hesitant to wear it, considering there's a nonzero chance she had it on when she died. I pretty much suspect that the contents of the pouch were all things taken out of her pockets or off her body while she still had one, prior to cremation. Also inside was a strange silver coin, some sage, a vial of clear liquid that I sincerely hope is holy water, and the key to a haunted house.

At least, I assume it's the house key.

I grab the key, and the sage and holy water because why not? I put them in my purse along with my cell, then head downstairs wondering whose car I'll "borrow."

"Morning. I made coffee." Dad sits at the kitchen table behind his open laptop, probably reading the news, an article about something depressing he'll tell us about later at an inopportune moment.

"Good morning, Daddy," I say, tying my hair up with a jumbo scrunchie. "May I borrow your car?"

"Don't go buy coffee," he says. "That's why I made some. Your generation wastes so much money on coffee."

"My generation is never going to be able to retire regardless."

"You're saving for retirement," he says. He knows because he set up my account and logs in sometimes to make sure I'm being a good girl. A responsible girl. "That seven bucks could go into your IRA."

I almost tell him I'm not going out to buy coffee, that I'm going to Edgewood, but decide it's better if he thinks I'm venturing to Starbucks. "Please, may I borrow your car to go buy a seven-dollar latte that will make me forget my troubles for all of ten minutes?"

He sighs. "Keys are next to the fridge."

There's a stretch of counter space in the kitchen that's used more as a desk, where the landline used to be. There's a stack of takeout menus and pens and a cell phone charger and photos of us. Dad's wallet. His car keys.

"Take my credit card. Get some for your sisters. And Amy. And what the hell? I'll have a mocha."

"A mocha?" I say, turning around with my pinky up.

"If I'm going in, might as well go all in," he says. "The blue one."

I reach for his wallet and get out the blue Chase card. "I have to run an errand first. I'll be back in an hour."

"Okay," he says. "Drive safe."

"Venti mocha," I say, opening the door to the garage. "With whip!"

"No whip!" he calls out as the door shuts behind me.

He won't be getting that mocha for a while, if at all. It's about a half hour drive to Edgewood from here, and I want to look around.

I'm excited about it.

It's a new project. A new opportunity for content creation. The chance to make something pretty, curate an aesthetic. My favorite.

I get to take the setting of the worst time in my family history and transform it into something else. Make it unrecognizable as the place where Mom lost her mind, the place where she died, the place where her demons lived.

It's the next best thing to burning it to the ground.

9

IT'S exactly as I remembered it. The long driveway sneaking off the cul-de-sac. It needs to be paved; it's needed to be paved for the last twenty years.

The house is set back, surrounded by woods. The front lawn is pale and patchy, covered in dead leaves and twigs. I park and step outside. It's chilly, and I'm grateful for the hoodie and to whomever it once belonged.

The roof is all angles, which gives the house character, I think. There's a tall brick chimney that runs along the side. A working fireplace—another feature. The siding is an ugly rusty red, which doesn't exactly help with the house's reputation as a demon lair. But paint it white or a dark navy, and suddenly it's chic and modern instead of evil and dated.

I dig the key out of my bag and watch my step as I head up the stone path toward the house. The pavers have sunk into the earth, thick moss between them. It's the smell of the rickety wooden stairs that lead to the front door that gets me, that resurrects a sentimentality, a nostalgia, that I didn't know I had. It's such a distinct scent, these stairs. I'm surprised they haven't collapsed by now.

There are parts of these stairs in me and my sisters. Parts of the back deck, too. Splinters we couldn't dig out, that we gave up on, impatient after sitting for too long on the bathroom floor with tweezers and a flashlight.

This is a reunion.

I get to the top of the steps, slip the key into the lock, and twist.

The landing is brick, but not nice brick. Loose chipped brick. There are carpeted stairs that lead down to a hall, off that hall a bathroom, my old room, Mom's room, and the garage. There are also carpeted stairs that lead up to the living room, kitchen, Mom's office, the second bathroom, a linen closet, and then Leda and Daphne's room. As expected, the carpet hasn't been replaced—the gross beige shag persists. The wall to the left is wood paneled, all the way up to the cathedral ceiling. To the right are vertical wood posts that leave the space open, allow a peek into the living room from the stairs. My sisters and I used to have fun weaving in and out of these posts, jumping down onto the landing, until Daphne sprained her ankle and ruined it for us.

The wood paneling is, unfortunately, orange-toned, but the wooden posts are a darker stain, along with the wooden beams that cross the high ceiling.

I hold on to the banister, black wrought iron, not totally ugly but not ideal, and make my way to the top of the stairs. There's barely any furniture. A beat-up leather couch set in front of the clunky brick fireplace, a round glass dining table with three old cane chairs over by the tacky saloon doors to the kitchen. The table is a relic from our time here. The couch is a relic from the sad back room of some discount furniture store, probably.

The ceiling fan hangs low, big blades like the propellers of a jet. I stare up at it. And I watch as it slowly starts to spin.

I swallow. Something hot and dense squeezes down my throat,

landing heavily in my gut. Fear? Dread? The feeling has yet to crystallize, to reach its final form.

The blades travel at a lazy cadence. Did I accidentally hit a switch? Is it just the circulation of air in the house stirring the fan? There's a breeze coming in from somewhere. It's here, stroking the back of my neck.

I turn around and walk over to the wood posts, peek down into the foyer. I left the front door open.

I'm tempted to shimmy through the posts and jump down onto the landing for old times' sake, but I don't have rubber kid knees anymore, I have prematurely achy former dancer knees, so I go around, down the stairs, and close the door. I listen to make sure I hear it latch, then turn to lean back against it, rest my head, take a moment to think.

The carpet needs to go, needs to be replaced with hardwood or quality vinyl. The brick replaced with tile. The ceiling beams can stay, but the paneling can't. I could keep it mid-century, incorporate some funky retro accent pieces. Go for a neutral color palette. Use mirrors to make it seem bigger, brighter.

I head downstairs to visit my old bedroom and check out the state of the lower level. It's dark. I feel around the wall for the light switch. The fixture on the ceiling above me flickers on, the bulb humming.

Every door down here is shut, the framed artwork knocked off the walls, and there are muddy footprints on the carpet.

They lead to my room.

I lean down and run my hands over the footprints. The mud is dried, crusty. They appear to have been left by bulky man boots. Could belong to Roy or the paramedics or the coroner or whatever. No one offered up any other details about Mom's death, and I don't really care to know. She had a massive heart attack. She called 911. She died before they got here. Any specifics beyond that aren't for me; they're for the kind of morbid weirdos who look at photos of dead celebrities on TMZ or spend their lives on true crime forums obsessing over blood spatter. I'm curious, but not curious like that. Dead is dead.

One thing I do know now, whether I want to or not, is that she clearly died in my room. I follow the footprints there and open the door.

Someone left the light on.

There's my twin bed, in the corner, with my pink floral sheets. Unmade. The bed is unmade.

"Did she die in my bed?" I ask aloud to no one. It would make sense, why Leda and Daphne and Helen would choose to omit that particular detail.

A squeaking interrupts my train of thought. I pivot, chasing the sound. I listen, but it's gone. Now I face my double dresser. My closet. The dreaded closet.

My hot pink beanbag chair is opposite the closet, under a lamp that looks like a giant tulip, and there are books and magazines piled up beside it. Pictures I cut out of those magazines are tacked to the walls, along with some drawings I made at school and photos from disposable cameras.

She left it the same. It's a bug in amber. A time capsule.

The lone window is in a weird spot between the bed and the beanbag chair, too high on the wall inside and too low to the ground outside to let in decent light. It's covered by a white lace curtain that Mom made from her wedding dress. There's a matching one in Leda and Daphne's room upstairs.

I approach the bed, study the impression in the covers, the curve of the sheets, the shape made by her, the shape she left in her absence. If I believed in ghosts, I'd wonder if hers was lying there.

Another *squeak*.

I whip around, not sure where it's coming from. I hold my breath. Wait. Stay completely still.

There's nothing but quiet.

When I turn back toward the bed, I notice there's a book on the nightstand. One I've never read, that never belonged to me when I lived in this house. I pick it up and realize it's torn along the spine; the binding fragile. There's no back cover, nothing past page 137. Part of it is missing. I open it, and another page comes loose, fluttering to the floor. It's falling apart in my hands.

I'm about to look around for the rest of the book when I see it. A flash of writing in blue pen. There's a handwritten note on the title page.

For my Clio—

My troublemaker. My fireball. May you always be brave.
Don't ever let anyone extinguish your light.
I hope this helps you understand.

Love forever,
Mom

I trace my fingers over her words. I forgot her perfect handwriting, the beautiful loops of it. I continue to flip through the book gently, careful not to damage what's left. There are notes on almost every page. She annotated this copy. Annotated it for me. When? This thing is beat to hell.

Did she leave it here for me to find? Did she know she was about to die?

PLAY NICE

Squeak!

There's movement. A flash of fur. I'm screaming before my mind catches up, before my brain comprehends there's a mouse scurrying across the top of my sneakers.

"Oh my God, oh my God, oh my God!"

I kick my feet and run. Down the hall, up the stairs, to the landing, wishing I hadn't shut the door only a few minutes ago because now I'm fumbling to get it open, to dash through it and escape mouse house.

Out of the corner of my eye, I see the ceiling fan in the living room spinning fast, like it's caught in a hurricane. I turn toward it, and it stops. Suddenly, all on its own. Unless it wasn't spinning at all, and I imagined it. Unless I didn't see what I thought I saw.

I stand staring, arrested by confusion.

A blood-freezing cold grabs me by the back of the neck. Icy fingers press hard into my skin with the promise of bruises. I shake, throw my hands up, spin around. There's no one, nothing, but it doesn't matter, because I still feel that terrible chill on my neck and in my bones. Feel little mice crawling all over me, their claws scoring my skin.

What I don't feel is alone. I don't feel like I'm alone in the house.

I bolt through the door and pull it shut behind me, lock it with trembling hands.

By the time I get to the car, I've managed to take a few deep breaths, steady myself enough to drive. As I go to buckle my seat belt, prepared to speed to Starbucks, then go home and take an infinite hot shower, I find my mother's book in my hand. I don't remember it being there a second ago. I don't remember carrying it out of the house. But here it is, and now I can't seem to put it down. It sticks to me like it's covered in glue, like it's an extension of my hand, my body. Like it belongs.

One visit to the house, and I'm entertaining the possibility that maybe a place can make you crazy.

I open the book.

DEMON OF EDGEWOOD DRIVE:
THE TRUE STORY OF A SUBURBAN HAUNTING

-1-
New Beginnings

I bought the house sight unseen. I needed a place to live, for my three daughters to live, that was close enough to their father, my ex-husband, who had recently purchased an ostentatious brick Colonial in a wealthy town in a notoriously wealthy county. Coming off the divorce, I wasn't in the best financial position. So it goes. Beggars can't be choosers.

The house had belonged to an elderly couple who had already moved to a retirement community in Florida. Though I'd come to learn that the couple, who had built the house in 1972, had never lived there full-time. Their story is not mine to tell, but I will say this. Shortly after moving in, a series of family tragedies prevented them from spending more than a few months at a time in the house. Why they waited thirty-plus years to sell it is a question for them,

Dramatic license. He had a secret second family that she found out about when his mistress showed up at the door late one night. She moved in with her mother, he moved in with his other family. They reconciled several times but couldn't make it stick, not until after his mistress's funeral. As far as I know, they lived happily ever after in Florida. At least as happy as two people can be when one betrayed the other. Maybe she just wanted to be around to watch him die.

though I suspect you'll be able to intuit the answer by the end of this book.

The house was priced very low, but that didn't raise any suspicion on my part because I was told by my agent that it wasn't in the best condition. It passed inspection, I could afford it, the girls wouldn't have to change schools, and I could move in right away.

I packed up the home I'd made with my ex-husband and my daughters, the home I'd once hoped would hold a happy future, and moved into Edgewood Drive piecemeal, making so many trips I lost track.

My first impression of the house was that it was in a nice neighborhood. Perfect for trick-or-treating, for making friends with neighbors. I was struck by the color of the house—an intense red—and how different it was from the other houses in the neighborhood. More angular. Harsher.

It was surrounded by woods, and I worried about ticks.

Inside was dated, a little musty, the layout a bit odd, but overall I thought it would work. A big open living area, a small kitchen. The appliances were old, but I was never much of a cook, so it didn't bother me. Four bedrooms, two full baths. A split-level.

There were two bedrooms upstairs and two downstairs, and they were awkwardly sized. One big, one tiny on each floor. I decided I'd let the girls pick their own rooms. I decided it was going to be a new beginning for all of us. A house full of women. A safe place for us to be. I'd paint it pink. It'd smell like vanilla and nail polish remover. It'd be ours.

My fantasy didn't last long.

I hired two college-aged kids with a van to help move the bigger pieces of furniture. One of them lived down the street. He was polite, but I couldn't help noticing he was acting strange. He seemed anxious. His eyes darting around, his skin going pale.

I overheard the other teasing him, using language I won't repeat here.

"Whatever, man," he responded. "I hate this house."

When they were done, I thanked them and paid them their fifty bucks each. The kid who lived down the street started to walk home, and I called out his name.

"Why do you hate the house?" I asked him.

He stuttered.

"It's okay. You can tell me," I said.

"Just stupid kid stuff," he said, shaking his head. "Empty house at the end of the street."

It wasn't an answer, but I nodded and thanked him again, and he picked up his pace.

I went inside and unpacked for a while, then poured myself a glass of wine and put on a record. *Little Queen* by Heart. My girls and I loved Heart. I'd play their favorite music when I missed them, when they were at their dad's.

You might not realize, but I was very conscious about playing you and Daffy and Leeds music by female singers and musicians. I wanted you to know you could be rock stars, or whatever you wanted to be.

But the record kept skipping. It had never done that before. I was beside myself, worried my record player had been damaged in transport. I couldn't afford another. I got up to look at it. I put on a different record, I forget which one, and it did the same thing. It would start to skip, and then make this noise. Almost a hissing. Like a hot kettle with something to say, trying to form words out of steam. It was utterly bizarre and frustrating, and after a long day, and an even longer year, I'd had enough.

I finished my glass of wine and put myself to bed, lying on my naked mattress that I hadn't had the time or energy to make. And I cried. I let loose. Loud, hopeless sobs. I was in an empty house—so I thought—there was no one to judge me. *Bottle. I will be honest with you here.*

I don't know how long it took for me to hear it. Or perhaps I didn't hear it but sensed it. The other sound. The other voice. It was almost as if it were attempting to harmonize with me. Or intentionally hiding beneath my sobs, obscuring itself. I bit my lip, covered my mouth to silence my own voice, to listen for it. But when I was quiet, it was quiet.

When I let go, fell back into my wailing, surrendered to my grief, to my tears, it came back.

Laughing. Throaty, hideous, soul-chilling laughter. *Evil.* Someone, something, laughing at me as I cried.

10

My phone rings—a jump scare. It's Daphne. The book unsticks from my grip, and I pick up the call.

"We were promised coffee," she says. She's mildly annoyed, which is my favorite Daphne. She gets a little plucky when she's pissed. "Why does it take you forever to do anything? Where the fuck are you?"

She drops her voice to a whisper. "Dude. Are you at the house?"

"Yes." I'm too rattled not to tell her what happened.

"So, I was right. Only it was a mouse instead of a spider."

"You're focusing on the wrong thing. I felt . . . it felt . . . *off* in there."

"The house doesn't need an exorcism, Clio. It needs an exterminator and an electrician," she says. "You just freaked yourself out."

"Yeah, but when's the last time something freaked me out?"

She's quiet for long enough for me to ask if she's still there.

"If you changed your mind after seeing how shitty the house is, you can just say that. No one will care."

"Forget it." I start the car. "I'll be home soon. What do you want from Starbucks?"

"Nothing. There's a better coffee place near Dad's," she says. "I'll text you. But pay attention to the road. You suck at driving."

"I'm a Manhattanite."

"Whatever. Bye."

"Love you with a cherry on top! Byyyeeeee!" I turn around in the driveway so I don't have to back out. I peek in the rearview to make sure that the front door is shut, that I didn't imagine closing it behind me. There are smart locks now, something else I can add to the list, after an exterminator and an electrician. Or maybe I'll just get a boyfriend.

I don't think I'm ready to give up on the house. Not yet.

WHEN I arrive back at Dad's almost an hour later, it's with coffee and pastries from the local place superior to Starbucks, which sufficiently distracts my family from noticing the book-shaped thing tucked into my hoodie.

I didn't tell Daphne about the book.

I smuggle it upstairs, hide it inside my suitcase, take a long shower, put my sneakers in the washing machine, and join everyone after all the Danish are gone.

"Returning your credit card with witnesses so no one can accuse me of stealing it," I tell Dad, slipping his blue Chase card back into his wallet.

"You probably have the number memorized," Daphne says.

"If I did, I'd be in head-to-toe McQueen right now," I say. "Which reminds me. I have a brand campaign scheduled to shoot in Chelsea on Tuesday."

"I can drop you," Daphne says. "I should get back to the restaurant."

"Tom and I are headed out first thing tomorrow," Leda says.

"No!" Amy says. "Stay forever. All of you."

"You're all still coming for Memorial Day?" Dad asks. "I'm getting ribs and hot dogs from the butcher."

"Maybe. I'll see," Daphne says, such a tease. She's too busy for us. She doesn't get paid time off. She knows she's not coming, but she gives us maybes to see if we beg. A test. If we fail, she won't make a scene or outwardly mope. She hoards her hurt feelings like a squirrel with acorns. Feeds off them on cold nights, uses them as fuel. But she never makes them our problem. That's Leda's thing.

"We'll be there," Tommy says, smiling, poppyseeds wedged between his teeth.

"It's nice out," Leda says. "Let's go for a walk."

I doubt she ate a pastry, but merely being in their presence is enough to set her mind to burning calories.

We all suit up for a neighborhood stroll. My sneakers are still in the wash, so I borrow a pair from Amy. They're neon green and leopard print, and it pains me to wear them in public, but whatever. We fall into our typical formations. Leda speeds ahead with Tommy jogging at her heels, then it's me and Daphne, trailed by Dad and Amy.

But then Daphne stops to tie her shoe, Dad and Amy catch up, and there's a switch. It's me and Dad now pulling up the middle, Daphne and Amy hanging back, admiring a neighbor's daffodils. It becomes immediately apparent that this was a deliberate swap.

"I know you went to Edgewood," he says. "You could have told me."

"Why would I tell you when my sisters would inevitably do it for me?"

"I'm not upset that you went. I'm upset that you felt like you couldn't be open about it with me. We don't keep things from each other in this family. We talk."

"Not everything needs to be a conversation, Dad."

"You don't think the house warrants discussion?"

"Obviously not, since no one thought to mention it was still in the family. Not Helen. Not you. You kept that from us."

"I didn't. I didn't know. How could I? I hadn't spoken to Alexandra in years. She cut off all contact after—"

"I'm perfectly aware of the situation, thank you. Whatever. If you don't want me over there—"

"I didn't say that. Your sisters told me that you want to put some work into it. That's fine. I think it'll be good for you."

"Really?" I was ready for an argument. I might have even been hoping for one.

The sky is blue and cloudless, the sun high and yellow, and the entire world is incapable of telling me no. It makes me feel like a god. Powerful, bored, dangerous.

Dad puts his arm around my shoulders. "We can get into the finances of it. What makes sense to invest into the house."

"Whatever's invested I'll make back. I'm playing with house money, literally."

"Not necessarily," he says. "It adds up. You'd be surprised. That house wasn't in great shape when Alex bought it almost twenty years ago. Probably needs a new roof, HVAC, et cetera. It's not all fun stuff, like paint and furniture."

"It isn't?" I ask, all Pollyanna.

He shakes his head. "You'll see."

"Then I'll see."

"I'm proud of you for wanting to take this on. I don't doubt you can do anything you set your mind to. But this is *your* project. Not mine. Not Daphne's or Leda's."

"I know," I say. Amy's shoes don't fit me right, and I feel a blister forming at my heel. The friction siring something ugly.

"I don't want them over there. I worry about that."

"You don't worry about me?"

"You're less sensitive than your sisters. Emotionally, I think it would be hard for them to be back there in a way it won't be hard for you."

"What if it's haunted?"

He laughs.

He laughs so hard and so loud that it fills the whole neighborhood. So hard and so loud it occurs to me that I might not have been joking.

Usually, I love the sound of his laughter. Usually, making my dad laugh is my favorite thing.

It's not my favorite right now, though.

He pulls me in for a hug, kisses me on the forehead. Daphne and Amy catch up to us. We encounter a neighbor walking their sweet, slobbery golden retriever. Dad and Amy argue about adopting a dog as we circle the block and get back to the house. Everyone gathers in the family room to play a board game. I lie and say I have a headache to get out of Monopoly or Clue—it hasn't been decided. Amy insists on making me tea. I take it upstairs with me, close my bedroom door, lock it for the first time since I was seventeen and would make out with Natalie Ruggerio when we were supposed to be doing homework.

Dad and Amy were cool about Daphne, but I always suspected they would take my not being totally straight as proof that Alexandra turned us into man-haters. Which she tried. But I love men. I just don't trust or respect them.

I take the book out of my suitcase, climb into bed, and start to skim the second chapter, titled "The Girls." She doesn't use our names, which I suspect was less about protecting us and more about not wanting to end up back at odds with Dad, who likely would have made it an issue, threatened legal action. We're referred to as Elle, Dee, and Cici.

Elle and Dee pick the big upstairs bedroom to share. Cici wants the downstairs room across the hall from Mom.

Thinking back, that's not how I remember it.

I remember wanting to be upstairs near Daphne and Leda. They're closer in age, and when we were kids, before Leda's teenage angst, the two of them were thick as thieves. They played with me like a doll, but I was never in on any of their jokes or secrets. They left me out on purpose, an older sibling power move. I eventually retaliated by feigning independence, which then calcified into legitimate independence.

But, yeah, I remember wanting the room next to theirs, the room that would become the office. There was more natural light upstairs, a bigger window with a better view of the front yard, the green of the trees.

And I remember Mom guilting me, saying something like "You're going to leave me all alone downstairs?"

Conveniently, she left this out of the book. Or maybe what's written is faithful to her recollection, to how it played out in her mind. One person's truth is another's fiction.

All I have is a fraction of a memory, edges frayed. I don't recall agreeing to the downstairs bedroom, but that's where I ended up. Did I do it to make her happy? Did I do it to show my sisters that I didn't care about being part of their little club, even though I did? I don't know, will never know.

The book in my hands becomes a bad idea, a piece of half-rotten fruit. Do I eat around the dark, mushy parts? Do I throw the whole thing out? I'm not sure that I even want to read it, that I care about her version of events. The uncertainty frustrates me.

But I can't help myself. I can't stop now that I started.

The first night with my girls in the house, I made peanut butter and jelly sandwiches for dinner and let them eat in front of the TV—something they weren't allowed to do at their father's. I knew they would report back and that he wouldn't approve. For as long as I'd been a mother, I'd been made to feel like I was a bad mother. My relationship with my ex-husband shifted after Elle, our eldest, was born. I couldn't get her to latch, and my failure to nurse her became indicative of my failure as a parent. I appreciated that he loved our daughters, but it came at my expense. I was never good enough for them in his eyes.

I also, apparently, wasn't good enough for him. He began an affair with our daughters' dance instructor, spent a year denying it, accusing me of being crazy and insecure, and then one day I woke up to him packing a bag, telling me he was leaving me and taking the girls. He promised I could still see them. He told me it'd be better for everyone if I didn't fight.

But I fought. Of course I fought. Eleven months later, I was in the new house with my daughters, but as far as he was concerned, custody still was not settled.

There were stakes to feeding them peanut butter and jelly for dinner and allowing them to watch TV. It didn't

He'll continue to deny this till the day he dies. He'll tell you that I never recovered from my postpartum with you. That I became reliant on alcohol. That I was paranoid and mentally unstable. And that accusing him of cheating was my way of tarnishing his reputation while redeeming my own. I know you love your father. He's a great dad. But he was horrible to me. This is the truth. I know you're smart enough to see it, if you look back, and look closely.

matter that I was exhausted from the move, physically and financially. There was no room for me to fail, to open myself up to ridicule.

The pressure put me on edge. It made me vulnerable.

So when I went into the kitchen to find all the cabinets open and peanut butter smeared on the walls, even though I knew in my right mind, in my heart of hearts, that it wasn't my daughters, I called them into the kitchen.

"Who did this?" I asked.

They looked confused.

"Is this supposed to be funny?"

"What happened?" Elle asked, anxiously shifting her weight, shuffling back and forth.

"You tell me," I said.

"We were in the other room," Dee said. "It wasn't us. But I can clean it up. I'll clean."

"Cici?" I asked. "Was this you?"

She wasn't tall enough to reach the cabinets. Not unless she climbed up . . .

"No," she said. Then, very matter-of-fact, added, "It was probably the thing that lives in my closet."

We all looked at her.

"What?" I asked, kneeling so we could be eye to eye.

She repeated herself in her sweet little voice. "The thing that lives in my closet."

There was no trace of her typical impishness, no wink in her eye. I knew my daughters, I understood them. I saw them. And I knew Cici was being serious.

"What thing?" I asked.

She shrugged. "I dunno. It doesn't have a body yet."

"Cici," I said, standing. "This is our new house. Why

would you make a mess in our new house? Do you not like it here?"

"I didn't do it," she said, her cheeks going red, eyes welling with tears. "I didn't do it."

"She didn't," Dee said. "She was with us the whole time."

"Fine," I said. "Then you can all clean. Clean it up, and then go to bed!"

I stormed out of the kitchen, down the stairs, and into my room, slamming the door behind me. I regretted my behavior instantly and wanted to run back upstairs to apologize, but I couldn't bear to face them. I was too ashamed.

An hour later, I emerged from my room to find the kitchen wiped clean, cabinets closed, and the girls asleep in their beds. I kissed them all on the forehead and prepared to make it up to them in the morning with French toast.

> I know I was crueler in the moment than I recounted here. I will be sorry about this until the day I die, and probably even after.

Too upset to sleep, I decided to light some candles and run a bath. The downstairs bathroom had a sunken tub, which was novel to the girls. They liked it, so I liked it.

I set out the few candles I had, switched off the lights, and leaned down to turn on the faucet. At first, I couldn't tell, since the room was dark. But by the soft flicker of candlelight, the water looked wrong, only I couldn't determine why. Or perhaps I just struggled to wrap my mind around it, to accept that the water was black as ash. And that it smelled. That it stank of sulfur.

I pulled up the drain, blew out the candles, and told myself that I'd call a plumber first thing.

Needing fresh air, I sat on the back deck with a glass of wine, looking out into the woods, listening to the crickets and to the wind rustling the trees.

I had thought moving into the house marked the end of my nightmare, but it was only the beginning.

THERE'S a smell. Peanut butter and Coca-Cola. An anxiety hot and sharp, and it cuts straight through my chest without resistance, like I have no substance, like I'm nothing at all.

There was an incident in the kitchen. Something spilled. A mess made. Mom angry. Daffy attempting to defuse the tension. A sound. *That* sound. Hitting is so oddly distinct. Daffy holding her cheek. Mom yelling, *Clean it up, and then go to bed!*

That's the cruelty she alluded to in her footnote, what she wouldn't commit to paper for the masses, only to me. Because she had to. Because I was there. Because I remember.

But I have no memory of blaming a vague, formless, closet-dwelling entity for the mess.

I close my eyes, and I think back, and I try to summon that night, that moment. My fingers sticky from the sandwich. My teeth gritty, coated with sugar from the soda. The chitter of cartoons on the TV in the living room. My mother in front of me, hair wild, eyes wide, mouth purple, breath sour. My sisters beside me. A shadow in the corner with no eyes, no face, looking right at me—not there, not real. Memories are so easily manipulated.

There was a malevolent energy in the kitchen with us, but I'm pretty sure it's the kind that exists in every house, in every family, in all of us on our worst nights. Mom surrendered to it, to her worst, and couldn't take responsibility.

I imagine her tiptoeing into my room as I slept and kissing me on the forehead, an apology. I imagine my eyelids fluttering at her touch. I imagine a shape in the dark. I see it.

Not her.

My heart drops as it stares back at me, this shape, this shadow, this faceless thing.

I open my eyes.

11

"OF course the house is haunted," Veronica says, eating the olive out of her martini. "Like, come on."

"You should get it checked for carbon monoxide," Hannah says, discreetly gluing and reapplying a press-on. "A lot of times people think their house is haunted, and it's actually carbon monoxide."

We're at the launch of a new skincare line from a big makeup brand, hosted at some swanky bar on the Lower East Side. Veronica is dressed in all gold, still promoting her Shine Inc. partnership. She's in sparkly stark contrast to Hannah, who is goth. She's in a fishnet dress, matte black lipstick, and thick kohl eyeliner. Hannah is a vlogger and special effects makeup artist who's married to an indie film director. They share a one-year-old son named Morpheus. She and I used to drop Molly together and go to Bushwick raves. She's still fun, but it's not the same.

"I have an exterminator coming," I say. "I'm going back next weekend. I don't know. The idea of it excites me, but it might be more trouble than it's worth."

"Are you kidding me? Everyone loves a home makeover. Document the whole process. People will eat it up!" Veronica says, reaching over and petting my neck, the snake charm. Before, I suspected that she was either jealous of me or had a little angsty, confused hetero girl crush on me, or both. But my genuine love for her charm has brought us closer, I think, our friendship now grounded in mutual gratitude.

"Haunted home makeover. I'd watch that shit," Hannah says.

"As much as I love a gimmick, I'm ultimately trying to *sell* this house. I'm not exactly looking to advertise its supernatural associations. So *shh*. Let's keep the ghosts quiet."

"A good general rule," Hannah says. She lives across from Green-Wood Cemetery. We go there for walks occasionally.

"I had mice in my old apartment," Veronica says. "The worst. Oh my God. You can hear them in the walls . . ."

She shudders.

"New subject," I say. I fish the lemon twist out of my glass and down my cocktail. "Did anyone actually like these products?"

The consensus is no.

An hour goes by, spent enjoying complimentary drinks and gossiping and taking the obligatory photos—the price of admission. Hannah taps out and calls a car back to her apartment, where she has a husband and a baby and probably a sink full of dishes waiting for her. Veronica and I stand on the sidewalk blowing her kisses as she climbs into her Uber, and I wonder if she misses her old self the way that I do. If part of her wants to stay out late, come traipse around the city with us, but feels like she can't because she's a mother now.

Motherhood irrevocably changed me. Years in, and I was still getting to know this new self, the ways my daughters had reconfigured me from the inside out. But motherhood had also irrevocably changed how others saw me, how they spoke to me, and it was consistently unmooring.

"Everything looks fine to me, ma'am," the plumber said, after the water from every single faucet in the house ran clean.

"I don't understand. The water was black, like tar."

He looked at me like I was crazy. "If you're worried about it, don't let your daughters drink from the tap."

"Clio?"

"That's me!" I say, snapping out of my head, which is stuck in Mom's book, which is back at my apartment, hidden under my pillow, because it feels wrong to have it, to read it. Because I said I never would.

Veronica puts her arm around my waist and pulls me into her. "Let's go dancing."

"I know just the place," I say, taking her hand and leading her to Second Avenue.

"By the way, what happened with you and Ethan? I saw you leaving my launch together."

"Nothing. I'm keeping him on ice."

"Laurie always said he was good in bed."

"I don't trust Laurie's standards. Think of the lipsticks."

Veronica laughs, stumbling into me.

I take her to SMOKE—a dive bar with a not-so-secret basement club. The dance floor is sticky, as are the velvet couches pressed up against the concrete walls, and the lighting sucks, but the DJ is great. It's packed like a Saturday night on a Thursday night, and everyone here is hot and smells like Santal 33.

The music is so loud I can't think, and it's a blessing. A most welcome escape.

We drink vodka tonics and run up a tab that Veronica pays for. We dance together, and she keeps stroking my collar bones, my chest, where the charm rests. The snake with shining eyes.

"I love it on you!" she shouts over the thumping bass.

"I love it on me, too!" I shout back.

"Everything looks good on you," she says, her arms around my neck. "I hate you."

"Yeah, but you're on me," I say.

"Then I must look good."

Later, when I kiss her on the street, she suddenly turns shy.

"I can't," she says, pulling away. "Johnny."

Her boyfriend.

Normally, I wouldn't care. I've historically kept a pretty laissez-faire attitude about cheating. Monogamy is for suckers. And yet, after resurfacing my mother's claim that my father stepped out on her with Amy, a claim I'd never previously given any real consideration because it's one he so adamantly denied, infidelity has suddenly become a more sensitive subject. One I'd rather avoid. Because now, as a world-wise adult, I'm confronting the legitimate possibility that my dad and Amy are committed, perpetual liars. Of course they would deny it. They have nothing to gain by admitting guilt and everything to gain by stripping my mother of all credibility.

Veronica giggles, touching her lips. Then she turns around and pukes all over the sidewalk.

I get us an Uber and drop her off first in Boerum Hill. When I get back to my apartment, I change into sweatpants and a tank top, eat cold lo mein on my couch, and wait for the world to stop spinning.

I consider calling Ethan, since he's been oh-so eager, or any one of my reliable hookups to come over and distract me. To stop me from doing what I've been doing, from crawling into bed with a version of the past—my past—that doesn't belong to me.

But I've never been any good at controlling my impulses. It's not in my nature. Apparently, it's genetic.

PLAY NICE

Weeks passed without incident, and we began to settle in, establish a new routine. The girls and I built forts out of old blankets and duct tape and cardboard boxes left over from the move. Our most impressive fort was surprisingly sturdy and comfortably fit all four of us, so I allowed them to leave it up indefinitely.

Then one night, after I'd put my daughters to bed, I was alone on the couch reading a magazine, and out of the corner of my eye I saw the blanket draped over the entrance to the fort pull back. A second later, the fabric released, sweeping down, concealing the interior of the fort.

> It was <u>Us Weekly</u>. It had Britney Spears on the cover. This was shortly after she shaved her head. The world will drive a woman insane, then point at them and laugh.

The magazine dropped into my lap. I leaned forward, wondering if that had just happened, if I'd truly just seen what I thought I'd seen.

Maybe it was the wind? Only no windows were open. It was April. The heat wasn't on either. No air was moving through the vents, circulating through the house. I called out my girls' names, keeping my voice low. At least, at first.

"This isn't funny," I said, hoping one of them would wriggle out of the fort laughing. Cici was a practical joker, my little jester. She loved to hide in strange places, then pop out to scare me and her sisters. "Cici?"

There was no answer.

The blanket moved, undulating as if in a breeze. As if there were a giant mouth behind it, breathing in and pulling the fabric back, breathing out and releasing it. Inhale. Exhale. Inhale. Exhale.

I stood up and took a step closer. I could see it. A vague shape. The outline of something there.

In that moment, I remembered what Cici had said after the incident in the kitchen.

It doesn't have a body yet.

"Cici," I said again, more sternly. "Cici, come out right now!"

The blanket stopped moving.

"Cici?"

"Yeah, Mommy?"

I turned around to see my daughter at the top of the stairs, rubbing the sleep from her eyes.

Seeing her there disturbed my center of gravity. I was unbalanced, untethered from reality. I ran forward and ripped the blanket off the fort. There was nothing behind it, not that I could see, but that did nothing to reassure me. They say that seeing is believing, but I believed that something lurked there in the shadowy emptiness. I believed with my gut. My intuition. I believed with a protective maternal response that is ordained by nature.

The destruction of the fort was quick but took some effort, some force. I stomped the cardboard flat. Tore through the old blankets. Then it was a pile on the floor, and I was panting so loudly that it took a minute for me to hear the girls.

Elle and Dee had come out of their room, joining Cici. They held each other, looks of sheer horror on their faces. They were terrified. Terrified of *me*.

I couldn't stand it.

"Go back to bed!" I screamed. I'd never screamed at them like that before. "Now! In your rooms!"

Elle and Dee turned and ran down the hall to their room. I heard the door slam. I heard them crying.

But Cici didn't move. She stood there with her little hands balled into fists.

"Go!"

"I'm *thirsty*," she said, and marched into the kitchen.

I heard her climb up onto the counter, a cabinet open, and then the fridge whirring.

I backed away from the ruined fort. I didn't want to be near it, to be reminded of what I'd done, of how my daughters had looked at me. What had made me do it in the first place.

So I followed Cici into the kitchen.

She had her favorite cup—the pineapple cup. I'd gotten a set of three plastic cups at a garage sale years earlier that were all shaped like fruit. Dee liked the strawberry, Elle the apple. Cici filled her pineapple cup with the water from the Brita filter, which I'd purchased right after the plumber left.

"Cici."

She didn't look up. She wouldn't make eye contact. She was seven years old but acted seventeen. Or seventy, depending on the day. So much personality. So self-assured.

"Cici . . ."

"Why would you do that?" she asked.

I poured myself some water and sat on the floor. She sat down across from me, and I wanted to pull her to me,

I didn't have water, I had wine. Wouldn't you want a drink after seeing what I'd seen?

hug her, squeeze her, never let her go. But I was afraid to touch her. She was too precious, and I was falling apart.

"I thought I saw something inside the fort. It scared me," I told her. I'd always been honest with my daughters. I respected them too much to lie or sugarcoat.

"Oh," Cici said, nodding. Her demeanor changed. She wasn't angry with me anymore. I was forgiven.

"You said . . ." I hesitated. I worried about bringing her into my fear of the house. It was important to me that my daughters wanted to be there. To be with me. If they didn't, if they decided they would rather be at their father's, I could lose them.

"You said there was something in your closet."

"Yeah," she said, sighing and rolling her eyes. Annoyed.

"Why did you say that?"

"Because there is," she said. "I don't know what it is."

"How do you know it's there?"

"I hear it."

"What does it sound like?"

You asked for a dollar before you told me. I was impressed by your savviness, that you knew how to barter. That you knew your own value. I gave you one.

She shrugged, and it occurred to me that maybe she was hearing normal house sounds, nothing out of the ordinary. The pipes. Her sisters moving upstairs, the floorboards creaking. Maybe there was nothing wrong with the house, I just wanted to believe there was, instead of accepting that something might be wrong with me. Cici finished her water, put her cup in the dishwasher, yawned, and gave me a hug.

"Good night," she said, and went downstairs.

I stayed in the kitchen. I finished my water and made the girls their lunches for school the next day. I stuffed the cardboard from the ruined fort into the recycling bin in the garage, tossed the sheets and blankets into the washing machine.

After, on the way to my bedroom, I passed by Cici's, and I heard her. Awake. Whispering.

I pressed my ear to the door, but I couldn't distinguish any words. I couldn't hear what she was saying. I assumed—I hoped—she was just talking in her sleep.

The next morning, I drove the girls to school. I dropped Elle and Dee off first. When it was only me and Cici in the car, I asked her.

"I heard you talking last night," I said, turning down the radio. "Who were you talking to?"

"Hey!" she said, kicking the back of my seat. "I like this song!"

"Cici."

She huffed and crossed her arms. "I wasn't talking."

"I heard you," I said.

She stayed quiet.

"Okay," I said. "Never mind."

A moment passed, and I turned the radio up again.

Then she said softly, so softly I almost didn't hear, "It thinks you're funny and wants to be my friend."

"What?"

"Nothing."

I pressed her, but she wouldn't repeat it. She claimed she never said anything.

THE pineapple cup. The fort. I drank out of that cup. I played in that fort.

But the fort's supposedly traumatic destruction? Bartering for a dollar over demon info? *It thinks you're funny and wants to be my friend*? No recollection. Mom must have made all that up for the book. I almost text Daffy but think better of it.

Which leaves me to sit with myself. Which leaves me alone with a bad question.

If we don't remember something, how can we be sure it never happened?

12

"EDGEWOOD Drive, huh," says Danny, my Uber driver, and suddenly I regret not asking Dad to pick me up from the station and take me to the house.

After reading Mom's book and her frankly quite compelling footnote allegation, I found it difficult to hold my tongue around my father, to pretend like the seed of doubt hadn't been planted in my mind.

It made perfect sense why he hadn't wanted us to read the book. When I looked at him now, his halo was askew.

"What's with you?" Daphne had asked me when she dropped me off at the train on her way back to Hudson. "You've been acting weird since yesterday."

"I don't know what you mean," I'd said, going through her glove compartment, where I discovered a bag of mushrooms. "Shrooms? What else am I going to find in here? A flower crown? A tie-dye T-shirt?"

"Stop going through my shit," she'd said, slamming her glove compartment shut. "Is it the house? Because I told you. Leda and I don't care if you don't want to do it anymore."

"I'm still going to work on the house."

"Okay. Is it Alexandra? Are you all right to go back to the city? I'm sure you could stay with Dad. Or you can come up and crash on my couch."

Sometimes, I loved my sister so much I felt like I might explode.

"Thanks, Daffy." I kissed my fingers and touched her cheek. "Do you think Dad cheated on Mom with Amy?"

Daphne almost ran through a stop sign. "Dude! Why are you asking me this? Did Aunt Helen bring it up at the fucking funeral?"

"Yes," I'd said, because I wasn't ready to cop to reading the book. My sisters would see it as a betrayal, and it'd become a whole thing. I didn't have the energy to puppy-eye my way out of the doghouse.

"Yeah," she'd said. She didn't seem surprised. "Figures."

I sat up in the passenger seat. "I know this tea isn't, like, piping hot, but it's still tea."

"It's bullshit, is what it is. Dad and Amy only got together after he and Alexandra split. After he started taking us to dance."

"They never met before then?" I'd asked as we pulled into the station.

"Maybe once or twice." She paused. Shrugged. "For, like, a minute when he picked us up. Do you have any memory of Dad chatting up Amy after class? Because I don't. Not until well after he'd moved out and we were getting carted back and forth. It's just something Alexandra wanted to believe. Nothing was ever her fault."

"Yeah," I'd said, unbuckling my seat belt as I heard the train whistle in the distance. We hugged goodbye, and I wanted to leave my suspicion in the car with her, but it followed me to the train, back to the city. Tenacious. Parasitic.

It has me avoiding Dad. Other than having coordinated with him to install the smart lock and deal with the visit from the exterminator at Edgewood last week. And the electrician.

"I'm done after this," he'd said. "You can take it from here."

"Promise," I'd said.

So I hadn't even told him that I was planning on being here this weekend. Which is how I ended up in this Uber with Danny, who is desperate to talk to me.

"Number six Edgewood, yeah?" he says. We make eye contact in the rearview.

"Sir, yes, sir," I say, smiling.

"You know it's haunted, right?"

"I've heard. It's also got mice. And the worst carpets you've ever seen. A real house of horrors."

"Ah," he says, returning his eyes to the road. "It's your house?"

Sometimes men are so dumb I envy them. Why would I confirm that information for a stranger? Might as well give him the code to the door and tell him I'll be alone all weekend while I'm at it.

I don't respond, and he doesn't say anything else for the rest of the ride. When we get to the house, he pulls into the driveway, but barely.

"Hate to disappoint you," I say. "But the house isn't haunted. Can you pull up, please? I have a lot of stuff to carry in."

"Oh, right. Sorry," he says, his voice dropping an octave. "No, I don't believe in any of that."

"Of course you don't," I say, flashing him another smile in the rearview as my fingers find the door handle. "Me either."

The code to the house is a mix of our birthdays. Leda's, Daphne's, and mine. The lock whirs and turns on its own. I carry in my bags and the boxes of stuff on the stoop, things I ordered and had sent directly.

It's obvious from the smell of bleach that Dad cleaned.

I text him **Thank you**, and a second later he's calling me.

"You're at the house?" he asks. "I would have taken you."

"You said you were done helping," I say, looking up at the ceiling fan.

"I would have happily picked you up from the train and dropped you off," he says.

"My hero!"

He goes on to report—in exquisite detail—what the exterminator and the electrician had to say. He's already told me this once, but I wasn't paying attention the last time, so I welcome the reiteration.

Essentially, there was no evidence of an infestation in the house, but there were droppings in the garage, where there are now glue traps that I need to check, that I absolutely do not want to check.

The electrician did find some issues, but he fixed them, and it cost, in Dad's words, "not an insignificant amount of money." Which could be any amount. He doesn't specify, and when I ask, he says, "We'll sit down with a spreadsheet."

There are few things on this earth that interest me less than Microsoft Excel.

"I'd get someone to look at the deck and those front stairs," Dad says.

"Who?" I ask. "Who's someone?"

"I'll get you some names," he says. "How long are you staying there?"

"I don't know. I'm taking some before photos and video today. Then maybe tomorrow I'll go get some paint samples."

"Do you need me to take you?"

All this angst for the past two weeks wondering if he cheated, but even if that were true, what would it change, really? Why inconvenience myself over it?

"Yes, please," I say.

"Did you notice the door?"

"What about it?"

"It's a different door."

I turn around and look. It is. It's white, generic. There's a window in the center, a flower etched into the glass. It's not my favorite. I'll probably end up replacing it again. Partner with a brand to shill some cute but overpriced babydoll dresses to cover the cost. How much are doors, anyway?

"The frame was damaged. Uneven," he says. "If it wasn't locked, it'd swing open."

"Really?"

"It was a lot of work, Clio. Big project. Luckily, Pete was around. He's handy."

"Who's Pete?"

"Pete. My friend Pete. You know Pete."

"Oh, yeah. *Pete*." I'm sure I've met him but doubt I could pick him out of a lineup.

"You should thank him next time you see him. He'll be at the barbecue on Memorial Day."

"Okey dokey, smokey."

"All right, all right. Pick you up tomorrow? One o'clock?"

I trace the flower in the glass with my fingers. A feeling washes over me. It's brief but unambiguous. There's someone behind me, standing over my shoulder. It happens to me all the time. At bars. On the subway. Some stranger hovering closer and closer, their looming presence prodding through whatever narrow space is left between us. Wanting to be near me, to touch me. For me to acknowledge them, which I rarely do.

"Clio?" Dad asks.

"Yeah," I say, spinning around. There's no one here. "Thanks, Dad. Sounds like a plan."

I spend the afternoon taking photos and video of the house. The "before" state. I sketch out design ideas with my freshly sharpened colored pencil set. I blast music from my new portable speaker. I cruise Pinterest.

The ceiling fan only spins when I turn it on. It stops when I turn it off. The new front door remains shut and locked. I don't encounter another mouse, though I'm still on edge.

I find dead flies on the kitchen counter, on the windowsills—icky but not mouse-level icky. I use paper towels to pick them up and drop them into a giant black trash bag. I didn't realize when I ordered the bags how big they were. Good for contractors, serial killers, and apparently, moi.

I find the fridge empty except for a box of baking soda. I find a bottle of vodka in the freezer.

I don't find the back half of the book. It's not in my room. It didn't fall behind the nightstand or under the bed like I'd assumed. It's not in Mom's room. It's not anywhere. I decide I don't care. I don't want to finish it. The whole thing is derivative, and I resent being cast as the creepy little girl.

Reading it hasn't invoked a grand swell of memories, but some things have come back to me, and I do think I have a vague memory of Mom asking me about my closet. I probably realized validating her got me attention, my one true love. I buy that over me whispering to myself and claiming there was an entity in my closet unprompted, over seven-year-old me originating the idea of the demon.

I don't trust her version. How could I? And my own might be so faded that it's basically useless, but I do trust myself. I know myself. I don't know my mother. I never will.

PLAY NICE

I order takeout, enjoy watching the delivery kid squirm on the doorstep. I eat eggplant parmesan at the dining table while watching DIY home renovation videos on YouTube.

The sun goes down, and I anticipate the darkness turning the house into somewhere I don't want to be. But it's fine.

I get the bottle of vodka out of the freezer and set myself up on the couch under a thick blanket, another new purchase. I balance a sketchpad on my lap and experiment with color palettes, periodically reaching over to the coffee table for different colored pencils and for the bottle. I take a few swigs and feel like a rebellious teenager, drinking vodka straight. It's disgusting but I love it. The burn of it reminding me how alive I am inside my body, inside this moment. In the present. The past is over, and the future is overrated. *Now* is my favorite.

My eyelids go heavy, and I'm comfortable and content enough to doze off, which feels like a win until I'm awoken by a low, slow creaking.

I sit up, groggy, my throat sore. The sketchpad slides off my lap and flaps like an injured bird down to the floor. The overhead light is on, and it's not particularly bright, but it still takes my sleepy eyes a moment to adjust. My vision is spotty, so the shadow standing in front of the sliding glass doors isn't anything at first. Just another smudge. An inkblot.

Until it isn't.

Until it's something. Some*one*. Someone standing there.

Until it screams.

Until I scream.

It flees through the open sliding glass doors out to the deck, fast footsteps. *Thud thud thud thud.*

I'm up, and I'm wild, and I'm chasing the figure onto the deck. *Thud thud . . . thud-thud-thud-thud.*

There's an awful *crack*, followed by a morbid groaning.

I reach inside and flick the back light on, then look over the banister to see there's an adolescent at the bottom of the deck stairs, splayed out on the yard.

"What the fuck?" I yell.

"I'm sorry," the boy says, his voice breaking. "I'm sorry. I didn't know anyone lived here."

"Are you hurt?" I ask.

A beat. "Yeah."

"Good," I say. "Remember this. This is what breaking and entering feels like."

"Hey! Hey!" I hear. There's a guy running over.

"Hasn't anyone ever heard of private property?" I ask.

"Baker. Baker, are you okay?" This guy is older. Around my age.

The kid, Baker, punches the older guy on the arm. "You asshole! You said the house was empty!"

"It was," he says. "I'm sorry."

"It wasn't," I say. "Clearly."

The guy squints up at me. The light on the back of the house is ruthlessly bright, illuminating the yard out to the perimeter of the woods.

"Shit," he says. "Hey, I'm sorry about this. I'm Austin. I live down the street. This is my nephew. I, um . . ."

He pauses to laugh.

"I dared him to break into the house."

He takes a step to the side, and I get a better view of him. Curly brown hair. Pretty face. Tall.

"That so," I say, tilting my head so my own curls fall forward. I give him a grin.

13

TURNS out Dad left a first aid kit in the upstairs bathroom, with a note on top reminding me to be careful, to be safe. I bring it outside, down to where Baker sits in the yard.

"It's not broken," Austin says, checking Baker's ankle. "Just sprained."

"Here," I say, handing over an antiseptic wipe and a Band-Aid for the scrape across the boy's forehead.

He's a sweet-looking kid. Big eyes, mouth full of braces. On the verge of puberty, poor thing.

"Thanks," Austin says, his gaze lingering. I return his stare, give him the up-and-down. He's dressed in gray sweatpants and a black tank. He has a delicate gold chain around his neck. The uniform of a douchebag. His saving grace are his Vans. If he had on Nikes, it'd be game over.

Also promising—his sweatpants look like they could be from Costco. They're not designer sweatpants. There's a direct correlation between men who wear designer sweatpants and men who can't make me come. I've done the unfortunate research.

He has muscles, but they're not gym muscles. He's not wearing the tank top to show off his shoulders and his biceps. He's not trying too hard. All the guys in the city are trying too hard, especially the ones who pretend like they aren't.

"Don't thank me yet," I say. "I'm suing."

Baker's already big eyes go huge.

"Relax, baby. I'm joking," I say, sitting on the deck stairs.

"Actually, *we're* suing," Austin says. He gestures to Baker. "Look at this."

"A tragic accident," I say.

"Did you fall, or did she push you?" Austin asks Baker. "Be honest. You're under oath."

"I . . . I fell," Baker says.

"Hmm. You're off the hook, miss. For now," Austin says. He unwraps the antiseptic towelette and brings it to Baker's scrape. "When did you move in?"

"I didn't," I say.

Baker winces. "There's no car out front."

"I don't have a car. I'm a city girl," I say. "I'm not here full-time. I'm just fixing it up. It was my mom's house."

"Oh shit," Austin says, standing up straight. "I knew you looked familiar. Daphne?"

The shock of hearing my sister's name knocks me back. I bang my elbows against the stairs.

"No. Clio?" he asks. "Not Leda."

"How . . . ?"

"Like I said, I live down the street. I grew up here. We hung out a few times, as kids."

"Did we?" I think back. Toward the end of our short tenure in the house, my sisters and I were so desperate to get out, we did end up making friends with some of the neighbor kids. There were games of capture the flag, freeze tag. The rest of the kids all knew each other better because they went to school together, rode the same bus, but not us. The Barnes girls went to private school. I'm sure it added to our mystique.

Austin presses the Band-Aid to Baker's head.

"Ow!" Baker says.

"My brother Jackson helped your mom move in," Austin says.

Mom wrote about him. The scared teenager who denied saying that he hated the house.

"Did he think the house was haunted?" I ask, swatting at a mosquito. "Your brother."

Austin crumples up the Band-Aid wrapper and puts it in his pocket. "Don't think so. No one thought that until after the book came out."

"Interesting," I say. "But you think the house is haunted? That's why you sent your nephew to break in? On a dare?"

He hangs a hand on the back of his neck. His cheeks go red. "What can I say? I'm a bad babysitter."

I look at Baker. "I think you're the bad babysitter."

"Ha. Yeah. Maybe. Yeah," he says.

"You don't remember me?" Austin asks.

"Sorry. You must not have made much of an impression."

He laughs. "I was shy. You and your sisters were intimidating."

"Still are."

"Clio, right?"

"That's me," I say, reaching out and offering him my hand to shake. He takes it. His hand is warm, his skin soft. "Next time you want to come over, knock."

"Next time, huh?"

"I'm going inside now," I say, standing up and collecting the first aid kit. "Good night, Baker. Good night, Austin."

"Sorry again," Baker says. Austin helps him to his feet.

"Me, too, kid. A rocky start to your life of crime," I say, climbing the stairs up to the deck. I step inside and close the sliding doors behind me, lock them.

I flop back onto the couch and pull the blanket up to my chest. I text my sisters on our group thread.

Do you remember a neighbor kid named Austin?

Neither responds. Not surprising: it's late. Daphne must still be working, and Leda must be asleep—she and Tommy probably share a nightcap of MiraLAX and pass out by nine thirty.

I turn onto my side. My sketchpad is on the coffee table next to the bottle of vodka.

Something nags at me, but I can't figure out what.

I sit up and look over at the sliding doors. I left the back light on.

I get up to turn it off, then go to the bathroom to brush my teeth and do my p.m. skincare routine.

Earlier in the day, I'd made up one of the twin mattresses in Daphne and Leda's room for me to sleep on. I don't want to sleep in my room because the combination of boot prints on the carpet leading in and the rumpled sheets imply the disturbing possibility that Mom might have died in my bed—something I still don't care to confirm—and that's where I saw the mouse, so just overall it's not ideal. I also don't want to sleep in Mom's room because it's too weird. She probably had sex with demonologist Roy in that bed. Daphne and Leda's room is really the only option other than the couch, which isn't particularly comfy.

I retrieve my new favorite blanket from the couch for extra warmth, drape it over my shoulders, and waltz down the hall. It feels wrong to be in Leda and Daffy's room without them. Like I'm breaking a sacred law. Like at any moment they'll burst in and scream at me to get out.

It makes it difficult to relax into sleep. And it's way too quiet. Even quieter than at Dad's. The crickets around here must be bashful.

Half an hour passes before I give in and get up, trek back to the living room for my portable speaker. I bring it into my sisters' room, connect to Bluetooth, and pull up "City Sounds Ambience for Sleep" on YouTube. I shimmy under the covers as the generic city sounds stretch to touch the walls, fill the space. I close my eyes and wait for sleep.

I'm almost there when I notice it.

Among the chorus of traffic and faraway conversations, there's a distinct voice. It comes and it goes, like it's part of the loop, but it doesn't totally match the rest of the track. It's a whispering that's somehow loud enough to hear over the car horns. Always the same, saying the same thing.

Hello hello.

It's so good to see you again.

Hello hello.

It's so good to see you again.

It's unnerving at first, but eventually the repetition becomes hypnotic. Lulling me to sleep.

Hello hello.

It's so good to see you again.

Hello hello.

It's so good to see you again.

Hello hello.

Hello hello.

"Hello."

The entrance to the attic was in Cici's closet. A small rectangular opening covered by a plank of painted wood. You needed a ladder to get up there, and I didn't have a ladder.

One rainy Saturday, when the girls were at their father's house, I dragged a dining chair downstairs to Cici's room, stacked some books on top of it, and climbed up to the attic.

The attic was essentially a crawl space over the garage. Not enough room for me to stand up, not even hunched over. There was old insulation, white like snow. Cobwebs hung from the rafters. It was cold, so much colder than the rest of the house. There was no explanation, no reason for it, because even outside, it was warm and pleasant—mid-May. But in the attic, it was winter. Desolate and freezing.

I could tolerate being up there for only a few minutes at most. I shuddered and lowered myself through the opening. My feet found the stack of books. They came out from under me, and I fell.

My head hit the wall and my knee smashed against the doorframe.

I lay there in shock. I reached up to my head and my hand came away bloody.

That's when I knew with certainty. Crystal clarity.

When your father dropped you off the next day, I was incoherent, still bleeding. He assumed I had fallen because I was drunk. He called his lawyers as soon as he left. The truth is I had been drinking. I needed the liquid courage to look up in the attic, to confront what I suspected was there. But that's not why I fell. And I had only done it to keep you girls safe. That was my reason for everything.

PLAY NICE

That's where it lives.
It lives up there.
There's something living in my house.

Then I heard it again, like I did that first night. It's awful, evil laughter.

But it wasn't trying to hide this time. It made no attempt to conceal itself, to sneak. It was glad that I knew. It wanted me to know it was there.

Because it understood something, something that I did not.

No one would believe me.

14

I WAKE up facing the opposite direction in bed. My head is where my feet were, my feet are where my head was. The blankets are piled up on the floor.

This has never happened to me before. It's disorienting. Unpleasant.

I rub my forehead. I'm hungover even though I didn't drink that much. I don't think.

"Straight vodka," I say, shaking a loose fist at the sky.

I turn off the city sounds. I forgot to set an alarm, and it's almost eleven a.m. Such meager sunlight comes through these windows. The cursed wedding dress curtains certainly don't help.

New window treatments, a fresh coat of light paint, some strategically placed lamps, mirrors. A crystal chandelier, maybe. The ceilings aren't quite high enough.

I start a list in my Notes app of all the things I want to buy today. I text Dad and ask him if he can come pick me up now and we can get lunch.

He's at the house twenty minutes later, Amy in the passenger seat. The three of us go to our favorite deli for sandwiches, then spend far too much time and money at Home Depot, then to Benjamin Moore because I want bougie paint, then to my favorite antique store in Chester for inspiration. I buy some tin ceiling panels, a few mirrors, a pair of art deco wall sconces, and a beautiful brass banker's desk lamp.

"I would never know what to do with any of this stuff. I'm so amazed by your creativity," Amy says, popping a stick of gum into her mouth. She offers me the pack. "You have *vision*."

"Thank you, Amy. For the gum and the compliment."

I have her take photos of me in the antiques store. She's better at it than Dad.

"What about me?" Dad says as we head out to the car. "Where's my thanks? Sacrificing my Sunday."

"Please. You love this," I say. "Quality time with your favorite daughter."

"I don't have a favorite. You're all my favorite."

"Sure." I wink at him, and he bursts out laughing.

"Subtle," he says, shaking his head. "What am I going to do with you?"

On the drive back, we have a sing-along to some Journey, some Whitesnake.

A half hour later, we pull up to 6 Edgewood.

"You sure you don't want to come over for dinner?" Amy asks.

"I have leftover spaghetti in the fridge," I say. "And the other half of my sandwich from lunch. I'll be fine."

"Okay," Dad says, parking and getting out to open the door for me. He helps me carry my spoils into the house. Amy stays in the car.

"Never took Amy for superstitious," I say to Dad, punching in the code to the front door.

"It's not that. You know she doesn't believe in that crap," he says. "This place caused a lot of pain and suffering. She was the one who put us all back together. Your sisters, especially."

Daphne and Leda confided a lot in Amy. I loved her, but most of the time growing up, she just felt like my dance teacher. One who happened to live in my house and be married to my dad. Maybe because I was a legitimately talented dancer and did it competitively and spent more time with Amy in that capacity than my sisters did.

My relationship with Amy is about as deep as a baby pool. But it's sweet and easy, and I think I prefer it this way.

I pop my gum.

"Don't do that," Dad says. "I hate that."

I do it again.

We carry the rest in, and he says he'll come by tomorrow during his lunch, then he gives me a big hug and leaves.

I paint some swatches on the wall in the living room, but there isn't enough daylight left for me to determine a favorite. I pick at the other half of my deli sandwich and drink a bottle of kombucha while sitting on the couch, editing and posting the antiques store photos.

The knock at the door is so jarring I just sit there after it happens, wondering if it actually happened, until it happens again.

I check my phone to see if Dad called. Maybe he accidentally left something or has something to drop off? But no missed calls. No texts—not from him, anyway.

Phone in hand, I step cautiously down the stairs. I see someone through the glass panel in the door, but the flower obscures them. Is it a delivery? Did I order something and forget? It's a little late for UPS.

I open the door just enough to poke my head through.

"I knocked this time," he says. It's Austin. He's got a six-pack of beer and a tray of cookies.

"You're learning," I say. "How's your nephew?"

"A narc," he says. "Try to be the fun uncle and suddenly you're a bad influence."

"It's a thin line."

"Exactly."

"You want to come in?" I say, stepping back and holding the door open.

He looks past me into the house.

"Unless you're too intimidated," I say.

"I am intimidated," he says, crossing the threshold, bringing his pretty face close to mine. "But not by the house, to be clear."

"Duly noted," I say. "We can go upstairs."

I follow behind him, checking out the view. He wears jeans and a generic black sweatshirt. His Vans.

"The cookies are from my mom. The beer is from me," he says.

"That's sweet," I say.

"She remembers you. And your mom. They had coffee . . . a few times," he says, setting the cookies down on the dining table. He looks around.

"That surprises me. My mom would often lament her status as the outcast divorcée."

"Well, my mom's a widow, so . . ." He crosses to the wall, studying the array of paint colors I swatched.

I don't want to hear about his dead parent any more than he wants to hear about mine. "Did you bring a bottle opener?"

He takes a set of keys out of his pocket and walks back over, opening a beer for me. Then he opens one for himself.

"Cheers, neighbor," he says.

"Cheers," I say. We clink bottles. "So, you live at home with your mom."

He laughs. "You're direct."

"Your powers of observation know no bounds." I grin and take a swig of beer. In theory, drinking a lukewarm Yuengling in the suburbs on a Sunday evening with a mommy's boy isn't exactly my idea of a good time. In practice, it's not so bad. "You want to sit outside? It's a nice night."

We go out through the sliding doors and sit in the two plastic Adirondack chairs on the deck. I immediately go back inside and get my blanket. It's a little chilly for May. But the stars are out, and the moon is full and bright.

"I do live at home with my mom," he says. "Just turned twenty-six, living in my mom's house."

I shrug. "My dad still pays for my cell phone."

He laughs again. He laughs a lot. I like that about him.

"Yeah, well. My mom has MS," he says. "It's hard."

"So you're a good son, not a fuckup?"

"Oh, I'm both," he says.

"I'm neither."

"Not a good son?"

"No," I say. Thinking of my dad this afternoon, I add, "But I am the favorite daughter."

"I could see that," he says. He takes out a joint. "Mind?"

"Go for it."

"Where are your sisters?" he asks, lighting up. "Are they helping you?"

"No. They're too traumatized," I say, taking the joint from him and hitting it. "Not by demons or whatever. By my mom."

"Ah," he says.

Because I can't tell my sisters, or Dad or Amy, and because he's here and I feel like it, I tell him, "I found a copy of her book in the house. She wrote little notes in it, for me."

"Had you read it before?" he asks.

"Nope. My dad didn't want us to. He made us promise. Link pinkies. Cross our hearts."

"Makes sense. He's not exactly the hero of the story."

"You've read it?"

"A copy got passed around my high school."

"I only read the first few chapters. I only *found* the first few chapters. The copy was so old it was falling apart; the glue in the binding was disintegrated or whatever," I say, offering up the joint. He accepts it. "I can't find the rest."

"You could download it, if you're curious."

"Nah. It's not available in digital. And it's out of print. But it's fine. I don't care. Like, I'm not going to go out of my way to track down another copy. It's not a particularly pleasant read. Not exactly a good time."

"Huh. Yeah," he says. "It's fucked-up."

"You're going to have to be more specific, if you're referring to my childhood."

"No, just that, a lot of the second half of the book is about you."

I take another swig of beer. And another. "And here I'd assumed the demon got top billing."

"You're up there," he says. "I don't know how much of it is true. But . . . fucked-up."

The conversation isn't fun anymore, but it's an easy fix.

"Why did you come over here?" I ask him.

He leans forward, elbows on his knees. He turns his head and looks over at me. I want to run my tongue along his jaw. "To do this."

"To sit outside and drink beer and get high under the stars while we talk about sad things? Poor us."

"No. Well, yes. But mostly to look at you. And do this." He reaches over and gently pulls one of my curls straight. "I've wanted to do that since I was a kid."

It's my turn to laugh. I let my head back and giggle like crazy. Then I grab his face and kiss him.

WE stumble inside. He lifts my dress over my head, kicks off his Vans while I unbutton his jeans. They slide down to his ankles, and he trips. We fall back onto the couch.

He's an excellent kisser and knows exactly how to use his hands. What luck to have him show up on my doorstep.

"Can I touch you?" he asks me. He waits until I say yes, until I whisper the word into his ear, then he slips his fingers between my thighs.

He doesn't talk to me, which I appreciate. The next person to ask me, *Yeah, you like that?* is getting a firm no.

He makes me come with just his hands, and I could leave it at that, but I like him enough to go down on him. He weaves his fingers through my hair. He doesn't pull, he's not rough with me, but he's not so gentle to turn me off. He warns me before he finishes.

All in all, a great hookup. No notes.

We get dressed and he opens two more beers for us. We drink them on the couch this time, my legs draped over his lap, his hands skimming my shins, my knees, my thighs. I play with his hair.

"Your hair is curly, too."

"Not curly like yours. Not springy."

"That's true," I say.

"What's in there?" he says, pointing to the sketchbook.

I reach over and pick it up, hand it to him. He flips it open.

"Well, shit. You're talented, too," he says. "Hot and talented."

"They're just sketches."

"Get outta here," he says. "There's shading."

"So?"

He turns the page. "All right. This one's a sketch."

"Can I see that?" I ask, taking the sketchpad from him.

PLAY NICE

I'm staring at something that I clearly drew, only I have no memory of drawing it.

It's just the word "Hello" in bold cursive lettering. It's my go-to scribble.

"What is it?" Austin asks. "What's up?"

"Nothing," I say, closing the sketchpad and setting it down on the coffee table. My palms are suddenly sweaty. I want to put the sketchpad somewhere else, somewhere out of view. In another room. In the trash. Set it on fire.

I don't know why.

"It's late," I say, standing.

Austin nods. He gets up, takes the empty beer bottles to the kitchen.

He comes back and kisses me on the lips. "Good night, Clio Barnes."

"Good night."

He's down the stairs, door open, and I wait for him to turn around and say something. He doesn't, so I do.

"If the lights are on, I'm around."

He turns, smiling. "I'll still knock first."

He closes the door behind him. I lock it from the app on my phone.

I eat two cookies while I check my socials and respond to comments, then get ready for bed.

Instead of city sounds, I put on basic white noise.

When I get into bed, I put the pillow at the bottom, so I'm in the position I was when I woke up this morning, the opposite of how I fell asleep last night. I must have reversed in the night, deciding I was more comfortable this way.

I settle in and pass out instantaneously.

When I wake up the next morning, I'm on the floor.

15

"I STARTED painting," I tell Daphne over elderflower gimlets. She's in the city for a work thing and got us reservations at an insane restaurant on the Upper West Side where we're eating for free because she knows the chef.

"Like, you picked it up again? Oils?" she says, studying the menu like she's going to be tested on it. Her brow is furrowed; she gnaws on her lip.

"The house. I started painting the house. Priming. You have to prime first. I've done Mom's office, the upstairs hall, and the downstairs hall. I've done the cutting in in your old room. Not the kitchen yet, because I think it's going to be a gut job. And I'm doing wallpaper in the bathroom. Look." I get out my phone to show her the wallpaper I picked, but she shakes her head and both hands, dropping the menu.

"I don't want to see," she says.

"You don't want to see wallpaper?"

"I'm sorry, Cli. I'm glad you're enjoying yourself, but I don't want to think about it."

A waiter comes by and saves the day. Daphne chats them up,

and the chef sends over oysters and potato chips with caviar and crème fraîche.

Later, when we're back at my apartment wearing sheet masks and sipping adaptogen soda through straws, Daphne says, "I didn't mean to snap at you earlier."

"What?"

"About the wallpaper," she says, suddenly morose. "I had a dream about the house the other night. A bad one."

I don't know what to say, so I say nothing.

"I haven't had an Edgewood nightmare in forever. I used to have them all the time. I'd wake up Amy and she'd make me hot chocolate. Those fucking gross packets with the freeze-dried mini marshmallows. Woof."

"Why are you telling me this?" I ask, unreasonably annoyed at her harshing my mellow. "How does this affect your ability to view floral wallpaper."

"Because all this shit is coming up again. I was in a good place with everything before Alexandra died. Now you're at that house, and I'm having nightmares about the time she chased you down the stairs with a knife."

A flash. A vision.

A memory, buried deep, now bursting through the dirt like a zombie.

My back to my locked bedroom door, bracing it against Mom's pounding. *I will bleed you out! I will bleed you out!*

My breath hitches. I clear my throat and stand up, peel the sheet mask off my face. I toss it in the kitchen garbage, gently pat the remaining serum into my skin.

"You know I appreciate some dramatic flair, but if you want some woe-is-me hot chocolate, just ask," I say. "I'd make you some.

I'd even go out and get you some real marshmallows. Fresh and gooey."

She narrows her eyes at me. "That's not . . ."

"Not what?"

She seems surprised that I'm being a smidge bitchy while she's trying to be vulnerable and open with me, and I wonder if she knows that she's being manipulative. She's typically pretty self-aware.

"Never mind," she says, getting up. She goes into the bathroom, shutting the door a little too hard behind her.

I make up the couch for her to sleep on while she gets ready for bed. The toilet flushes, the faucet runs. I hear the swish of her toothbrush, the spritz of toner. Resentment. How can something silent be so damn loud?

When she's done in the bathroom, she comes over and sits on the edge of my bed. I get under the covers.

"You love to tell me how you and Leda won't care if I abandon the house. Won't hold it against me if I change my mind. But I'm not the one who changed my mind. Just admit you don't want me there," I say. "Don't plant seeds and pretend you're not. I'm smarter than that."

"Okay. You're right," she says. "I don't want you there. I don't like it. It bothers me. I didn't think it would, but it does."

"You're having nightmares about the place while I'm there getting finger-banged on the couch by the hot neighbor," I say, smiling so big it pushes the tension out of the room.

"Dude. Stop," she says, shuddering. "And how come this shit always happens to you? It's so unfair. Where's my meet-cute?"

"It wasn't a meet-cute," I say. "No meet-cute involves Yuengling and oral."

She clicks her tongue. "Mine would."

"Yours would be in an orchard, on a beautiful fall day, reaching for the same apple."

"Fuck. Yeah, that's true," she says. "All right. Show me the wallpaper."

"Are you sure?" I ask, pulling up the image on my phone.

She crawls over to where I am, puts her head on the pillow next to mine. I show her the picture.

"That's stunning. Damn."

I show her some of the YouTube tutorials I've been watching. She falls asleep as we watch time-lapsed kitchen remodels.

She snores and steals the covers, so I end up on the couch.

I came back to the city earlier this week for work and for some appointments—facial, personal training session, trim and blowout—and to have dinner with Daphne. But ever since I got here, I've been anxious to return to the house. The progress is addicting. And the potential. Looking around at all that raw space. There's just something about being there.

What would Daphne say if I told her about waking up on the floor with the bedding all piled up beside me like a soft cairn? If I told her about the sketch that I don't remember drawing?

Probably blame emotional distress or lack of sleep or alcohol. Probably be right. Definitely tell Dad and Leda. And they would change the locks and put the house on the market.

So I won't tell her, even though it justifies her having concerns about me being there. I won't tell her *because* it justifies her concerns.

I won't tell her because I'm starting to suspect that part of me wants to believe the house is haunted, wants the place to prove to me that it is.

How could I forget the bedroom door incident? How is it

possible I could just block something like that out? Mom locked outside, holding a knife, trying to get in. Screaming.

No.

No, it's not that I want to believe the house is haunted.

It's that part of me wants to believe she wasn't crazy.

The closest church was St. Ann's. Catholic. I'd been raised Greek Orthodox, but our family had never been particularly committed to the church. My ex-husband wasn't religious, and so our girls weren't brought up in faith.

Any belief I'd had in God as a child had waned over the years. If there was a God, he was at best apathetic, at worst cruel. Why would I worship such a being?

But after falling from the attic, I was desperate. I needed help and I would seek it anywhere, from anyone.

I attended mass on a Friday evening while the girls were with their father—he was taking them out to dinner and to the movies because he could afford to do fun things like that with them. They would whine on the weekends they were with me about how bored they were.

Catholic mass was a solemn affair, but I found something soothing about it. A peace I hadn't ever experienced before. I was grateful for that hour, sitting in the mostly empty pews, the divine words echoing through the space.

The church itself was beautiful. Outside, a statue of the Virgin Mary stood surrounded by flowers. The exterior of the church was simple—white and square with a tall steeple. Inside, the walls were painted pale yellow. There were elaborate stained-glass windows all around.

The ceiling was high and curved, and the floors were cherrywood except for the green runner down the aisle. There were statues on either side of the altar, the Virgin Mary again—one with her holding Jesus as an infant, the other her holding him after he died. Beyond the pulpit, Jesus was alone on his cross.

After mass, I lingered, waiting for an opportunity to speak to the priest, Father John. He was an older man with gray hair and a soft face. Kind eyes.

"Hello, Father," I said.

"Hello," he said, extending a hand. "I don't believe we've met. Welcome."

"I recently moved to the area with my three daughters," I said. When I slipped my hand in his, a shadow passed across his face. His hand was warm; mine was freezing. He held on to it. He didn't let me go. He could sense something was wrong, and I think he wanted me to know that I could confide in him. "It's been a rough start. I . . . I was wondering if you could come and bless our house."

"Of course," he said. "I would be glad to."

I gave him the address, and we settled on the following Wednesday at one o'clock. I told my boss I had a doctor's appointment, an excuse to leave work early.

I couldn't have Father John at the house while my girls were there. They would tell their father, who would ask me why I had a priest at the house. I wouldn't have a good answer, a good lie, and the truth wasn't an option. If my ex-husband knew that I suspected there was a presence in the house, he would take it as further proof that I was crazy. It infuriated me how he would revel in my agony. How he would wield my vulnerabilities as weapons against me. Any opportunity he had to exploit my very human weaknesses, he would take.

I hung my hopes on Father John's visit. Whatever evil was in the house, I thought he could cast out. It was *something*.

I went to sleep on Tuesday cautiously optimistic.

I woke up on Wednesday to a sick daughter in my bed.

"My stomach hurts," Cici said, and proceeded to vomit all over my sheets.

She was too sick to go to school. I had to call out of work, my boss suspicious since I'd already taken a half day.

I stripped my bed and did a load of laundry, set up Cici on the couch with ginger ale and plain toast. She watched cartoons and colored. I was grateful that whatever she had didn't seem to affect her sisters, who were their usual surly preteen selves.

Though all my daughters were daddy's girls, Cici was still my baby. She liked to follow me around, sit in the tub while I did my hair and makeup in the morning, pick out my clothes with me. There was a chance I could get Cici to keep Father John's visit a secret, but I realized it would likely involve bribery. Cici was clever enough to know when she held the cards.

"I'm having a visitor come by this afternoon," I told her after I'd dropped the older girls at school.

"A boyfriend?" she asked, perking up.

> I'd read and loved Jane Eyre as a teenager. As a grown woman, my perspective on the novel changed. I was Bertha Mason. Rochester was not a romantic hero; he was a criminal asshole.

"No," I said. "His name is Father John. He's a priest."

She scrunched up her face like she'd just caught a whiff of something rotten. "Why's a priest coming over?"

"He's going to bless the house," I said. "Make it nice for us to live here."

She blew a raspberry. "I don't know about that."

"What don't you know about?"

She turned back to her drawing—the sky at sunset. She didn't give me an answer.

"Can I have more toast?" she asked.

"Feeling better?"

She shrugged.

"How would you like to go hang out in your sisters' room?" I asked her. "We don't have to tell them."

She cracked a mischievous grin.

Father John arrived promptly at one o'clock. I'd made coffee, plugged in the electric kettle in case he wanted tea instead. I'd even bought shortbread cookies from a local bakery.

I opened the door, my palms sweating. "Hello, Father."

He was dressed in all black, save for the white of his clerical collar. He removed his wide-brimmed hat and bowed his head. "Hello, Ms. Barnes. How are you today?"

"Very well, thank you, Father. Please, call me Alex. Come in."

As he stepped over the threshold, he began to cough.

"Are you all right?" I asked, closing the door. "Some water?"

He nodded.

There was a noticeable shift in his demeanor as soon as he set foot in the house.

He followed me up the stairs, and I asked him to have a seat at the dining table. I went into the kitchen to get him a glass of water and the cookies. But when I came out, he was gone.

"Father?"

I set the water and cookies down on the table and repeated his name.

I heard him coughing. Horrible, violent, hacking coughs. I followed the sound toward the stairs, peering down to the landing. The front door was open. It slowly swung itself wide.

Had he left?

"Father?"

The door slammed shut.

"Father!" I ran down the stairs and went to open the front door. The knob was hot to the touch, so hot that my hand came away sizzling, steaming. "Ah!"

"Mom?" I heard. Cici.

"Go back to your room!" I shouted. I pulled my sleeve down over my hand—which was still burning, throbbing—and twisted the knob. It was hot even through the fabric.

Father John sat on the front steps, hat in hands, staring straight ahead.

"Father? What happened?" I asked.

"Please, sit," he said, and so I did. I sat on the step beside him, the wood creaking beneath our weight. "Alex. Why did you ask me here?"

He was white as a ghost and his voice was now hoarse.

"I . . . I'm afraid in the house," I said. "Of the house. I feel . . . unsafe. I don't know how to explain it."

He nodded. He took a handkerchief out of his pocket and wiped the sweat from his brow, then turned it over and dragged it across his tongue, which I thought was strange. "I have a colleague who may be able to help you. He's more experienced with these . . . phenomena."

"What phenomena? What . . . why did you leave? What happened?"

He patted my knee. "I shall put you in touch with him. Father Bernard."

"Father," I said. He wouldn't look at me. "What is it?"

He stood up. "I will pass along your address. He will come by at his earliest convenience."

"Earliest convenience? Why? Why can't you bless the house? What's wrong with it?" He wouldn't answer. He put his hat on and began to walk briskly toward his car, cutting across the lawn. I was at his heels, begging him to stay. "Please, Father. Don't leave. Wait. Tell me. Tell me!"

"I'm sorry," he mumbled before getting into his car and closing the door. I banged my fists on the driver's-side window as he started the engine. I could see myself reflected in the glass, my hair a frizzy mess, my eyes bulging. I looked desperate. Exhausted. Deranged.

"Please!" I said, chasing his car down the driveway.

It had started to rain, and I just stood there dazed and hopeless.

When I finally turned to wander back inside, my clothes were soaked.

I saw it near the foot of the stairs on my way in. Something small and gray and red. A dead mouse. Half a dead mouse. It'd been ripped in two, straight down the middle, its guts spilling out, its little face shriveled. It was wet, covered in mucus. In spit.

It didn't occur to me then that Father John had coughed it up. Why would it?

I went inside and heard Cici softly singing to herself in her room. By dinnertime, she would be cured of whatever ailed her.

I went to the kitchen and drank the coffee I'd made for Father John. My hand was burned from the doorknob. It had already started to blister.

Over the next few days, the blisters ballooned with yellow puss. They were so painful I worried they would erupt. I had to drain them with sterile needles. Then came the disinfectant. It stung and I cried alone on the bathroom floor. As I applied my own bandages, I ached in my loneliness. I didn't miss my ex, who wouldn't have helped me anyway. I missed someone who didn't exist. An empathetic partner who would take care of me, listen, understand, believe.

I needed help. And soon, it would come. But it would come at a cost.

I poured the coffee down the drain and poured vodka into a mug. That's what I drank. I knew I was drinking too much, but everyone copes in their own way. Alcohol was never my problem. It was a response to my problems.

I missed Roy, though I hadn't met him yet. It's difficult to regret everything that happened because it led me to him. My great love. I tried to be honest with you girls about what to expect from men. Had I known Roy back then, maybe I would have been less cynical. Maybe. There are exceptions to every rule.

16

AUSTIN walks up the driveway toward me, where I rinse paint brushes with the hose. There's a utility sink in the garage, but I'm avoiding going in there, afraid there will be dead mice stuck to the glue traps.

"Come to borrow a cup of sugar?" I ask him.

He waits to reply until he's right in front of me.

"Yeah, actually," he says, kissing me on the lips.

"Don't be cute," I tell him. "It's a turn-off."

"Can't make any promises," he says, following me inside. "How you been?"

"Busy," I say. "I was hoping you'd come by."

"Oh yeah?"

"I need someone to hold the ladder."

He laughs. "You're putting me to work?"

"The door is behind you," I say. "Should you choose to use it."

He won't. I'm wearing cutoff jean shorts, tube socks, and a white tank top with a pink bra underneath. I'm covered in paint and sweat. My hair is in space buns. I'm a girl-next-door fantasy.

He helps me prime the living room, and as a thank-you I order us Thai food.

"Do you do this for a living?" he asks, gesturing to the house.

"No," I say.

"Really? You seem like a pro."

"I'm just good at everything."

"I'm gathering that," he says. "What do you do?"

"I'm a stylist," I say. "And a fashion influencer."

I expect him to pull a face, like most people do at the word "influencer." But he doesn't.

"What about you?" I ask him.

"I'm a nurse," he says. "I work at a senior facility."

"Then why did you tell me you were a fuckup?" I've hooked up with NHL and NFL and MLB players, with actors and models, with professors and archaeologists, with New York's leading brain surgeon, but senior care nurse might be the hottest job of all time.

For some reason, I'm now thinking about Mom and Roy. Wondering if she was attracted to him because of his weird job, or if it was just him, if it wouldn't have mattered if he was a gym teacher. I imagine it's probably the former, because if you believe in demons, what hotter job is there than demon expert?

"I was going to be a doctor," Austin says, mouth full of spring roll.

"Close enough," I say. If he wants to tell me what happened, why he's not a doctor, he will. I'm not going to ask.

He laughs. "Glad you think so."

"I love old people. They have the best stories. Give great advice. No filter, no ego," I say. "Very old people and very young people. They're the most fun."

"They're always asking me to get them drugs," he says. "Drugs and chocolate. And butter."

"You're a mule."

"I don't do it," he says. "I'd lose my job."

"Not ever? Not once?" I ask, getting up and taking his hand, leading him over to the couch.

"Plead the Fifth," he says, grabbing me by the waist. He kisses me.

We undress slowly until we're both naked except for my tube socks, which I leave on intentionally. I straddle him on the couch.

"Do you want to?" he asks me, his hands in my hair, his lips on my neck.

"Do you have a condom?"

He tells me he does.

I bite his shoulder. "Presumptuous."

"What can I say? I'm an optimist."

I put the condom on him with my mouth—a trick I learned from one of my dancer friends who went on to be a Wall Street CEO's sugar baby—then I slide on top.

"Fuck," he says, his breath hitching, fingers pressing into my hips.

It lasts longer than I expect it to. It's the best sex I've had in a long time. Might make it into the Hall of Fame.

When it's over, we're both spent. We pass out on the couch.

I wake up in the morning to the sound of the front door closing. I've got a blanket draped over me, still naked save for my socks. There's a page ripped out of my sketchpad. He left me a note on the coffee table.

> *Had to go to work.*
> *Last night was something...*
> *See you again tonight?*

His phone number is scribbled at the bottom.

I yawn and set the paper back on the table. I order some coffee and a breakfast sandwich, scroll on my phone while waiting for them to arrive.

Veronica invites me to brunch with two of her other photogenic friends, Tara and Simone. It's hard to know sometimes if people want to see me only to *see* me. The purpose of the outing is to document the experience. We can enjoy the experience while we're there, but that's not what matters. It's veneer.

I tell her I can't make it, that I'm at the house.

Did you see that guy again? she asks, probably with a twinge of jealousy. I wonder if when she's mad at her boyfriend she daydreams about me.

Who knew if you wanted good dick you had to come to the suburbs? I reply.

OMG!!

There's a knock at the door, and I forget about Veronica. I wrap myself in the blanket and go down to answer. The delivery kid turns a lovely shade of magenta, realizing I'm naked underneath.

I drink my coffee and eat my egg sandwich and then prepare to take a shower. I'm so filthy, but I'm just going to get dirty again. Sweat more.

Caffeine-buzzed and highly motivated, I decide to clean up around the house first before I clean up myself.

I put on yesterday's clothes. I dust. Pick more dead flies off the windowsills. Vacuum.

Finally, I brave the garage.

As soon as I open the door, I smell death.

It's nauseating.

PLAY NICE

I stand there, torn between abandoning ship, running to call Dad, or confronting the poor mice in the glue traps. Which, now that I think about, I only consented to in a moment of weakness. I didn't want the mice in the house, but I never wanted them dead either. I wanted them to move out into a tree stump, where they could dress in aprons and serve each other tea in cute mouse-sized cups.

Racked with guilt about my role in their untimely end, I step deeper into the garage, letting the door shut behind me. I hold my nose, my breath. I flick on the light, a horrible fluorescent that makes it look even more like a crime scene.

I anticipate having to search for the traps, thinking they must have been strategically placed in dark corners, behind a snow shovel, whatever.

They have been strategically placed. They're right in front of me, in a line snaking across the middle of the garage floor.

And they're covered in mouse parts.

Not whole mice. Just parts.

A tail. A claw. A head. A half.

There's no other half. No rest of the body.

Can a mouse survive in pieces?

Are these parts of the same mouse? Or different mice that all suffered the same brutal demise?

It's disgusting. Baffling.

A massacre.

Dead mice in front of me. A dead mouse on the page of a book, in a scene that I dismissed as an Amityville-style embellishment. But now . . .

I step forward on tiptoes, my hands over my mouth and nose to protect me from the death smell.

There's no blood. Wouldn't they leak?

The tail, the claw, the other small and unidentifiable pieces . . . it's possible the mice chewed themselves free. But the head? The half?

WHEN I call Dad, he tells me to calm down and that he'll come over after work.

I take an hour-long shower. I paint. I online-shop. I distract myself. I do not go back in the garage. I do not reread that scene in *Demon of Edgewood Drive*.

We'd find dead mice and chipmunks and squirrels and the occasional baby bunny near the stoop sometimes, courtesy of the neighborhood's stray cats. That's what Mom saw. Nothing that came from the throat of a man of God in some freak supernatural episode.

And what's in the garage now—that's not supernatural either. Just proof of a long-standing infestation. Just weird and gross.

Rationally, in my right, bright, shiny mind, I know this to be true. I know it.

I know it.

I hear Dad's car pull up around five thirty.

"You were supposed to be checking every day," he says as soon as he comes through the door.

"Good to see you, too, Daddy."

"Hi," he says, hugging me and kissing the top of my head. He hands me a grocery bag.

"What's this?"

"Food," he says. He takes off his suit jacket and hangs it on the banister. "All right."

He goes downstairs to the garage, and I take the groceries up to the kitchen.

He bought me kombucha, bananas, bread, peanut butter, jelly, granola bars, frozen burritos, and White Claw. He must think I'm still a college student.

I hear the garage door open, which I hope means he's disposing of the massacre.

The door closes a few minutes later, and then he's up the stairs, hands on his hips.

"They got spooked," he says. "Happens."

"What does that even mean?" I ask, opening a White Claw. "How does a mouse decapitate itself?"

"Trying to wriggle out of the glue," he says. "I can get the exterminator back here. Have you seen any others in the house?"

"No, thank God," I say, crossing myself. Father, Son, Holy, Spirit.

Dad hates it. I've only seen him lose it a handful of times in my life, and one of those times was when he found out about Father Bernard and Mom taking us to mass.

"Okay," he says. "I'll give him a call tomorrow and see what he says."

"Thank you. I appreciate it. Sincerely."

He nods. "Let me see what you've done so far."

I take him down the hall and show him all my expert priming. Then back into the living room.

"It was difficult in those corners. See?" I say, pointing.

"You had some help."

His tone turns me around. He stands near the coffee table, holding up Austin's note.

"Did you want me up on the ladder all by myself?" I ask. Somehow, I failed to notice until just now that the condom wrapper is still on the couch, peeking out of the cushions.

"Is this a boyfriend?" he asks, likely already knowing it isn't, because of the phone number at the bottom of the note. If we were dating, I'd have his number.

It's a point of contention for us that I don't have long-term relationships. Dad wants me to settle down, like Leda. Not because he's aiming to pawn me off—he loves that I need him, rejoices in my need, wouldn't know what to do without it. It's that he wants me to be "normal." To provide him with nice, innocuous photos that he can send to his friends and coworkers of me with a husband, the two of us smiling, looking like we're in a toothpaste commercial that would air on the Fox News Channel. He doesn't care about Daphne getting married, which is telling.

"Is it your business?" I ask, tilting my head to the side, batting my lashes.

"Clio," he says scoldingly.

"How about we just forget it?" I say, taking the note from him and putting it back on the coffee table, letter-side down. "How about you look at what a good job I did in the corners?"

"I should get home to Amy. She's got dinner going."

He makes toward the stairs, clearly upset at being reminded that I am an adult woman with a sex life. He can't get away from me fast enough. His excuse is total nonsense; no one on earth would ever be in a rush for Amy's cooking.

"All right. Bye, Dad."

"Bye, Cli," he says, opening the front door. "I'll let you know what the exterminator says."

"Okay. Thank you! Love you!"

He doesn't say it back.

17

"DAD slut-shamed me," I tell Leda an hour later as I make myself a peanut butter and jelly sandwich.

"What?" she asks, frazzled. I don't know why she called; I just picked up and said the thing I want to talk about. That's why I picked up. If I had nothing to say, I would have ignored her call. She's not fun on the phone.

"I hooked up with the neighbor and he left me a note. Dad found it and got all dad about it."

"What did the note say?" she asks.

"Had fun last night, let's do it again," I say. "Basically that."

"You shouldn't have had it out for him to find. And what was he doing at the house?"

"Pest control."

She sighs. "You said you would handle the house yourself."

"I am," I say.

"You're not. You're involving Dad. How many times has he been over there?"

"Not a lot. There were dead mice in the garage. Stuck in glue traps. Not whole mice either. Parts of them. Wouldn't you ask

Tommy or Dad for help disposing of a mouse head stuck to a glue trap? Head only, Leda. Just a head. No body."

She doesn't say anything. I don't even hear her breathe. I check to make sure we weren't disconnected.

"Leeds?"

Still nothing.

"Leda, are you there?"

"You're reading the book," she says. She's not angry, her tone isn't accusing. That's what makes it so scary.

"What are you talking about?" I ask, going with denial, because how would she know? There's no way. "What do dead mice have to do with the book?"

I, of course, know about the priest coughing up half a mouse in *Demon of Edgewood Drive*. But how would Leda know said incident was featured in the book if she never read it?

"What aren't you telling me?" I ask her.

"Nothing," she says, her voice going high and squeaky. "Nothing. Just . . . we all agreed you would do this on your own. Part of being an adult is cleaning up your own messes."

"Did you call to lecture me or . . . ?" I ask, taking a bite of my PB&J. It tastes like nostalgia. Sweet at first and then whatever. I swallow and wash it down with White Claw.

"I was checking in," she says.

"So, yes," I say. "How's Tommy? Tell him I miss him."

"I will," she says. "Actually, I called to tell you about Holly."

Leda loves to gossip, but being so risk averse, she can do it only with me, someone who doesn't know any of the people she knows in Boston. Apparently, Holly is cheating on her husband with her hot tennis instructor. I don't really know if he's hot, but it makes the story more interesting if I imagine he is.

"He was hiding in the closet. Like in a movie!" Leda says. I picture her sipping white tea on her white couch while Tommy does a crossword puzzle in the other room.

I don't envy her life, but sometimes I envy her contentment in it. What must it be like to get so much out of so little?

"Good for her," I say. "Our time on this earth is but brief. Here for a good time, not a long time."

Leda scoffs. "Please. She's having her cake and eating it, too. She's selfish."

"She's your friend."

"Not a close friend," she mumbles. "Of course you'd take her side."

"As a fellow slut?" I ask.

"That's not what I meant," she says. "You're a deviant for the sake of deviance."

"I am not," I say. "I just don't see anything wrong with being selfish."

Mom's voice, crystal clear and razor-sharp, its arrival as jarring as a blow to the back of the head. A vision of her sitting on the stairs here at Edgewood after Dad just threw his epic fit about Father Bernard. He'd called her selfish. Among other things. Worse things.

I approached her, and she took my face in her hands.

Men are never selfish. They're smart. Women are always selfish. You want to be single? Selfish. You're a wife and mother and do anything other than dote on your husband and children? Selfish. I want you and your sisters to learn to take that word as a compliment. Anyone who says that to you is trying to discourage you from doing what you want. That's how you know you're doing something right.

Did this happen? Did I read it in the book? I close my eyes and try to picture the words on the page, but I can't. All I see is *her*.

Is it a fictional scene that inspired a false memory? Maybe the book has reshaped my recollection, etched details into an amorphous slab of clay. Maybe there are no truths in memory. Maybe, when we look back, we see only what we want to see, what suits us in the present.

"Cli?" Leda asks.

"Yeah?"

She huffs. "You're not listening."

"I am."

"Never mind," she says. "I'm going to go catch up on reading before bed. You're still planning on going to Dad's for Memorial Day, right?"

"Think so," I say. "Unless a better offer comes along."

"You're impossible," she says.

"Love you, with a cherry on top!"

"Love you." She hangs up.

I take my White Claw to the stairs, sit in the same spot as Mom did when she maybe shared her thoughts on selfishness with me. I could revisit that chapter of the book, read it again, but what's the point when I don't know if the book is uncovering authentic memories or creating false ones or contaminating the few I have. Or all of the above.

I close my eyes and take a deep breath in. Exhale. Take another sip of my now flat hard seltzer.

My moment of reflection is rudely interrupted by a noise.

I can't tell where the sound is coming from. I only know that it's there.

It's strange. Almost like a sliding. A dragging. Like something heavy is being pulled across the floor.

I stand up and step down to the landing, attempting to figure out if it's coming from upstairs or downstairs. But now it's gone. Quiet.

I'm on the verge of wondering if I imagined it when there's a *thud*.

Something fell. Something substantial. Upstairs. The ladder?

I run up to find the ladder standing tall in the corner. I look around, but nothing seems out of place. I push through the saloon doors into the kitchen.

The jar of peanut butter is on the floor. It landed upside down.

I pick it up and put it back on the counter.

The countertops are a horrible white laminate, which have yellowed over the years.

The kitchen is in desperate need of a deep clean, but I can't motivate myself since I'm seriously considering gutting it all anyway.

I stare at the ugly countertops. At the jar of peanut butter. How did it fall? Did I leave it right on the edge? I must have.

At least it didn't spatter everywhere.

Like it did in that scene of Mom's book.

Who did this?

Is this supposed to be funny?

"It was probably the thing that lives in my closet," I hear myself say, reaching for the jar and tucking it away in a cabinet. I roll my eyes at the idea of a demonic entity with a love of nut butter.

The more I think about the demon or whatever, the more I entertain the idea of its existence, the more real it will become. If I allow myself to attribute every noise, every odd occurrence, every chill in the house to a boogeyman, I will have a boogeyman.

Two years ago, Veronica went on a meditation retreat and came back saying she had this epiphany that the universe sends her butterflies as signs that she's on the right path. Now she sees butterflies everywhere, all the time. She'll be getting day drunk at a bottomless brunch, see a butterfly, and think, *Wow, the universe is so happy I'm on my fourth Bloody Mary—good for me.* It's a sweet belief, albeit a little self-aggrandizing, but who am I to judge?

It just makes me wonder about belief and delusion. What's the difference there, really?

Maybe delusion is an eagerness to believe. A desperation for it.

Did Mom ever think about any of this? Did she ever ask herself these questions? Not Mom in the book, in her memory, or mine. Mom in life. Back then, in real time.

I'll never know.

I yawn and step out into the hallway.

The dragging noise is back. It transforms quickly into a scraping. An ugly racket. Nails on a chalkboard. Coming from . . . below me? Beneath my feet?

It's like someone's downstairs pulling a rake across the ceiling.

This isn't a matter of belief or delusion. It's happening. It's happening.

The temperature drops. My heart plummets into the pit of my stomach. My knees buckle. I'm dizzy, and nauseated, and . . . and I don't know how to be scared like this. My body doesn't know what to do with this fear. My mind either.

I have no fight-or-flight reflex. I'm a creature who has existed in comfort practically all my life, and the supreme discomfort of listening to this scraping is maddening. My hair is in my fists. My back against the wall.

Are the walls bending? Is the floor tilting? I can't get my footing.

The scraping stops, and the world holds still, and it's brief but it's there.

Laughing.

A split second of it as the lights flicker and then go out.

In the dark, it's quiet again. I reach out as my eyes adjust, stumble forward, totally disoriented.

What I feel is skin. Hot skin at my fingertips.

The lights fizz back on and there's nothing in front of me.

I stay where I am, hoping in vain to steady myself. After a minute I make my way over to the couch on Bambi legs.

I sit and stare straight ahead. I listen.

The silence is somehow more menacing than the strange noises—than the dragging, the scraping. The laughing. This silence isn't calm; it's waiting. There's something coiling inside it, I know. I can feel it. I *believe* it. If I were to close my eyes, I would see it.

Sometimes silence isn't peace; it's war.

I'm afraid to blink.

I keep my eyes wide. I move them everywhere.

My sketchpad is open on the coffee table to the page with the sketch I don't remember making, the word I don't remember writing.

Hello.

I couldn't sleep after Father John's visit. That night, once I'd put the girls to bed, I wandered through the house, room to room. I was manic. I felt silly for inviting him over, foolish for thinking I could get help from any man, even a holy man. Perhaps especially a holy man.

In the eyes of the Catholic Church, all women are sinners. We invented the enterprise, after all. Eve plucked the fruit from the tree.

I poured myself a glass of wine and sat outside on the back deck. I called my sister, Helen.

"I think there's something wrong with the house," I told her. "That or I'm losing my mind."

"What are you talking about? What do you mean?" she asked. I could hear her smoking through the phone, and it made me want a cigarette. Our parents smoked, so we smoked, but I quit when I met my ex-husband, at his insistence. He said it was a nasty habit. I craved one that night as I sat alone on the deck shivering.

"I hear noises."

"Houses make noise. You'll get used to it," she said. "You've been under an incredible amount of stress. Consistent stress for years. You must be exhausted."

"I am. But it's not that. Not just that, anyway," I said. "I swear. I hear it laughing at me. It's mocking me. It moves through the house. It wants me to know it's there, but it doesn't want anyone else to know."

"Lex. Slow down."

"I don't know if it wants to hurt me. It . . . it wants me to hurt myself," I said. I'd spoken a truth I hadn't been fully aware of until the words freed themselves from me, escaped into the night. It was frightening to hear that truth out loud.

"I'm going to talk to my boss tomorrow. I think I should come down there," she said.

"No, Helen. Don't . . . don't listen to me." A moment passed. I heard her light another cigarette. I took another slow sip of wine. "I had a priest come to the house."

"Come again?"

I did speak to Helen on the phone that night, but I don't remember the specifics of our conversation. I made this part up. She already knew that I suspected the house was haunted. She already knew about Father John. I spoke to her almost every day, as I'm sure you speak to your sisters. I could tell she did not believe me, and I felt some resentment toward her. She thought I was crazy, but she was at least sympathetic. I did have a few friends at that time. Rebecca was one of them, the closest one. I lied about her not picking up my calls. While my other friends shunned me after the divorce, Rebecca was unbothered and unthreatened. But I feared if I told her about the hauntings, she'd cut me off. Then I'd really have no one. The neighbors were friendly, but they all liked to embroider and bake cookies. They sold Mary Kay and had Tupperware parties. I didn't fit in. I didn't want to. It depressed the hell out of me. I didn't think the average reader would understand, but I think you will. I don't know. Maybe I hope you don't.

PLAY NICE

"He left. He didn't stay a minute. Not a minute."

"What about Rebecca? Have you seen her at all lately? Have you met any of the neighbors? Anyone friendly?"

"I lost everyone in the divorce!" I snapped. "You know that."

"You said Rebecca—"

"She won't return my calls. I'm alone, Helen. I'm alone, and it's glad."

"You keep saying 'it.' What's 'it'?"

"I'm not sure. The priest said he was sending someone else, but I don't think he meant it. I feel . . . I feel hopeless." I broke down in tears.

She offered again to come down, but I told her not to bother. I didn't want to get her involved in whatever was happening inside the house.

There was a beep, indicating a call on the other line.

"Helen, I have to go." I promised to call her in the morning, told her I loved and appreciated her, and then switched lines. "Hello?"

"Ms. Alexandra Barnes? This is Father Bernard. I have reason to believe you and your daughters may be in grave danger."

> I doubt I said I loved her. I do love and appreciate Helen, but we rarely said such things to each other. It wasn't how we were raised. Your father was always telling you he loved you, and you girls always said it back, said it to each other. I was never good at that. So much of my life I've felt like I'm pressing my nose to the window, watching everyone else be happy beyond the glass.

> He didn't say that. He didn't call. He showed up at our door the next morning with a Bible, a crucifix, and an attitude I didn't care for. But I needed something punchy to end the chapter, instead of me crying into my wine on the deck.

18

WHEN I dream, I hear my mother's voice. That's how I know I'm dreaming, because even asleep I know she's dead.

Father Bernard arrived the next morning before I could get the girls to school.

Elle, Dee, and Cici were at the kitchen table eating oatmeal when the doorbell rang. They perked up, curious.

"This is my visitor and my personal business," I told them. "No one likes a busybody."

"What's a busybody?" Elle asked me.

I suspect she's the one who told your father.

"A gossip."

I went down and answered the door.

Father Bernard was an old man, well into his seventies. He was completely bald but had long, dark, bristly eyebrows, like black widows glued to his face. Like Father John, he was dressed in all black, except for the white of his clerical collar. Unlike Father John, he came without a hat. And without manners.

"Good morning, Father," I said.

He grunted. "Ms. Barnes."

"Alexandra. Please, come in," I said.

Our call the night before was short. He didn't provide details other than he'd spoken to Father John about the house and that he would come by in the morning.

He crossed himself before coming inside.

He winced the second he stepped into the foyer. Then he sniffed the air. Two exaggerated inhales, crinkling his nose.

It was incredibly, unabashedly rude.

"Sulfur. Excrement."

"Excuse me?"

He shook his head. "I'm not welcome here. The presence is making it known. Trying to repel me. It's powerful."

I was shocked to receive such immediate validation.

"'The presence'?" I asked.

He ignored me, waving a hand as if I were a gnat. He looked past me, down the stairs, then up the stairs, then down the stairs, as if debating which way to go. A sort of purgatory there on the landing.

He clutched a Bible to his chest and started upstairs.

"My girls," I whispered, following at his heels. "They don't know."

"Very well," he said.

When we reached the top of the stairs, we found the

girls gathered around the dining table. They'd moved their chairs closer together and were glowering at us like a little pack of wolves.

"Hello there," Father Bernard said, his tone artificially cheery. I was grateful he wasn't as brash with the girls as he was with me but knew they would be able to see right through him. I'd taught them to be skeptical of strangers, done what I could to nurture their intuition.

Sure enough, they narrowed their eyes at him.

Cici, in particular, was never afraid of being perceived as ill-mannered. "Who are you?"

"I'm Father Bernard," he said. "I'm here for a quick visit, to see your new house."

Cici made a face. "Like that other guy?"

"Father John, yes. He's a friend of mine."

"He had a pretty bad time," she said, and returned to her breakfast.

Elle and Dee said nothing. They exchanged looks and then got up and went to their room.

Cici stayed at the table, occasionally poking at her oatmeal while doodling on a notepad.

"It's better if I explore the house alone," Father Bernard said. "Without your influence."

"'Influence'?" I asked.

> So often we're trained to ignore our intuition. That it's impolite or irrational to be anything but sweet and nice, arms open, ankles crossed. I was scolded by my parents, by teachers, by friends, by ex-lovers, by your father. I was told so many times that my intuition was wrong when it was right that I didn't know how to trust myself anymore. Men love a beautiful fool. Weak men, rather. I didn't want you girls to suffer the way I did.

He waved me off again and started to wander around, muttering prayers to himself.

I sat beside Cici at the dining table with my coffee, now gone cold.

Father Bernard moved through the house. He was slow, methodical. With his Bible and his prayers and a vial of holy water.

Cici drew. I finished my cold coffee.

Elle emerged from her room. "We're going to be late to school."

"You can be late," I told her. What could I do?

She huffed, clenching her jaw, her fists, and stormed back into her room, slamming the door.

I looked over at Cici. She was drawing a picture of the house.

"That's very good," I told her, because it was. Not just good for a seven-year-old. She was a prodigy. A very talented artist.

"Thanks," she said. "I know."

There was a crash downstairs.

I gasped, but Cici was unfazed. She raised her eyebrows, shrugged.

"Father Bernard?" I called as I got up and went over to the stairs.

He was coming up to the landing, patting his head with a handkerchief.

"Alexandra, I need to speak with you," he said sternly. "Outside. Now, please."

"I'll be right back," I told Cici.

"Ooooh, you're in trouble," she singsonged, grinning at me.

I met Father Bernard outside. He paced on the front pathway. It was a hot, sticky day. Impossibly humid. He was drenched in sweat.

"I have known Father John for a long, long time. We were altar boys together, before you were even a twinkle in your father's eye. When I received the call from him, I knew the matter at hand must be urgent. You see, all priests are aware of and educated on the subject of occult phenomena, but only some are specialists in dealing with such matters. I am one of such specialists, which is why John reached out to me. He relayed his concern of a possible infestation. Diabolical interference."

An awful expression in general, but especially from the mouth of a priest, and this priest in particular.

"I'm sorry. What does that mean?"

He looked at me with a solemn expression and said, "I am sorry to inform you. I believe there is an entity living in your house. And I believe it may be demonic."

I never could have anticipated what would come next

It was the single most terrifying moment of my life up until that point. It was also the most liberating.

Here was someone who was substantiating my fear, confirming what I had known all along.

There was evil lurking inside my home.

"What do I do?" I asked him, practically on my knees, pleading.

"It is very rare, though not impossible, for such an entity to inhabit a home. Possession of places and things are often means to an end for such entities. It is their ultimate desire to possess the flesh. A body. A mind. A person.

That is why I believe you and your daughters may be at risk. But for my own integrity, I will need to be sure before I perform the rites of exorcism on your home. It is my recommendation that we have an outside investigative research team confirm that this is in fact a demon we are dealing with and not, say, a ghost or poltergeist. I have some names. In the meantime, I suggest you take some precautions."

"Like what?"

"Do not underestimate the power of prayer. The power of God. Are your daughters baptized?"

I remember Father Bernard in the abstract. I see him, a man dressed in black, but where there should be a face, there's nothing. An indistinguishable smear of features. My mother's description of him wasn't enough to resurrect his image, what he looked like.

I see my sisters in their school uniforms. I see the kitchen table, the paper in front of me, a box of colored pencils, a sharpener, neat spirals of pencil shavings, my drawing of the house not yet complete.

I see my mother. See her, hear her. But I can't touch her, and she can't touch me, can't hear me, see me. She looks past me. Beyond me.

Behind me.

I wake up on the couch to the sun streaming through the windows. I don't remember falling asleep. There are four cans of White Claw on the coffee table. My sketchpad is open, with a new doodle.

The words "Leave Me Alone" floating in space, with stars and planets all around.

I do remember drawing this.

I check my phone. It's past noon. I have two contractors coming today to look at the kitchen and the bathrooms, to give me a quote for those and the floors. The first will be here in forty minutes. I wanted to get up early and start priming downstairs. I wanted to do yoga. Shower. Have coffee. Post photos I took in Brooklyn last week. Now my content posting schedule is off. Now I'm tragically uncaffeinated.

I gather up the cans of White Claw and put them in the recycling bin under the kitchen sink. I change into a long Oxford shirt that I wear as a dress and slip on a pair of loafers, make myself presentable for company.

I brush my teeth, rinse with Listerine. I can still taste the fear in my mouth, even after my valiant attempts to wash it out.

There are mice. They're living in the walls. That's what I heard. The scraping. There's a lingering electrical issue. The flickering lights. There's me, more worn than I maybe realize. All this back and forth. Brooklyn. Penn Station. New Jersey. Leda. Daphne. Dad. Amy. Mom. Past. Present.

Or maybe it is the demon that my mother was so convinced lived here with us, who wasn't exorcised after all. The ultimate freeloader. The unwelcome guest.

The part of me that wanted my mother vindicated had been much bigger and braver back in New York. Had been much bigger and braver before last night.

The first contractor is fifteen minutes late and calls me "hon," which isn't my favorite, but I play into it and get a better quote than the second contractor, who is the consummate professional and calls me "Ms.," which apparently comes at a cost of seven thousand dollars.

The first is condescending when I ask questions like "What if I did the demo myself?" and "Would it be possible to take out this wall?"

The second sighs and puts his hands on his hips a lot as he looks around.

I was always going to pick the one who charged me more—I trust a bargain only in a thrift shop. It's just so satisfying that I get to reject the one who clearly thinks I'm incapable.

To be fair, I *am* incapable. Painting is one thing, but I've come to realize there's no way I can replace a countertop or put in hardwood floors by my lonesome. Those Instagram Reels are deceiving, but there's no deceiving a deceiver.

If I'm doing this, I want to do it right. Hiring a professional will pretty much decimate my savings, but I consulted with a few Realtors who assured me it'll be well worth it. No risk, no reward. The satisfaction of leaving this place unrecognizable will be so sweet, the scent of it wafting toward me like a pie left to cool on a windowsill.

"Thank you for coming by. I'll be in touch. Appreciate your time, *hon*," I say, closing the door on contractor number one.

I tell the second I will call him by the end of the week. I know I'm going to hire him, but I don't want him to think me too eager.

After the contractor appointments are done, I change out of my Oxford dress and into my paint clothes. My suitcase is on Leda's bed, zipped shut because I have zero confidence this house is rodent-free. It's definitely not bug-free either. Every day I'm here, I discover at least one dead fly.

I open it up and unzip the inner compartment, where Mom's book is.

I take it out carefully. I empathize with the binding of this fifteen-year-old paperback, in how it's struggling to keep it all together.

There's a tear in the front cover that I don't remember being there before. It must have happened in transit. I run my finger over it, tracing the damage.

A thought. A conspiracy.

Did Daphne find the book? Did she go through my things when she was at my apartment? Is that how the cover got torn? Is that why Leda asked me about it?

I kneel on the floor, chew on my thumb for a minute. I wouldn't put it past Leda, but I'd be surprised if Daphne invaded my privacy in that way. The three of us never crossed those lines, read each other's diaries, anything like that.

I flip the book over and over in my hands, then open it up to the last chapter—of what I have, anyway. I still haven't found the back half of the book anywhere in the house, and I still haven't been able to bring myself to track down another copy. I'm afraid of the empty margins, the blank spaces without my mother's notes to me. Afraid of her absence on the page. I'm afraid of what I don't remember. Afraid of the truth. Afraid of the fiction.

I've read this part already. More than once.

But I read it again.

———◆———

At Father Bernard's insistence, I began taking the girls to church. I prayed with them at night. They were reluctant. Confused. Dee was openly angry. Elle was more measured in her disapproval. She wrote me an essay arguing against the Catholic Church, which she slipped under my door one morning.

Cici was unbothered. She seemed to genuinely enjoy mass. When I asked her why, she said, "It's like a show. They wear costumes and sing."

PLAY NICE

I was frustrated with my daughters, and they were frustrated with me.

They couldn't see that I was trying to protect them. Nothing I did seemed to be working.

My sleep was plagued with bad dreams. I'd be running through the house, looking for my daughters, and they wouldn't be there. I'd look around and there'd be blood on the walls, the floor, my hands. I'd scream for them until my throat was raw. I would wake up to that cruel, horrible laughter.

The house began to smell, to stink of rot. The girls complained. I burned candles. I burned sage.

Three weeks went by until the inevitable. Until my ex came to the door when he dropped off our daughters, red-faced. I could see every vein in his neck, and the angry one on his forehead was in danger of bursting.

"You're taking them to church?" he said.

"They're my daughters, too." I'd been preparing, so why did I feel so unprepared? "I want them to learn about faith. About goodness. Have values."

He balked. "They *are* good. They have values. I've taught them values. They don't want to go. You're forcing them."

"I'm their mother," I said, because I had no other argument. Not one that I could remember in the moment, with *He would always do this. Twist my words. Of course you were good. That wasn't what I meant, and he knew it.* him there in front of me, screaming. I was paralyzed by him, by his anger.

"You're not even Catholic!" he said, throwing his hands up. "I don't know what you're playing at. Is this for the judge? To position yourself as some pious, God-fearing

> Believe it or not, this depiction of your father is generous. This conversation was far worse than I portrayed it.

mother? You're not doing this for the girls; you're doing this for yourself. You're so fucking selfish!"

He took a moment to catch his breath. "No more church. No more forced prayers. You'll be hearing from my lawyer."

MY stomach churning, I set the book aside, realizing I just used it to ruin my own day. What a thing, in retrospect, to watch the dominoes fall.

The house is quiet, and it occurs to me that I'm waiting for something to happen, some disturbance. I'm fine with being alone in the house, but I don't want to wonder if I'm alone in the house.

I get up and go look for Austin's note with his phone number. The note is where I left it, on the coffee table.

Beside it, my sketchpad is open to the drawing I did last night. My cosmic "Leave Me Alone."

There's a new addition. Small, in the bottom corner, in the center of a constellation, floating in the galaxy.

A response.

19

"HEY," Austin says, walking up the driveway. I sit on the front steps with the last two cans of White Claw. My can is already empty. His is probably warm. I've been out here for the last hour. I couldn't keep staring at the sketch. At that word, the little smiley face. Playful and defiant. Exactly my style. I might be charmed if I weren't fucking terrified.

I texted Austin to come over. Now here he is.

"Thought you might be . . . Are you okay?" he asks, brow furrowing. His concern is endearing. He wears jeans and a plain black V-neck T-shirt. His chain. I can see some chest hair. Just enough. Not too much.

The only way I'll go back in the house is if he's with me, which is so pathetic it makes me want to scream.

"Clio?"

"Yes," I say. "And no. Yes, I'm Clio. No, I'm not okay."

He kneels in front of me, pushes my hair out of my face. "You want to talk about it?"

I shake my head and offer him the White Claw. "Here. I saved this for you."

He accepts the can. He pops the tab and takes a sip. "Mm-hmm. Warm."

This makes me laugh. It's a miracle I can find anything funny right now, and it makes everything funny.

A demon drawing a smiley face? Hilarious.

My laughter turns manic.

"I'm sorry," I tell Austin, attempting to catch my breath.

He takes it in stride. He sits beside me on the stairs. "No need to apologize. I'm just glad you texted. I was waiting."

"Aw. Say, do you have any weed?"

"I feel like I'm at work."

"Only I'm full of youth and vitality."

"You'd be surprised, the vitality in that place," he says. He takes another sip of warm White Claw. "You're using me."

"You're letting me."

Another sip. "All right. I'll be back in five. You can finish this."

He hands me the can.

"Wait," I say, accepting it. "I'll come with you."

He raises an eyebrow. "You want to come over?"

"What? Do you not want to introduce me to your mother?" I ask, grinning.

He reaches his hand out. I give him mine. He says, "I wanted the drink back, but okay."

I pull my hand away.

"I was kidding. Give me your hand."

"You lost hand-holding privileges."

"You told me not to be cute. You said cute was a turn-off."

"That was then," I say, standing. "This is now."

The two of us walk down the driveway, and by the time we get to the end, we're holding hands.

It feels good to step into the cul-de-sac. To put the house behind me for a little while. Out of sight, out of mind.

"Molly Ericson lived in that house. Do you remember her at all?" he asks, pointing to a house on the left with a red door and blue shutters, a flagpole out front sans flag. "Braces. Glasses."

"Nope," I say.

"Not just me, then? You don't remember anyone?"

"No one specifically. I . . ." I reach for my snake charm, slide it back and forth along the chain. "I don't know. I don't remember a lot from that time. Is that weird?"

"I guess it was—what?—eighteen years ago? Shit. And you weren't here for that long."

"No. No, not really," I say, finishing the White Claw and tossing it into a neighbor's recycling bin.

"It felt long, though. To me, at least. When you're a kid, a week is forever," he says, turning down a driveway. "This one."

Austin lives in a generic Colonial. Brick up to the awning that covers the narrow concrete porch, yellow siding at the top. Wide windows with brown shutters.

He leads me in through the two-car garage, which is crowded with cobwebbed bicycles and cracked plastic snow sleds and deflated soccer balls and broken hockey sticks—like a sad museum of a happy childhood.

There's a single stair up to the door, which he opens for me.

His house smells like cheap candles. It's decorated like it's the set of a family sitcom. There are pictures of him and his brothers everywhere. His brothers on their respective wedding days with their standard blond brides. Baker with two other kids that I assume are his siblings or cousins.

"Hey, Mom," Austin calls out. "I've got Clio with me."

I follow Austin through the living room to the kitchen, where his mom sits at the table with her laptop open in front of her. She closes it and looks up at us.

Her chestnut hair is cut into a bob. There are gray streaks in her bangs. She wears drugstore reading glasses, a black zip-up cardigan, and baggy light-wash faux denim pants. No jewelry apart from a pair of gold heart-shaped studs. There's something so comforting about her appearance. I never had a mother who looked like a "mother." Mom never wore an outfit without ample cleavage, and Amy still dresses like a Y2K teenager. But this woman in front of me is straight out of the catalog. Classic Mom.

"Hello," she says. "I'd stand but . . ."

There's a cane leaning against the table.

"That's all right. I'll join you," I say, pulling out a chair and sitting to her left.

She takes off her glasses and sets them down. She studies me for a moment. "You're stunning. You look so much like her. Alex."

"Thank you," I say, smiling.

"You want some water?" Austin asks. "Mom? Clio?"

"Some tea?" she says.

"Yes, please," I say. "Tea."

"I was very sorry to hear about her passing," she says.

"I appreciate you saying so. I'm sorry, I don't know your name."

I don't even know Austin's last name, so I can't call her Mrs. Whatever.

"Dawn," she says.

"It's nice to meet you, Dawn," I say. There's a bouquet of pink and yellow tulips on the kitchen table. I take a moment to admire them. "Austin mentioned you and my mom had coffee a few times?"

"Oh, yes," she says. "Back then. And recently. She would come to the house every so often, with Roy."

"You knew Roy?"

"I met him a few times. Nice man. Interesting job," she says. She's being polite but testing the waters, which I respect.

"From what I've heard, demonology is actually a very dull profession," I say. "A lot of paperwork, surprisingly."

Dawn laughs, and I think I love her.

Austin watches us from beyond the island. He leans against the counter waiting for the kettle to boil. His hair mats to his forehead. It's hot in here. Stuffy.

"What did you think of her?" I ask. "My mom."

It's too direct a question, and a wave of unease passes through the kitchen. Across Dawn's face. Across Austin's. The kettle whimpers, louder, louder, on the precipice of a scream.

I could justify my bluntness, add disclaimers, but I let it hang. I want her honest answer. I want her to meet me where I am. I think she will. I'm not fooled by her CVS reading glasses and Kohl's sweater. She raised three sons on her own and has MS. She's not some delicate flower, some vanilla suburban pearl clutcher. Especially not if she willingly had coffee with my mother more than once.

Austin turns off the burner just as the kettle shrieks. Another moment passes in silence.

Dawn tilts her head. Her eyebrows pinch together. Austin sets a ceramic mug down in front of her, one with a pastoral scene painted on the side. A deer in a meadow.

"She wasn't like anyone I ever met before. I found it refreshing. I went over to introduce myself after Jackson moved her in. I brought her cookies, and she thanked me but said she wouldn't eat them. She invited me in and poured me a glass of wine. It was four in the afternoon."

Austin brings me a matching mug, only instead of a deer there's a fox. He joins us at the table with a glass of water.

"She was very open with me. She told me about her situation with her ex-husband. Your father. She told me about you and your sisters."

"Her entire life saga, sparing no detail, I'm sure."

"Yes," Dawn says, watching her tea bag steep, deep in thought. "She didn't say anything about the house, though. I didn't know about any of that until the book came out. Then we had all sorts of traffic on the street. No one was happy about that. About the attention."

"That first Halloween was crazy," Austin says. "The cops showed up."

"I heard she lost custody and moved out. I waited for her to put the house up for sale, but it never happened. I didn't see her again until, gosh. I can't remember. Until Jackson was at Rutgers. You were in high school, I think," she says, turning to Austin. "I saw a car in the driveway one afternoon. She came over. She brought me cookies. And wine." She pauses, smiling at the memory. "Told me how she was living with Roy in Connecticut, but she couldn't sell her house in case the possession was . . . dormant? I think that was the word she used. That's the first time she spoke to me about any of that. Maybe because the book was out, there was no point dancing around it. But I wondered . . ."

"If she made it all up?" I ask.

"Yes," she says. "She wrote in the book about Jack, but it wasn't how he remembered it. And he was sixteen at the time, not in college. He has no recollection of saying anything, alluding to anything. There was nothing funny about the house until, well . . . as frustrating as it was to have the commotion on the street, I never held it against her. She had a tough time. I related to that. And I can't imagine what it was like to lose her children. If it knocked a few screws loose . . . I understand."

"Thank you," I say. "There aren't many people who knew her who I can really talk about her with. Alexandra is a touchy subject with my dad, my stepmom, even my sisters, honestly. I have my aunt, but that's complicated, too. And then demonologist Roy and the rest of the occult society of Connecticut or whatever. Everyone has their biases. It's difficult for me to trust anything they have to say, wondering if they're trying to sway me, to get me to see her the way they want me to. And then there's her book, which is fiction. Of course."

She nods and takes a cautious sip of tea.

There's something she's not telling me.

I wonder if Austin senses this or if he's just anxious to grab the weed so we can head back to my house, get high, and get naked. He stands up. "Be right back."

"I appreciate your honesty," I tell her. A thumb on the bruise.

She gives me a quick closed-lip smile. Limited eye contact.

"Dawn," I say, reaching out and tapping her mug. "You can tell me. Whatever it is. I want to know. I can handle it. I'm tougher than I look, but you know how that goes."

A real smile this time. Though a bittersweet one. "You're a real spitfire, aren't you?"

"A blessing and a curse."

She takes a slow, ragged breath. "I think . . . I might have been the last person to see Alex alive. I don't think she was well . . . at the end."

"What makes you say that?"

"She came over earlier that day. I went out to get the mail. It takes me a while to get up and down the driveway. She saw me and came hurrying over. She seemed out of sorts, but I didn't want to say anything. She was sensitive to people thinking she was a nut."

"'Out of sorts'?"

"Disoriented. She was slurring her words. She might have been drunk. I'm sorry, Clio. Maybe I should have called someone. I don't know."

"Who would you have called? It's not like her getting day drunk was a rare occurrence," I say. My reassurance is genuine. My resentment unfounded. Yet they exist in tandem, threads of the same rope. It's not Dawn's fault that my mother is dead. But if she had acted on her intuition, her concern, maybe things would have turned out differently. Maybe not.

"I asked her if she was all right, and she said . . . she said, 'Our demons get us all in the end.' Then she told me she would see me later and walked off. Turned around and went home. I didn't follow her. I wish I would have. I keep thinking about it."

Austin comes back into the room, hands in his pockets.

"I was going to help Clio paint tonight," he says, his clever excuse for us leaving.

"Oh," Dawn says. "Oh, all right. That sounds like a very productive evening."

I get up and give Dawn a hug. "It was so lovely to meet you."

"You, too," she says.

When we get out to the garage, Austin reaches for my hand. I pull away.

"Take me somewhere," I tell him. "I don't want to go home just yet."

20

WE get stoned and have sex in the back seat of his car like we're sixteen. Then he takes me to the local diner, and we order breakfast even though it's nine p.m. We sit quietly across from each other in a booth, waiting for our food. He makes a pyramid out of those little packets of jam. I fidget with my necklace, make the snake dance.

I could attempt conversation, but I'm beginning to wonder if there's anything left for us to talk about. Maybe we've exhausted our chemistry. Maybe we're too high. Maybe I'm too tired. Maybe I'm busy wishing I could think about something other than Mom's demons, both figurative and literal.

"Here we go," says the waitress, dropping off plates of pancakes and eggs and bacon and a giant Belgian waffle. "Enjoy."

"This is a ridiculous amount of food," I say to Austin, who looks disappointed at the destruction of his jam pyramid, which was knocked over by the plate of scrambled eggs.

"Well, seemed like a good idea twenty minutes ago," he says. "Now I want disco fries."

"Shh. Don't let the bacon hear you. You'll hurt its feelings."

"Sorry," he says. "Didn't mean to offend."

"We made our choices and now we must live with them," I say, stabbing a pancake. "Be adults."

"Nothing about this is adult," he says. "We're eating breakfast after dark at a shitty diner because you don't want to go home. Don't want to deal with what's there."

"That took an unexpected turn to earnestness," I say, reaching for the syrup.

"I've grieved a parent," he says, looking me in the eye. I wonder if mine are as bloodshot as his. He's so pretty, even with his red eyes. His natural lashes look like the ones girls I know pay for. "You can talk to me. Tell me what's wrong."

I consider my responses. I could tell him how pretty he is, change the subject. I could be combative, say I'm not grieving because it's impossible to grieve someone I didn't know, whose memory is shrouded in lies. Or I could confess that I think my house is in fact haunted. That for all her mistakes, all her fictions, all the chaos she created, Mom might have been right about Edgewood.

But if I tell him that, and he doesn't believe me, this will be over. If I tell him and he does believe me, I'm not sure what then.

"It's not grief," I say, which is truth adjacent. "Nothing's wrong. I'm not avoiding the house because it makes me sad. I'm just used to the city. To constant movement. People everywhere. I'm a social creature."

"Fair enough," he says. He's not convinced, but he can take a hint. "Lucky for you the neighbors are friendly."

"Lucky me."

AUSTIN accepts my invitation to sleep over. I take him to Leda and Daphne's room, press the two twin beds together. It's not comfortable, but it's fine. More comfortable than being here by myself.

PLAY NICE

The house feels different with him here. It's smellier—he stinks of diner grease and weed and sweat. Louder—he snores. Warmer—he spoons me, which usually I hate but currently don't mind, and is also necessary given the size of the mattresses.

I drift in and out of restless sleep.

At some point in the night, the door creaks open, the hinges holding out the note, and I become aware that there's something in the room with us.

I keep my eyes shut tight, try to ignore the suspicion and go back to sleep.

I'm almost there when I feel the blanket slowly falling away. My feet are exposed. My ankles. It's cold in the room, though I swear it wasn't a second ago. Sweat freezes at the nape of my neck, at my temples. My toes go numb. A weird sensation travels up from my heels to my calves, a phantom tickling.

There's breathing that could be my breathing. That could be Austin's breathing. But then, why do I feel breath on my face? He's behind me, and I've been holding in an exhale for so long my lungs are burning.

I could be dreaming. I could be imagining things. I could be remembering.

One night, I woke up to Mom stumbling down the stairs, down the hall. Heavy footsteps. *Thud thud thud.* I never slept with my door all the way shut, and I opened one eye to see the slice of light from the hall was interrupted by her figure. She stood in my doorway, watching me, breathing intensely. Panting. I shut my eye and pretended to be asleep. But I could *feel* her watching.

Eventually, I opened my eyes, and she was gone.

I open my eyes now, anticipating nothing, an empty room. What I see are two giant pale eyes staring back at me.

The next thing I see is the floor. It comes up to meet me. The impact makes everything dark.

"Shit! Are you okay?" Austin gently turns me over onto my back. "Fuck. Did I knock you out of bed? I'm so sorry. Clio? Breathe."

I gasp. I only remember how to inhale.

"Clio," he says. "Breathe. It's okay. You're okay."

The exhale is cut short by a sob.

"Clio. Hey."

"I'm fine," I say, sitting up and pushing my hair out of my face. "Bad dream."

"How's your head? Your face? Do you want ice?"

"No, I don't want ice. I don't even have ice," I say, looking around the room to see where it went. If it went. Whatever might have been here. "I'm *fine*."

Out of the corner of my eye, I see a flash of movement. A shape. A shadow. A strange protrusion. Long and narrow. It moves like a serpent behind the wall. Under the paint. It glides toward the door, and then it vanishes around the corner into the hall.

"Okay," Austin says.

"Okay . . ." I don't want him to know that I'm afraid. He can't know. I manage a deep breath. Inhale. Exhale.

"But just in case," he says, tilting my face so he can look at me. "I want to make sure you're not concussed."

"Is that it? Or do you want to look deep into my eyes because you're a hopeless romantic."

"Both," he says. "How's your vision? Blurry? Any double vision? Shadows? Squiggles?"

"What? No," I say, defensive.

"All right," he says. "Okay."

He helps me up and back into bed. He props a pillow behind me.

"I have a queen bed," he says. "Just throwing that out there. It's a queen in my mom's basement, but it's a queen."

"Will Dawn judge me?" I ask, though I'm not sure I care. I'd take her judgment for somewhere else to sleep. "I like your mom. I don't want to scandalize her."

"Nah, she's cool," he says.

I get up and start to get dressed. "Let's go."

"Now?"

"Yes, now," I say, tossing him his shirt. "Take me to your queen."

WE wake up to his obnoxious alarm. He tells me I can stay in bed, and I take him up on his offer. I go back to sleep.

My phone wakes me up again sometime later. My group chat with Veronica, Hannah, Emma, Samantha, Kiera, and Kaleigh. Kaleigh just announced her partnership with SLIP, a loungewear brand. I congratulate her in emojis. I can't be bothered with words.

Veronica hits me and Hannah on the side, in our more exclusive group chat. **This is going to be a DISASTER! They sent me a sleep set once and it literally fell apart in the wash. Like literally dissolved.**

It's sweatshop pajamas, Hannah replies.

I almost ask them how much they think she got paid, but then I realize I don't care and that I have a terrible headache.

I have missed texts from Daphne and Leda on our sister thread. Daphne sent us a picture of the sun rising over the Hudson Valley. Leda with the sunrise over Boston. The sun is already up here; I have nothing to contribute.

They wouldn't want a picture of the sun rising over Edgewood Drive anyway. No matter how pretty.

I yawn and sit up, look around the room. Austin's room. It was dark and late last night, and he was with me, so I couldn't snoop.

Brave of him to leave me here alone.

Light pours in through the egress window. He has no curtains.

His sheets are plaid. Teenage boy sheets.

His furniture appears to be Ikea. He has a bookshelf with books on it, a good sign.

Framed artwork, also promising. If I found out a man with posters taped to his wall was giving me multiple orgasms, I might have gone into crisis.

I go through his drawers but find nothing offensive. His clothes are clean and folded. His pay stubs are sad but organized.

His laptop is password protected.

Once I've exhausted my search, I realize there's nothing to do but leave. Go back to the house.

I worry I'll run into Dawn on my way out and, lovely as she is, I don't feel like making small talk, not with this lump of dread in my throat and pounding inside my skull.

Thankfully, she's not around. My exit is quick and uninterrupted.

My walk down the street is a funeral march.

I catch myself playing with my necklace again, my snake charm with its bright diamond eyes. It occurs to me that maybe the reason why I'm so attached to it is because I received it the night Mom died.

It's not grief, I told Austin just hours ago. But it could be. I've never grieved before. Maybe I'm underestimating it. Maybe I wrote that response on the sketchpad. Maybe I didn't really see big pale eyes in the dark. Maybe I'm worrying about the wrong demons.

I imagine my mother drunk, walking toward me up Edgewood. Seeing her like Dawn saw her for the final time. Disheveled, rambling, slurring. It's not hard to picture—her three sheets to the wind, making no sense—since she's inebriated in about half of what memories I do have of her.

And I was stoned out of my mind last night.

My fear of the uncanny dissipates as I make it to the house, as I make amends with logic, as I swear off self-medicating.

I punch in the code, and the front door swings open.

I climb the stairs slowly.

The air in the house is stagnant.

With every step I take, the dread creeps back in. The fear. My neck prickles. I shiver, even as sweat drips from the thick nest of my hair, as it pools in the small of my back.

I reach the top step, and I'm suddenly disoriented, like I'm being held upside down. The world has capsized, turned on me. Nothing makes any sense. My hands slap to my face to hold it together so my jaw doesn't fall loose.

What am I looking at? What am I seeing? *How?*

There's paper scattered everywhere. Pages ripped out of my sketchpad.

I trip, land hard on my knees.

It's the same word scribbled on all of them, on all the pages.

Hello
Hello
Hello
Hello
Hello
Hello

I crawl forward, start to gather them up, crumple them. I want to set them on fire. Pretend this never happened. I want to scream, so I scream. I scream until I can't anymore.

Until I find the sheet with a different message, that shuts me up.

Remember? ☺

I go down the hall to Leda and Daphne's room. I grab my suitcase and I call a car to take me to the train station.

I wait outside.

It wanted my attention, and so it got my attention.

It's real.

It's real.

It's real, and now I know it. But I also know that no one will believe me.

21

DAD and Amy went all out for their Memorial Day barbecue. If I were to be cynical, I'd suspect it's because they can sense there's something rotten in Denmark and are trying to settle the kingdom and lift spirits with racks of ribs and expensive steaks and a variety of mayonnaise-based salads.

I've been avoiding my family for the past two weeks. It's not like me to be unresponsive, and it's got them in a tizzy.

I have to admit, I kind of like watching them squirm. Because the thing I want to talk about—the specter waiting patiently in the dark to emerge, hiding behind every word, every thought— is the very thing they don't want to talk about. Will never want to talk about.

So what is there to say?

I've been back to the house twice since the sketchpad incident, both times with Austin. We painted the office, Daphne and Leda's old room, and the upstairs hall.

There have been no strange happenings, no attempts at communication, which is almost disappointing. I'm being deprived of a witness.

Or maybe the lack of action has nothing to do with Austin's

presence. Maybe whatever is in the house is just waiting until I convince myself that it actually doesn't exist. When my doubt conquers my fear, then it'll reemerge. Pass me another note.

I haven't spent the night in the house. I sleep at Austin's.

I have successfully purchased another copy of Mom's book off eBay. I caved in the immediate aftermath of the note ordeal, whatever reluctance I'd had about finishing crushed by a newfound sense of urgent curiosity. My initial order was canceled, the seller skeptical of the shipping address. But it's on its way now. I told Austin, for some reason, and he offered to sit with me while I read. Which is pretty sweet, but I sincerely can't think of anything worse than reading about my fucked-up childhood in the presence of someone I'm fucking.

"I hear you have a boyfriend," Amy says, fixing us vodka lemonades.

"Clio! That's great!" Tommy says. He's got white splotches of sunblock all over his face. "Who's the lucky guy?"

"Your sources are mistaken," I say, pulling down the brim of my hat.

"You're not dating someone?" Amy asks, handing me a blue Solo cup with a bendy straw. A lemon wedge floats inside. I stab it with the straw.

"I don't even know what 'dating' means," I say. I take a sip. It's strong. "And I don't really care to."

"As long as you're happy," Tommy says, getting up and heading inside, probably to see if Dad needs help. He tries to be the son that Dad never had, but Dad doesn't know what to do with him.

"Thank you, Tommy," I call out after him. He gives me a double thumbs-up before closing the back door.

Amy sits next to me on the sofa. The patio furniture smells musty from being locked in the shed all winter, and Amy smells like candy, her cheap gourmand perfume. Then there's the distant scent of charcoal. Chlorine from the neighbor's pool. The citrus from the lemonade. Summer.

Leda is taking a walk around the block, and Dad is in the kitchen marinating meat or something. Daphne's not coming because she had to work.

There will be neighbors over at some point, friends of my dad and Amy, but for now it's just us under a blue, blue sky and tyrannical sun.

Amy stands up and adjusts the umbrella.

It could be my intrinsic proclivity for deviousness or just that the opportunity has so seamlessly presented itself. Or both. "Not everyone has a great love story like you and Dad."

"Aw," Amy says, blushing. She gives up on the umbrella and sits back down beside me, taking a sip of her vodka lemonade.

"Maybe part of me is holding out for what you two have. For romance," I say, resting my head on her shoulder. I drop my voice to a whisper. "He told me. He loved you from the moment he saw you. I know."

She puts her arm around me and draws me in close, starts to play with my hair. Says nothing.

"He wants me to find someone. You know he does," I say, vodka burning my throat. "He doesn't want me to be jaded because of Alexandra. And don't worry. I understand. Their marriage was over long before he met you."

She withdraws her arm, holds her drink with both hands. I wait for her to speak. She takes a series of small nervous sips. Somewhere in the neighborhood, a child cries.

"Amy. Relax. I couldn't care less. It all worked out, for everyone," I say, knocking her knee with mine. "Love is only a losing game for the losers, you know what I mean?"

"Clio, I have no idea what you're talking about," she says. The problem is she's got no poker face. I've caught her off guard. The sun beats down; that kid is still crying.

"Please. If anything, I'm jealous," I say, shifting to fabricated exasperation. "I want to find someone. I just get bored so easily. No one can hold my interest. I envy you. Not everyone meets their soul mate at nineteen."

"I was twenty-two!" she shrieks, spilling her drink onto her lap. "Shit."

"I'm sorry," I say, playing dumb. "Need a napkin?"

"I . . . I got it," she says, flustered. "Sorry."

She gets up to go inside, and I do some quick math.

Dad is sixteen years older than Amy. He was forty-one when they got married, meaning she was twenty-five. I can't remember how long she was around before the wedding, or when Dad sat us down and told us about them being together. Was she already living in the house when we moved in full-time?

Would she have gotten upset just now if she wasn't guilty?

"Where is everyone?"

It's Leda, the sun behind her like a fiery halo.

"Inside," I say, adjusting my hat again.

She sits down on the sofa and immediately gets up. "Ew! Why is it sticky?"

"There's no good answer to that question, is there?"

"What are you drinking?"

"Vodka lemonade," I say. "Want a sip?"

"No," she says. "What's going on? Something's wrong."

"Nothing is wrong," I say, tipping my hat back so she can see me smile. "Everything is perfect. Life is a dream."

She scoffs.

Then Tommy comes out with chips and salsa, followed by Dad

and Amy with a veggie tray, and then Bob and Lara Costigan from down the street, and it seems like there's real potential here for a pleasant afternoon.

But as I sit with this smile plastered on my face, accepting compliments from Lara Costigan on my dress, chatting with Bob about what the rental market is like in New York, I keep Dad and Amy at the corner of my eye.

I don't smell summer anymore. Not the chlorine or the charcoal or the sweet, citrusy lemonade. I smell burning. Fire—the hot annihilation of what was, of a belief I once held about something in my family history being good and pure.

Is there anything good for me to believe in? Or are the demons all that's left?

I inhale.

Only smoke.

THE afternoon smolders on. The sun burns itself out eventually. More neighbors arrive for red meat and beers and small talk. No amount of vodka lemonade makes it more tolerable.

I miss Daphne. I go upstairs and call her from my bedroom, but she doesn't pick up.

Listening to the soundtrack of chitchat and Bruce Springsteen through my window, I decide that I prefer it up here. That I'm done for the day.

My body is tired, but my mind is awake and needs occupying.

I undress and take a picture of myself. I send it to Austin.

He responds within five minutes, which is both too slow and too fast. "You're trying to kill me."

I leave him on read and scroll through socials for forty-five minutes, until Leda knocks on my door and lets herself in.

"Put some clothes on," she says. "Come back down. You're being rude."

"I'm not. You just miss me," I say, getting out of bed and stepping back into my sundress. "Zip me up."

"Amy's drunk," she says, being too rough with my zipper. "She keeps asking me if I still love her."

"Good thing the answer is yes," I say, spinning around so my dress floats up. "So you don't have to lie."

She narrows her eyes at me. "What's going on with you?"

"I'm getting bullied by my big sister."

"I'm not bullying you."

"Then leave," I say.

She puts her hands on her hips. "You're so mean. Being a brat will only get you so far in life, Clio."

I sit back on my bed, cross my legs. "It's gotten me pretty far so far."

She frowns, and I can tell that she is, unfortunately, legitimately upset.

"I don't want to go back down there," I say. "The small talk gets so exhausting. And you know Dad will get mad if I try to mix things up, make it interesting. Bring up Area 51 and see what happens. It's no fun. I'm not having fun."

"I'm not either," she says, turning to the door. "I'm not having any fun at all."

She slams it behind her in a very Mom move.

Our mother's presence is everywhere, her influence. Her ghost is us.

After a lazy moment, I get up to go chase after Leda.

I make my way downstairs with every intention of rejoining the party.

But the light is on in Dad's study. The door is open. It's always open, but I'm not typically compelled to go in. The compulsion feels absolute, and I'm suddenly briefly above myself, watching as I slip inside.

It's rare that I'm alone in here.

There are bookshelves all around, a heavy oak desk, leather chairs, a filing cabinet. A giant Mac. I hover behind his desk and start to open drawers.

I don't even have time to wonder what it is I'm looking for before I find it. Half of a beat-up old paperback. An annotated copy of *Demon of Edgewood Drive*. The other half of *my* copy.

Did some part of me know that it was here? That he had found it when he went to the house without me, stumbled across it in my room sometime after I'd run out post–initial mouse sighting but before I returned two weeks later to look for it? Did some part of me know that he took it? Was hiding it from me, or keeping it for himself? Or did I piece it all together just now, before I came in? I don't know. It seems obvious in retrospect.

I reach for it. It's in my hands, and I hear heavy footsteps.

They're mine.

I'm storming out into the hall, through the kitchen, the sunroom. I'm standing at the back door. I'm yelling.

"Dad! Dad!"

Eventually, the chatter quiets until it's just me. Me and Bruce. Born to run.

"Clio?" Dad says.

"What the fuck is this?" I shout, holding up the book.

He beelines across the yard toward me.

"Clio . . ." he says, jaw clenched. He grabs the book from my hand and ushers me inside.

"Give that back," I say.

"Where did you find this?" he asks, leading me back to his study. He closes the door behind us.

"You know where. In your desk drawer," I say. "That's mine. She left it for me."

He flips it open, looking for something specific. He finds it. "Look. You want this? You wanted this?"

I step forward so I can read the page.

I'm glad you called us. With all our experience, I feel confident in our assessment," said Ruth. "We can help. But we shouldn't delay the exorcism. I believe the demon has taken an interest in your daughter, ~~Cici.~~ CLIO ☺

"Can't you see? She was out of her mind," Dad says, releasing the page. The book flutters shut. "Clio Louise. Come on."

I'm shivering, cold to my bones. I might throw up.

"I know it's upsetting. I know it's hard. But I didn't want you to see this. I found it when I went to meet with the exterminator. It was in the closet of your old room. She put it there on purpose so you would think . . . I don't know."

"It's the same handwriting," I say, reaching for the book. "Let me see."

"Clio. Stop," he says, pulling it away from me. He holds it behind his back.

"Dad. *Please.*"

"This is exactly what she wanted," he says. "Don't you see that?"

He's wrong, and it makes me so angry I could spit fire. "You cheated on her."

"What?" he says. He sighs and shakes his head. "Great. Perfect."

"You did. Just admit it."

"I won't. It's not true," he says. "She had no proof."

"Just because she didn't have proof doesn't mean it didn't happen."

He's looking at me like he's never looked at me before. With contempt. It's like he's wearing a different face. "You sound just like her."

He means it as an insult, so I'll take it as a compliment. "Good."

"Clio," he says. "You don't want this. I'm protecting you."

"But I don't want protection. I want honesty," I say, stepping toward him.

"You won't find it in here," he says, his eyes dark. "She's turning you against me."

He's out of the room.

"Dad? Where are you going? Dad . . ."

I step out into the hall and catch a glimpse of him turning the corner. I follow him.

He's going outside.

"Dad!"

I'm at the back door. He's stomping across the yard toward the firepit.

"Dad!" I scream, again interrupting the barbecue chatter. "Don't!"

His back is to me, but then he turns. He turns so I can see him feed the book to the flames.

22

Tommy's quiet in the driver's seat, both hands on the wheel, ten and two.

It was a scene. The book burning. Me screaming at Dad. Saying I'd never forgive him. Leda pursuing me upstairs as I gathered my things, asking me what was happening. I told her. Instead of being sympathetic, she was mad that I broke my promise. That I read Mom's book.

"No, you're just jealous because Mom left me a copy and not you," I said, which didn't go over too well.

Tommy offered to drive me to the train station, attempting to defuse the tension. I took him up on it. Now Leda's angry at him, too. She thinks he's taking my side. To be fair, he is.

"Actually, I don't want to go back to the city," I tell him. "I want to go to the house."

"I think that's a good idea. We can talk now that everyone's had a chance to calm down. I'm sure your Dad—"

"Not Dad's house. Edgewood. It's a left—here."

We sit at the stop sign. He doesn't put on his turn signal.

"A left, Tommy."

He goes straight. "Clio."

"Thomas."

"I don't know how I feel about bringing you there. Leaving you there. I'm taking you to the train."

"Then just pull over and let me out. I'll call a car," I say, rummaging around my bag for my phone. "No one listens to me. It's infuriating."

"I'm listening," he says. "I'm here."

"I can't trust you," I tell him. I put down the window, let some air in. "You'll tell Leda anything I tell you. And it doesn't matter anyway, because no one takes me seriously."

"Do you think that's true? Or are you maybe just feeling that way right now because—"

"Don't. You know it's true. They love me. They fear me. But they won't believe me."

"About what?"

I lean my head out the window, look up at the sky. Someone's setting off fireworks. "Doesn't matter."

He keeps talking, trying to comfort me with platitudes. I'm in no mood. I let him prattle on for a few minutes before I turn on the tears. "Are you going to take me to Edgewood or not?"

Fifteen minutes later, when we pull up the driveway, he says, "This is the place?"

"This is it."

"It's not so scary," he says, putting the car in park. He looks out through the windshield, pushes his glasses up his nose, clears his throat. "Will you be okay here alone tonight? It was a difficult evening."

"I'll call my boyfriend," I say, winking as I open the door.

"I thought you didn't have one," he says, popping the trunk for me. He won't get out of the car. Not because he doesn't want to help me with my bags, but because of Leda. If he steps foot on the property, she'll see it as a violation. Already, if she finds out he took me here, she'll be irate.

"Maybe I do and maybe I don't," I say. "Thank you, Tommy."

"You're welcome, Clio. I'm here if you need anything. Call me anytime. Okay?"

"Okay," I say, crossing my heart.

He waits until I'm inside to drive away.

I turn the lights on in the foyer and climb the stairs, then flip the switch in the living room.

Everything is where I left it. Nothing is out of place. No new notes. Though, I didn't leave out any paper.

"I'm home," I say. "You wouldn't believe the day I had."

I go into the kitchen and get a glass of water. Bring it to the couch. Kick off my shoes.

I could see if Austin is around—back from spending the day at his brother's.

Or I could sit here and try to communicate with the thing in this house, the thing that everyone in this world who I love and who loves me has told me doesn't exist, has told me in words or through actions that believing in its existence is a sign of insanity. Is an unforgivable offense.

I pull my legs underneath me, sit propped on my calves.

"Hello," I say.

Laughter. Low and inauspicious, like the distant rumble of thunder.

Behind me. Coming from the stairs or the hall?

I spin around.

My heart beats with this savage desperation; my eyes are two big fools scanning the room for something they won't find unless it wants to be found. They search in vain and go desert dry but will not close, not even to blink. They won't give up because they're too stupid to accept it's hopeless, to understand that even if they see what they seek, it won't be a victory.

So this is what the paranormal does to a person. It separates your mind from your body, severs your logic like a gangrenous limb.

It's a unique suffering. One that inspires more ridicule than empathy.

I think about Roy but am too proud to call him.

And I have a nagging suspicion he would gather the circus to come here. All the psychics and monster hunters with their glorified toys, with their iPhone cameras, with their sad YouTube channels. I can't trust that he'd deal with it quietly, that he wouldn't reveal my belief.

I can't make a joke of myself. My entire life is built around my image.

I wonder if the demon knows that.

I wonder if I'm giving it too much credit.

Now that it's quiet, I wonder how I know it's still here. That it's watching me. That it's behind me, standing in front of the fireplace. That no matter how fast I turn around, I won't see it, because it's faster. Because it's not in its body right now.

My shoulders roll back, my posture feigning bravery. I turn around.

The entire house shakes. The ceiling fan starts to spin.

The laughter comes again.

Behind me. Always behind me. No matter where I turn.

"Here's the thing," I say, slipping my legs out from under me and planting both feet firmly on the carpet. "I can leave anytime I want. I don't live here. If you want to play with me, you have to play nice."

I down my glass of water and start toward the kitchen, wondering if I have it in me to stay here alone tonight.

The sound of scraping stops me.

Four long, distinct scrapes.

It's during the fourth that I cave. That I look over my shoulder.

On the wall beside the fireplace, which I conscientiously primed with white paint weeks ago, are four giant scratches. Deep down into the drywall.

The scratches form a specific shape. An image. Big. About the size of one of those rusty old merry-go-rounds at a playground that guarantees skinned knees and Neosporin.

Yeah, there it is. A response.

AUSTIN'S hair is wet. He's in bed, on top of the sheets, in his boxers and nothing else. He left the garage door open for me and told me to let myself in.

"Hey," he says.

I slip off my shoes and my dress and crawl over to him. I rest my head on his bare chest.

He puts his arm around me, runs his hand over my back.

There's a mass in my throat that's so agonizing I want to scream it out. There's the smell of smoke in my hair that reminds me of the fire, of my father burning the book, watching flames turn it to ash, to nothing. The words she wrote to me that I will never get to read.

And when I close my eyes, there's a frowning face. A damaged wall. Something but not proof.

If I cried right now in his arms, Austin would comfort me. I wouldn't need to tell him why.

But I wield my tears like a weapon. They don't get to be sincere.

So I won't cry. I'll spite the urge.

PLAY NICE

I grin into Austin's chest and gently sweep my tongue across his nipple.

"I'M gonna be late for work," Austin says as I kiss his neck. I have no idea what time it is. His alarm went off and woke me up, and yesterday flashed before my eyes in quick cuts. I don't know what's more upsetting—the memories or how poorly my mind edited the montage.

I started kissing him to forget the rest, to be in the moment. It's not really working.

"Clio," he says.

"Call out," I say. "They'll live. And if not, is that your fault or just the cruel march of time?"

"You need to work on your dirty talk," he says, making me laugh.

I'm always surprised when he gets me to laugh, when he says something genuinely funny. All my friends tell me my standards are too high, but this is confirmation of what I've known all along. They're not high enough.

"Clio," Austin says, pushing my hair back.

"Austin."

"I have to go," he says. "I don't want to."

"If you didn't want to, you wouldn't," I say, sliding off him. Frustrated that he's not giving me what I want. Company. A distraction.

"That right?" he asks, climbing over me and stumbling toward his dresser.

As soon as my feet hit the floor, a memory grabs me by the ankles like a monster under the bed. I had a dream last night. About my parents. Not Dad and Amy. Dad and Mom. One of their fights. The memory, the dream, it drags me in before I can take a breath.

What else am I doing that's not up to your standards, hmm? Mom yelled. I was on the couch in the living room of our first house, wedged between Daphne and Leda. We held each other, listening to the screaming in the kitchen. *Why don't you write me a list?*

Is it so hard to look at a plate to see if it's clean? This is your job. What else do you do all day? Is it too much to ask?

The sound of a plate smashing. *Nothing is ever good enough for you!* I can't breathe.

"I wish I could stay in bed with you," Austin says, pulling on a pair of jeans. "Trust me."

I fold over, the edges of everything going dim. I finally manage to inhale. Exhale.

"Clio? Hey." He reaches out and touches my face. "You all right?"

"I'm perfect," I say, brushing him off. I get up and grab my dress off the floor, slip it over my head.

"Okay . . ." I can tell he's kind of annoyed, and I respect him more for it. It's so boring when someone will just put up with me.

I'm struck with this sudden malignant strain of curiosity. How far can I push him? Will he ever speak to me the way my father spoke to my mother? How broken would I have to be to allow it? Am I close? Closer than I've ever been?

"Can you drop me at the train station?" I ask.

"Sure," he says. "I'll even buy you coffee first."

"Won't that make you late?"

He shrugs.

I kiss him and then whisper something in his ear that makes his knees buckle. "How's that for dirty talk?"

23

WHEN I get to the city, I buy weed from an ex-fling and smoke it on my rooftop. I'm back to self-medicating. I stare out at the skyline. I scroll through Instagram. I Google "Roy Johnston" and end up on the website for the New England Occultist Society, which is so janky and pathetic I immediately X out of it.

I call Daphne, and she picks up right away. "Clio."

"Yes," I say.

"Dude. What the hell? What happened?"

"I'm assuming you already know, since I have eight thousand missed calls from you."

"I want to hear it from you. Your side."

"Say, do you remember Mom and Dad fighting about dishes? A fight about a dirty plate?"

"What?"

"I had a dream last night, but I think it was one of those dreams that's really a memory. The two of them were screaming at each other in the kitchen of our old house. He was mad because she didn't clean a plate. He said it was her only job, or something along those lines. Then she broke the plate. Smashed it."

"Alexandra broke a lot of plates. Glasses. Vases. She was dramatic like that," Daphne says. "What does that have to do with anything?"

"Nothing. Everything."

"What's with you? You sound . . ."

"I'm stoned," I say. "And tired. I'm beyond tired, Daffy."

"Why didn't you tell me?"

The clouds move so fast. "About what?"

"The book. You could have told me, and you didn't. You lied to me."

"I didn't lie. I omitted."

"You lied."

"Dad burned my book. Why isn't that the topic of this conversation? Why is it my fault?"

"That's . . . he shouldn't have done that. But you can't blame him for being upset."

"I can, actually."

"You crossed a boundary. You broke a promise. You lied," she says. "To all of us."

"What do I owe you?" I ask, looking out at the city. I'm more exasperated than angry. Disappointed that she's not more understanding. I expected empathy from her, and it stings that I'm not getting any. "I made that promise when I was a kid. When my classmates still believed in Santa Claus."

"Okay. Still," she says. "You should have come to us when you found the book. When you started to read it."

"I don't need your approval for everything I do."

She clicks her tongue. "Yeah, you've made that clear. But then you need to live with the consequences. Take responsibility for your actions."

"You sound like Leda."

"You're too hard on her. On both of us," she says. "And on Dad."

"What if I'm not hard enough?" I ask. The weed isn't calming me down. It's just making me more anxious. I turn my gaze down to the street below. What's that thing, when you feel the urge to jump off a building? Isn't there a name for that impulse? I don't want to die. I just want to know how it feels to fall. "What if Dad isn't who we think he is? What if he's everything Mom said he was? He cheated on her with Amy and lied about it."

"You don't know that."

"Wow. Whatever," I say.

She takes a deep breath. "You need to apologize."

"Apologize to whom? Captain Beatty?"

"Yes. And Leda. And Amy. Everyone's really upset."

"*I'm* upset," I say, my voice breaking. "I'm really, really fucking upset."

I close my eyes, and where there should be darkness, I see the scrapes in the wall. The frowning face.

"Please, Clio," Daphne says. "Listen to me. Alexandra being gone . . . it makes things confusing. Emotionally. But she hurt us. Don't you remember how she would scream at us? Chase us around the house. She kept us locked out on the deck during a fucking exorcism. She showed up belligerent, drunk out of her mind to our dance recital, embarrassed the hell out of us before crashing her car in the parking lot. I know we never talk about it, but I think about it. I think about how she couldn't see us if she didn't get sober, if she didn't stop ranting about demons, but she refused to do that. We weren't worth it to her, Cli. She wasn't well. She was abusive. What she did to us, it was abuse."

"Are those your words?" I ask, shaking my head, backing away from the ledge. "Or Dad's?"

"Stop. You don't get to question my memories. My experience. It's not fair. It's not all about you, Clio."

"It *is* about me. The whole family revolves around me. I'm the sun. That's why you need me. You need me to apologize and make peace so you can all go back to pretending we're normal and happy and that everything's fine and has always been fine. And I'm done pretending."

I hang up and immediately call Veronica.

"Hey, hey," she says. "What's up, babe?"

"Do you want to go out tonight?"

"You know it."

"Can we smoke up here?" A voice from behind me. It's my upstairs neighbor. 6B. He's got a buzz cut and baby face and no job, enabler parents who pay his rent. He stares at me open-mouthed whenever I walk by. Something about him reminds me of Daphne's old pet gerbil. Maybe in that he's very cute but seemingly incapable of making conversation.

"You can do whatever you want as long as you don't get caught. Smoke. Throw a rager. Set off fucking fireworks. Knock yourself out," I say, tossing him my lighter and giving him a wink. I head back inside. "Sorry, V. How's seven thirty?"

WE get drunk at dinner and then go barhopping, and somehow we end up at the cursed club Scorpio after midnight, which doesn't bode well.

We're with Kiera and Kaleigh. One of them does coke, but I can't remember which one. I follow each of them into the bathroom at different points of the evening, hoping they'll offer me something harder than liquor, but it doesn't happen.

The music is corny and so loud it's painful. No one's dancing. They're flailing.

"You want to go hit my vape?" Kiera shouts at me.

"Yeah," I shout back.

She takes me by the hand and leads me outside. It's raining a little. Misting.

"This place is the worst," she says, taking out her vape. "But also kind of the best? I don't know. I feel, like, alive. Like I'm seventeen again. Sneaking into clubs."

"Right," I say. It's too quiet on the street. Too empty. Apocalyptic. "Makes me want to do coke."

"I think Kaleigh has some."

"Hard drugs and child labor pajamas. She's a real kingpin." I take a hit of her vape.

She pulls a face. "What did you just say?"

I exhale the mint-flavored vapor. "Relax. I'm not judging her. I asked for the drugs, remember?"

"No. You said . . . 'child labor pajamas.'"

"Yeah. Her partnership with SLIP."

"That's *my* deal."

"Oh," I say. I must have misread the text thread. "Congratulations."

"I can't believe you would say that. There's no child labor," she says, snatching her vape out of my hand.

I raise an eyebrow.

"Oh my God!" she shrieks. "There's not!"

"If you say so. You would know, right?"

"I'm leaving," she says, storming off as fast as she can in her Balenciaga knife pumps. I remember when everyone was up in arms about Balenciaga's BDSM teddy bear scandal, for all of five minutes. No one in fashion cares about anything but fashion; they just pretend to to save face.

I'd call out to Keira and apologize, but what for?

I'm just bummed she took her vape.

"Scorpio," I say, shaking my head. I go back inside and downstairs to find Veronica and Kaleigh at the bar, their arms crossed.

"Why would you say that to Kiera?" Veronica asks me, yelling over the music.

"Because I thought Kaleigh was the one with the SLIP partnership."

"I would never. *Never*," Kaleigh says. "Never ever."

"She just texted the whole thread except for you," Veronica says. "It's bad. She's pissed."

I shrug. "She'll get over it. Besides, you know I'm not wrong."

"Yeah, but you don't *say* that." I hate when Veronica gets all high and mighty. She moved to New York from South Carolina with nothing but good looks and a box set of *Sex and the City* DVDs. She found a lawyer boyfriend who will soon be her husband, who will buy her a nice house in the suburbs, and after the wedding and the move, once the house is furnished, she'll realize she needs to pivot her content, so she'll start having babies, who will hopefully be cute enough to post.

Why is everyone so predictable?

"You should call her tomorrow and say you're sorry," Kaleigh says. "Avoid more drama."

"Why do I have to apologize for being right?" I ask.

The two of them exchange a look.

"If my friends don't want to side with me, I'm sure the general public will," I say, smiling as I make my veiled threat.

"Yeah, you're right," Kaleigh says. She fakes a yawn. "You know, I'm getting tired."

Coincidentally, Veronica is, too.

They say a quick goodbye and hurry out. I just broke an unspoken rule of influencer etiquette, and now they're uneasy. We don't sabotage; we support. If I were to publicly call out SLIP, what about

Shine Inc.? Where do they source their diamonds? Did Veronica ever ask? And what about the face-tuning? What about the Photoshop? What about the lie of the lives we sell?

I don't fully consider myself an influencer, since I have a career as a stylist. But I've done sponsorships. We all play in the same shallow, dirty sandbox.

I think about Austin at the nursing home. Doing something good with his life. Selfless. And where did that get him? His mom's basement.

I think I miss him. Which makes me hate him.

He's not good because he can't be good. Because no one's good. Not Dad. Probably not even Tommy.

I crawl out of Scorpio and start to wander. I want food but I'm not hungry, or I'm hungry but don't want food. I'm thirsty. I'm tired. I don't want to sleep. I want drugs. I want to scream. I want to go home. I want to be at the house, at Edgewood, staring at that frowning face. I want to stare for so long that it smiles back at me.

"Look who it is," I hear. I turn around, and there's someone familiar. Handsome. Right on time. Ethan. "My Lower East Side Cinderella."

I curtsy. "Maybe you could help me. I seem to have lost my slipper."

He approaches, breaking off from his group of drunken bros. "Last time I saw you, you were kicking me out of a car."

"What poor manners," I say. "Let me make it up to you."

He laughs. "Yeah, uh, I'm not falling for that again."

"For what?" I ask, hailing a lucky cab. I open the door. "Are you coming?"

"You don't respond to me. Not one text."

"I'm very busy," I say. "The meter's running. Time is money, Ethan. You know that better than anyone."

"If you kick me out again, I swear . . ." he trails off. He signals back to his boys, then follows me into the cab.

I give the driver my address, then inch closer to Ethan as he buckles his seat belt.

"Such a Boy Scout," I say, stroking his leg.

He looks me over, his eyes landing on my neck. He reaches out and lifts my snake charm.

"Did you get this at Veronica's party?"

"I did," I say. "Along with a lifetime supply of glitter."

"I was washing it out of my hair for weeks," he says.

We start going at it once we're across the bridge, after we've taken in the view of the river. We don't come up for air at all down Flatbush Avenue. He's not a good kisser, but it's something for me to do.

He moves my hand over his jeans so I can feel that he's hard.

It doesn't turn me on. It makes me nauseated.

What am I doing?

"Here is fine," I tell the cabdriver, fumbling for my wallet.

"I got it," Ethan says.

I let him pay, even though I'm pretty sure I'm about to ditch him again.

I open the car door and stumble out onto the sidewalk. I smell smoke. Fire. Is it me? My imagination? The phantom scent of the book burning haunting my nostrils?

But then I feel heat.

"Shit," Ethan says.

We turn the corner to flashing lights. Fire trucks. Flames—red and yellow, tall and reaching. Ruthless. Ravenous. The air is thick with ruin. It's hell on my block.

My building is on fire.

24

IT was the genius in 6B. He threw a party on the roof, and someone in his esteemed crew, probably high out of their mind, decided they wanted s'mores, so they constructed a makeshift firepit, which wasn't so much a firepit as it was just setting the roof on fire.

After two days, I was able to retrieve my laptop, my jewelry, my clothes, and my fire safe with all my paperwork—passport, tax records, et cetera. The fire safe was a gift from Dad when I moved in. He also insisted I get renter's insurance, which I'm now grateful for. The damage to my unit was minimal, thankfully. The top units weren't so lucky.

On the bright side, because of my fiery misfortune, my friends can't be mad at me for what I said to Kiera. She's forgiven me. Or has at least claimed to. They all took me out to lunch yesterday. Ethan got me a day pass at a spa. My sisters have been checking up on me. Aunt Helen sent me cash. Dad called. He offered to come get me, but I said no. He offered to put me up in a hotel in the city, and I said fine.

I'm coming up on a week in the hotel.

Everything I own—well, everything I could salvage—reeks of smoke.

This room now reeks of smoke.

I can't stay here forever.

I can leave anytime I want. I don't live here. If you want to play with me, you have to play nice.

That's what I said before I left the house. Before I came back to the city and smoked on my roof to alleviate some stress. Before I offered words of encouragement to my idiot neighbor, inadvertently inspiring him to commit arson.

This isn't the fault of whatever's there at Edgewood. Not directly. It's not a coincidence either. It's cause and effect. It's distress instigating poor judgment manifesting disaster. It's how all bad situations get worse. Give in to despair, let your demons win, end up like my mother.

I know better.

"You're welcome to stay with me," Austin says. I have him on speaker while I soak in the tub. "Work on your house during the day. Crash here at night. There's a guest room upstairs, too. If you'd rather."

"A guest room?"

"I'm giving you options."

"Interesting," I say. "Don't want to live in sin with me? You know, I never took you for old-fashioned."

"No? What if I am? Let's get married."

"Don't tempt me with a good time."

"Mom would be thrilled."

The joke isn't funny anymore. "I'll let you know when I figure things out. I have to go."

I hang up.

The thought of going back to Edgewood terrifies me, makes me forget how to breathe, makes me feel like I'm being constricted, squeezed to death by my own skin. And yet somehow the thought of never going back is even worse.

Because I want to go back. Even if it scares me. Maybe because it scares me.

It occurs to me that I now have an excuse I didn't have before. No one could blame me if I were to ditch the renovation project in the wake of this fire. There's no pressure for me to finish. When I want to be done, I'll be done. I'll have Leda put the house on the market—tell her I need the money for a deposit on a new apartment. She won't be able to argue with that.

Part of me still does want to finish, to show them, to spite my sisters, to spite Dad. But we'll see.

Part of me just needs to know what will happen. How could I walk away now? Just go on living with this half-baked supernatural mystery floating around in the back of my mind. Return to my old life, which seems, unfortunately, far less stimulating post-demon.

I had this boyfriend in high school—Kyle Matheson—who loved to go see horror movies. He'd pay for the tickets and the popcorn, and we'd make out in his car in the parking lot after, and he was beautiful and a great kisser, so I was game. I came home late one summer night to my sisters in the upstairs bathroom, Daphne helping Leda color her hair.

"Where have you been?" Leda asked.

"The cinema," I'd said, flipping my curls over my shoulder for some drama.

"What'd ya see?" Daffy asked.

"An art house film called *Cannibal Dinner Party*."

They'd both rolled their eyes. Horror wasn't the genre of choice among the Barneses, for obvious reasons.

"I don't know how you could sit through that garbage," Leda said.

"Kyle likes them," I'd said, spritzing some perfume to combat the scent of ammonia. "It's not so bad. They're fun."

"I never understood those movies," Daphne said. "I can't suspend my disbelief. Like, a bunch of stupid fucking teenagers are, like, there are rumored to be murderous cannibals or ghosts or whatever over there, we should go! Why would anyone do that?"

"Curiosity. Excitement," I'd said. "I'd go."

I remember how they looked at me. Like I was crazy. I shrugged and left the bathroom, understanding there was a fundamental difference between us. Some people jump out of airplanes, some people backpack alone across Europe, some people climb Mount Everest, some people swim with sharks, some people fuck hot strangers they meet on the street, some people do heroin, chase a high because they know what it's worth, despite the danger. And some people sit around thinking, *I would never.*

Yes, the house scares me. But nothing scares me as much as the idea that I might become one of those tragic, boring, would-never people.

So I pack up my hotel room, drop some things off in my storage unit, and take an Uber all the way to New Jersey. I put it on Dad's account. I hope he sees where I went.

THERE'S a package waiting on the doorstep when I get to Edgewood.

I take it inside and open it, my back to the wall with the frowning face.

It's the copy of Mom's book I ordered. It's somehow in even

worse condition than the copy she left me. The spine cracked, cover frayed. The pages are yellow, and it smells—top note of vomit, base note of BO.

I sit at the dining table and flip through the book, looking for the place where I left off. But I can't concentrate, can't focus with the frowning face behind me. I can feel it looking at me.

I change into my painting shorts and T-shirt and then get out my putty knife and some Spackle. I patch the deep gashes in the wall, trying not to think about what made them. Who made them.

I ruin my manicure in the process.

The utility sink in the garage would be useful to wash off my putty knife and scrub the Spackle currently crusting on my cuticles, but I refuse to go back in there after the mouse massacre. I wash my hands in the kitchen sink instead.

I catch a whiff of something rancid, follow my nose to the fridge.

I open it to find guts.

Purple gore.

Jelly. The jar is on its side, lid off. Smeared all over, spotted with fuzzy white mold.

I slam the door shut.

My eyes find the bread on the counter. It's also covered in mold, so much it's practically bursting out of the plastic.

It is horrifically humid, but even still, this is a freakish amount of mold. And without Dad, there's no one to call to clean this up on my behalf.

I tie a bandanna around my face to cover my nose and mouth, and then I toss the bread into a garbage bag, reluctantly move on to the fridge. I turn on some music while I scrub, but it doesn't make the experience any more tolerable. Moldy, sticky, disgusting.

I ruin two sponges and go through an entire bottle of lemon-scented Lysol. The fridge now legitimately sparkles, but as far as I'm concerned, it'll never be clean again.

When I finish up in the kitchen, I take a long shower. The water temperature fluctuates between piping hot and freezing cold. There's no comfort to be found, even after I towel off and get dressed and sit on the couch. I'm sweating, then I'm shivering, so I get a blanket, then I'm sweating again.

The humidity reaches its breaking point, and it starts to pour. I get up to close the sliding doors. I pause to watch the rain, listen to the meaty drops pound against the house. It almost conceals the sound. The long dragging footsteps. Almost.

I'm too afraid to turn around.

My eyes peel wide, won't blink. My neck is stiff. Head stuck. The only part of me that moves are my lips, my teeth, my jaw—they tremble and chatter.

I stare straight ahead at my own reflection in the sliding glass doors. Out of the corner of my eye, I notice something else. A silhouette. A shadow beyond me, in the room behind me.

I know this shadow is too big to belong to me, to be mine. And its shape . . . my brain can't quite make sense of it.

There's a flash of lightning, followed by a low rumble of thunder, and in its wake comes quiet. An eerie silence.

I finally turn, slowly, to face the other side of the room.

There's no one there. Nothing. Except for the book, which is still on the table. Though in a different spot on the table. Maybe. I'm not sure where I left it. I don't remember.

I walk over and pick it up. It falls open to a section I haven't read before.

This copy isn't annotated by my mother.

But it is annotated.

PLAY NICE

Father Bernard had given me a list of contacts to reach out to, to further inspect the house and corroborate his assessment of demonic possession.

The first call I made was to a team of paranormal investigators out of Baltimore. They agreed to take the case if I paid for their travel. I borrowed the money from my sister, not telling her what it was for. I was embarrassed, ashamed—which was made all the worse when the team arrived a month after my initial call. Four men with an excessive amount of "equipment," with muddy boots they didn't bother to remove.

They trampled through the house, holding up their devices, their toys.

"Well, there's definitely something here," one of the men said, pulling up his jeans. "Strongest in that downstairs bedroom. It's not aggressive enough to be demonic, in my opinion."

"What do you mean, 'aggressive'?"

"Demons scratch, bite, gouge. Growl, snarl. It's more targeted. Demons, they generally possess people, not places."

"But Father Bernard said—"

He held up a hand, the rudest way to interrupt a person. "He referred you to us for a second opinion. Priests, they only deal in exorcisms. We deal with all supernatural interferences. If you only eat chicken, everything is chicken."

The rest of his crew was already packing up.

"If it isn't . . . a demon, then what is it?"

WEAR ANY SKIN
WANT HOUSE SKIN

"Poltergeist. Restless ghost that forgets it was ever human. They're more mischievous than malignant," he said, patting my arm and staring at my chest. "This is good news. You don't want a demon, trust me."

"It doesn't feel mischievous. It feels like . . . like it wants to isolate me. Make me feel alone. And insane."

Hearing myself say it out loud, I realized I could be talking about my ex-husband and not whatever was living in my house. I wondered if I was projecting.

"Yeah, well," the guy said, shrugging.

"What do I do about a poltergeist?"

"We could take care of it for you . . ." He went on to quote me his services for thirty-five hundred dollars.

When I told him I didn't have that kind of money, he suggested I take out a loan.

"You don't want to put your daughters at risk, do you?" he asked.

"I thought you said it wasn't malignant?"

He shrugged again. "Still. Demons are more violent, but poltergeists are known to make physical contact. Yank hair, pull out your chair, things like that."

"I'll have to think about it."

He gave me his card. "Call me. For anything."

With a wink, he was gone.

The next names on the list were an older married couple from Maine, along with their son-in-law and another AV club–type lackey. They brought video cameras, and when I told them I would prefer it if they didn't film, they bristled. They'd planned on interviewing me and my daughters, on filming inside the house, the entire excursion. They were putting together a documentary about themselves, about their adventures in ghost hunting. They hadn't mentioned on the phone that their visit, their "services," were offered in exchange for this. Permission to film, to be recorded, to open myself up to public scrutiny.

I was already under the thumb of my ex-husband, whose constant criticisms of me and my parenting had put me in such a state of anxiety and paranoia that it seemed particularly cruel for me to have ended up in yet another situation where I was being interrogated. Questioned about something I knew to be true. Put on trial for my behavior, my choices, my beliefs.

I initially refused, knowing any footage they shot could be used against me, but eventually I relented. They were at my doorstep, and I was desperate.

I gave them permission, signed a waiver. I was explicit in my instruction for them not to talk to my daughters, who I'd sequestered in the upstairs bedroom with a promise of a trip to the mall if they didn't come out for an hour.

It didn't matter. Cici left the room to use the bathroom, and the husband interviewed her upstairs while I was downstairs with the wife, explaining the laughter I'd heard the first night in the house.

"It's obviously living in this room," the woman said, shuddering as we walked into Cici's bedroom. "Ooh boy. It doesn't like that I'm here."

She started to retch.

"What do you mean?" I asked.

"It doesn't want me here!" she screamed. Her eyes bulged, turning from green to yellow, then they rolled over white. She stuck her tongue out at me. It seemed to extend too far, beyond what was humanly possible.

I backed out of the room, and she followed me, tongue wagging.

She started to laugh, and it sounded just like the laughter I'd heard that first night. The laughter I'd just been describing.

Her son-in-law was filming the whole time.

Thankfully, due to a series of lawsuits and scandals that plagued the couple in the months and years following their visit, this footage and Cici's brief interview were never released. My ex did manage to get ahold of it, to show in court.

"Hi," the husband said, catching Cici in the hall while she was on her way to the bathroom. That upstairs hallway is dark without the lights on, and Cici emerged from the darkness wearing a blue dress with ribbons, one she picked out at Goodwill. She was blissfully unaware of the resemblance it bore to the ensemble of *The Shining*'s Grady sisters, something I'm sure was not lost on either the social workers or the judge.

She narrowed her eyes at the strange man in front of her. "Who are you?"

"I'm here to help," he said.

"No, you're not," she said. "Why do you smell bad?"

She was born with a sensitive nose and blunt mouth.

"Like rotten eggs," she said.

He turned to the camera, to the AV kid. "Sulfur."

"You should leave," she said, approaching the bathroom door.

"Why's that, sweetheart?" he asked.

"Don't call me sweetheart," she said coldly. "Did you hear me? You should leave *now*."

"I'm sorry. Why should I leave now?"

"Because it doesn't like you. Because if you stay here, it'll come out and get you. When you see it, you'll wish you didn't. Then you'll be sorry."

She gave a devious little half smile, one I recognized—she'd given me the same look a thousand times. But to anyone else, it could be interpreted as villainous. A sign that she was corrupted by the evil in the house. Or, according to my ex, by me.

She went into the bathroom and slammed the door in the camera's face.

"Go away," she said through the door. "Bye!"

LEAVE AND COME BACK NEVER BUT STILL I LOOK INSIDE THEIR HEADS AND DRINK THE GOOD THOUGHTS OUT ☺

The footage intersects as the wife runs up the stairs and out the front door. Then both cameras cut to static.

They left with what they came for, and I was left with nothing. Less than nothing. They used me.

After they drove off back to Maine, I brought my daughters to the mall as promised and allowed them each to pick out a reward for their cooperation. Elle chose a book from Barnes & Noble, Dee chose nothing, and Cici chose an expensive pair of earrings from Macy's. Once I'd made good on my bribe, I took them to the food court, where we split two plates of chicken teriyaki, and I told them the truth.

"That's why we're going to church?" Dee asked.

"It's a precaution," I said.

"I don't think the house is haunted," Elle said, crossing her arms over her chest.

I knew she would tell her father eventually. She was loyal to him. She resented me because I was there, because I was the one raising them. If I'd begged, maybe I could have bought myself some time. Delayed the inevitable.

Or I could have gone on lying, but I was exhausted, and I'd already kept so much from them.

How do you prepare your daughters for the world? How do you protect them?

Do you tell them every ugly truth so that they understand? So that they know what to expect?

Or do you fill their heads with dreams and hope for the best? Hope that they want more for themselves and don't settle for the way the world is, that they demand it to be better, and maybe because of that it will be?

"I wouldn't worry about it," Cici said, bending her plastic fork.

"What do you mean?" I asked her.

She shrugged. "It's happy with us, but it didn't like those people."

Her sisters looked at her. She ignored them.

"Does it . . . talk to you?" I asked her.

She rolled her eyes. "Not your business."

"It *is* my business."

"Whatever. Never mind," she said, shifting in her seat. I knew the harder I pressed, the more she'd hold back. She was stubborn in that way. So I let it go. I took the girls home.

Later, when I said good night to Cici, I sat at the foot of her bed for a while, waiting for her to tell me more about the presence in the house that she seemed to have some connection to. That she knew, as I did, was real.

"Elle's gonna tell Dad," she said, after about twenty minutes had passed. "He'll be mad."

"I know."

"He wants us to live with him. But it wants us to stay."

"What's '*it*'?"

"I don't know," she whispered. "*Shh*. It's listening. It's here."

"Cici. This is serious."

She started to giggle. This wild, erratic giggling that I'd never heard out of her before. "I'm the favorite," she said. She suddenly stopped her giggling and looked at me, now gravely serious. "I'm its favorite."

25

I FALL asleep reading, and when I wake up it's dark. It's night.

The house is different at night. Or maybe it's just harder to be brave in the dark.

I grab the vape I bought before I left the city, my phone, and my wallet, slip on my shoes, and walk over to Austin's.

It's no longer raining, but there's a dampness in the air, and it stinks of summer-ripe earth. Grass and mushrooms and geraniums and dirt.

I call Austin.

"Hey," he says.

"I'm coming over. Okay?"

"Okay." He hangs up first, which I don't like.

"Look who's back in the neighborhood," he says, meeting me at the end of his driveway a minute later.

I hit my vape, exhale into the space between us.

"Do what you want, but those things will destroy your lungs," he says, pointing to the vape.

"Appreciate your concern," I say, hitting it again.

He tosses his car keys up and catches them in the other hand. "Let me buy you some disco fries."

"My Prince Charming. My knight in shining armor."
"All right. I'll throw in a milkshake."

IT'S a rare occasion that I don't want to think or talk about myself, but tonight is one of those rare occasions. Instead, I ask Austin questions about himself. He shares and I listen. Really listen.

His father's death was unexpected and hard. His older brothers are overachievers, both assholes but in different ways. His mother was diagnosed with MS when he was a sophomore in college. He's got an insane amount of student debt that he's doing his best to chip away at. He's had two long-term girlfriends—one in high school and one in his early twenties who he thought he'd end up with. They lived together. He was the one to call it off, which he claims is worse because now he has to live with wondering if he did the right thing. She just got married to a guy in his second year of residency.

After they broke up, Austin moved in with his mom.

"It's not easy to meet people when you live with your mom," he says, shrugging, then sucking down the last of his milkshake.

Maybe, but women don't care. It's a confidence issue. Charlie Manson didn't own property, and he was only five foot two. But he had charisma. And good hair.

I think I might think about Charlie Manson too much.

"Are you on the apps?" I ask him, stabbing at a soggy fry.

"I was," he says. "It's demoralizing. Are you?"

"God no," I say, laughing. "I have no trouble meeting people."

The way he looks at me, I understand that he's sincerely invested in whatever this is between us. It'd be so much simpler if he wasn't.

I resent him for not being able to keep this casual.

Why, as a man, wear a slim gold chain if you're open to

commitment? That's the universal symbol for fuckboy. A chain like that comes with a box of ribbed Trojans and a habit of liking Instagram models' bikini pics.

I know what to do with guys like that. I don't know what to do with him.

Never fall in love. It'll ruin your life. More motherly wisdom. Funny, what memories stick.

"How's your milkshake?" he asks me. "I've never had a strawberry milkshake before."

"You're missing out," I say. "You want a sip?"

He shakes his head. "That's okay."

There's an awkward pause as I fiddle with my straw.

"Hey, can I ask you something?" he says. He doesn't wait for me to respond. "Are we hanging out because you like spending time with me or because you don't like being alone at the house?"

I take a beat. "Both."

He laughs. "Fair enough."

Another beat. "I . . . I got that other copy of my mom's book. I started reading it today."

"What's that like?"

"It's pretty . . . I don't know. It's whatever. I can't figure out if it's me, in the book, or some fictional character named Cici. I can't . . . I can't remember a lot from that time. I mean, I was seven. How much do you remember from when you were seven?"

"You. I remember you."

"Wow. Cute."

"Sorry." He looks up at the ceiling, runs his hands through his hair. "Um, I haven't really thought about it. Some, I guess?"

"Some. I have *some* memories. And then I have my sisters and my dad telling me what happened. I've been hearing their versions for so long, believing their versions for so long. And now, now I have my mom's book. And then, even if I said or did any of the things she wrote about, it could have just been for attention. But . . ."

A chance to tell him—to tell someone—the truth. Here and now. *It's not all fiction. The haunting is real.*

"But . . . ?"

"Nah. Never mind. The whole thing is so cliché," I say, throwing my hands up. "It's every trope. And I'm that trope of the creepy kid. The kid with terrible vibes. That's not me. My vibes have been impeccable since birth. And what's even more frustrating is that the footage, from the paranormal investigators or whatever, is nowhere on the internet. I checked. Mom was telling the truth about the lawsuits against them, that weird married couple. Their scandals are well documented. Plenty of detailed information available on how they took advantage of the mentally ill and financially desperate. But there's only one mention, one blog post on their website, about their trip to Edgewood. Our suffering must not have been interesting enough for them because it's a meager three paragraphs. And there's nothing specific about me. Nothing to prove or disprove how I really was. Woof. My bad. Let's talk about something else," I say, finishing my milkshake. He stares at me. "What?"

"Nothing. Just . . . I'm sorry. That's shitty. If it helps, I remember your vibes being good. That I remember. One hundred percent."

"Impeccable," I correct him. "Impeccable vibes."

He nods. "Not creepy at all."

"Thanks," I say. I always forget that he knew me back then, that he has some context. Limited context, yeah, but still. "It does, actually. Help. Thank you."

"Anytime," he says, grinning.

He pays the check and takes me back to his house. We have tea with his mom, and the two of them gang up on me for having never seen *Game of Thrones*.

"I'm just not into hobbits," I say.

"There's no—" Dawn starts.

Austin cuts her off. "She knows, Mom. She's messing with us."

"Oh!" Dawn blows a raspberry at me, and I give a devious little laugh. I fit in so well here, I wonder how my photo isn't already on the wall.

Austin and I go to bed around midnight, and it's the first time we've slept next to each other without hooking up. He kisses me good night and that's it.

He falls asleep right away, but I can't get there. Panic throbs through my body, rattles my bones, makes my heart ache. Right now, it feels scarier to be beside him than anything else I've experienced over these last two months. To be so close to someone who might care about me. Who might be trying to get me to care about them, who might be trying to earn my trust, who might be succeeding in those endeavors.

I'm losing my grip. On this. On the house. On my family. On my mind. My life.

I don't know how to not be in control.

I close my eyes, and I see the moldy bread, the mess in the fridge, the frowning face on the wall. I hear the echo of that horrible laughter. There's nothing to drown it out. It's inside my head.

Austin rolls over and puts his arm around me. He reeks of antiseptic and old lady perfume and diner, and I wish I could bottle it—his scent right now—and the way it feels to be held when I'm afraid.

THE morning is all sunshine and blue skies. Austin leaves for work, and I go back to the house. The first thing I do is search for signs of mischief, but nothing is out of place. Everything is exactly as I left it. The book is on the coffee table.

PLAY NICE

My heart sinks.

Wow. Am I . . . *disappointed*?

I realize some part of me was hoping for another grand gesture. For more proof. Maybe even more fear.

Fear is new and exhilarating. Addicting.

I walk over to the wall I patched yesterday, run my hand over the dried Spackle. I'll need to sand and repaint today.

All that awaits me are ordinary chores, ordinary problems.

I change into my paint clothes and touch up the wall in the living room, then start cutting in. I listen to the music Mom used to play for us. Heart, Linda Ronstadt, Sade, Kate Bush, Cher, Fleetwood Mac.

She used to dance around the kitchen while she was cooking, glass of wine in her hand. Back at the old house before Dad left. After Dad left, there was no more dancing. Only more wine.

One time I caught her here at Edgewood with a bottle of vodka and a pack of cigarettes out on the deck. Not dancing but swaying.

"Ya . . . ya should be . . . a . . . sleep," she said, slurring, lighting a cigarette with a hot pink Bic.

The memory begins and ends there.

But the lighter . . .

I look down at my arm, at my scar from the burn.

I step back from the wall, dripping paint on the carpet.

"Shit." My brush goes in the kitchen sink. I seal the can of paint using my new mallet, feeling like a Looney Tune for an amusing few seconds.

While the paint dries, I go out to the deck and call Daphne.

She doesn't pick up and neither does Leda.

Or Veronica. Or Hannah.

I suspect I'm being avoided because now I'm someone with problems.

No one wants to talk to someone with problems. Especially not the person they've always relied on to not have any. My brand is fun and glamour, so it's unsurprising this pivot isn't going over particularly well.

It's annoying nonetheless.

There is someone else I can call. Someone I was convinced not to trust by people I trusted. Since I was a kid, I was told to be wary of her biases, of her hatred for my father, of her version of events as told to her by my mother, her sister.

I'm beginning to understand that it's no longer about whether I trust her. I've just been afraid to hear what she has to say, afraid of what it could unravel.

But everything is already unraveling. So I call Aunt Helen. She answers.

"Hi, Clio," she says. "How are you doing?"

There's concern in her voice, and it bothers me. Between Mom's death and the fire, I've actually become more than just someone with problems. I've become someone perceived as a victim.

It occurs to me now that so much of my life and my persona has been constructed to war against this. I didn't want to be the sad woman on the deck with a bottle of wine and pack of cigarettes. I didn't want to be my mother. I also didn't want to be Cici, the child caught up in a horror story. Now I'm in danger of becoming both.

"I'm good," I say, artificially cheery.

"Good," she says, her voice leveling. Even through the phone she can read me, like she did at the funeral. She knows I don't want fuss. Pity.

"Thank you for the money," I say. "That was generous."

"You're welcome. I'm sorry that happened to you," she says. "I had a friend lose a place in a fire. Faulty electric. Awful. Just awful."

"Yeah," I say. "So, did Mom ever mention to you how I got my burn?"

A few seconds pass. I hear her breathing. "Where is this coming from?"

"I just remembered something," I say. "She had this hot pink lighter. I think that's what burned me. But I have no recollection of how it happened. Who did it. Dad said it was Mom. The judge seemed to believe him."

Another pause from Helen. "He wouldn't know because he wasn't there."

"Right," I say, sitting down in one of the plastic Adirondack chairs. The only time I remember him being in the house was when he yelled at Mom about the church thing. And she was so worried about losing us, why would she suddenly be so stupid as to abuse me in front of him?

Though she wasn't exactly operating on logic by that point. She was wrapped up in her demons.

"But," Helen starts, "your sisters were."

"What?" I ask, startled. I'd forgotten I was on the phone.

I hear her light a cigarette. I close my eyes and see my mother. "Clio, I have to ask. Is this a door you want to open?"

"It's already open," I say, wishing I had my vape. It's somewhere inside, but I'm too lazy to get up. "It's been open. Since . . ."

"Since Alex. Died. Since she died," Helen says, exhaling. "She wanted you to know the truth. I want you and your sisters to be able to forgive her. Understand her. Be able to move on. What I don't want is chaos."

"What's wrong with a little chaos? Keeps things interesting."

"Leda told me about what happened with your father and the book," she says, that seething anger of hers seeping through the phone, making it hot to the touch. "I wanted to call you, but I wasn't sure it was my place."

"Yeah," I say, relieved to finally be connecting with someone sympathetic about the incident. Someone to validate me. "I still can't believe he did that."

"I can," she says. "Clio, listen. There's no love lost between me and him, as I'm sure you're aware. He's perhaps the one person on this planet I can confidently say I despise. And your little stepmother . . ."

She takes a drag, composes herself.

"And still, it didn't bring me any comfort or peace to hear about what transpired between you. Even Lex, she never wanted you or your sisters to hold any animosity toward your father. She was grateful for the relationship you had with him. All she wanted was for you to see her and for you to know that she loved you."

"Okay," I say, irritated by this unexpected kumbaya bullshit.

"My point is, as much as I want you to come to terms with Alex . . . she's gone. Your dad, your sisters, they're still here. Those relationships aren't worth damaging in pursuit of truths of the past."

I push myself to stand, turn around to face the house. My gaze shifts to the sliding glass doors. The reflection of the deck, the surrounding woods. "All due respect, Helen, that's not your call."

She's quiet.

I move closer to the sliding doors. It's me in the reflection. But I look like her.

I repeat my initial question. Slowly, enunciating each word to make my point. "Did Mom ever mention how I got my burn?"

"She didn't know. Your sisters told your dad about the burn. They said they saw Alex do it."

"Oh. Okay, yeah. Wow. Let me call you back."

26

MY sisters continue to ignore my calls. I leave voicemails.
I read. Turn the pages too fast. Get paper cuts. Freakishly deep ones. I lick my wounds and carry on.
I read.

The third and final call I made was to a woman in Connecticut named Mariella.

"Hello, darling," she said when she answered the phone. "I've been expecting your call."

I learned Mariella was a psychic medium who was the head of a group she called "The New England Occultist Collective." She explained she'd met Father Bernard while investigating a haunting in the Hudson Valley in 2003.

"Most people find the supernatural very overwhelming," she said. "But I was born into a house of belief. The sky is blue, the grass is green, the veil is thin. It seems rather silly to me to deny the existence of other possibilities.

Seems far-fetched that we would be all alone in this world."

Mariella's views made sense to me. She was the first person to present the situation in a way that I could metabolize. She was warm and friendly, and I liked her immediately.

"I *am* overwhelmed," I admitted. "Whatever's here in the house with us, I fear it."

"Of course. We fear what we do not understand. I won't sugarcoat it, darling. Not all that moves in parallel to our reality moves with good intent. Try to think of it as this. Everything that exists, exists in need. In want. We operate with our own motives. Some more selfish than others. It sounds to me like you share your home with something that may be rather . . . egocentric."

[Handwritten margin note: THE SELFLESS STARVE PICK MY TEETH WITH THEIR BONES :)]

I laughed. "Wouldn't be the first time."

Mariella told me she would come by that weekend, along with a few members of her collective.

Thankfully, it was a weekend the girls were with their father.

I got off the phone with Mariella, and for the first time since I moved in, I felt like I could exhale.

That night, the girls and I had breakfast for dinner. We flipped pancakes to Fleetwood Mac, sang into spoons.

Thunder only happens when it's raining . . .

I woke up in the night to a crack of thunder. A brutish summer storm.

At the sound, my eyes flipped open. It took a moment for me to realize I couldn't move.

PLAY NICE

It felt as though something heavy was sitting on my chest. I found it difficult to breathe. My entire body was rigid, with pins and needles up and down my limbs.

I attempted to relax back into sleep, but a white flash of lightning warned of more thunder and put me on edge.

There's something terrible about that time between lightning and thunder. That cruel purgatory of anticipation, waiting for the universe to scream.

I realized I still couldn't move. I'd never experienced sleep paralysis before, but my sister Helen had. She went through a spell of it in her teenage years, so I knew what it was. I didn't immediately panic.

Not until something moved in my peripheral vision. My eyes followed the movement.

The door to my room. It swung open. Slowly. So slowly.

I expected to see one of my daughters. Cici.

Instead, there was a hulking shadow. It took up the entirety of the doorway.

A voice in my head. *Don't look.*

Sweat drenched my hair, my back.

Don't look.

It was there. It was there.

The house shook. Thunder.

It stepped inside. Inside the room. Inside the sound of the thunder, to hide its own noise. Its step.

Don't look.

How could I not?

The shadow moved in such a way that I knew it wasn't a shadow. It prowled, crawling along the walls. Into the dark spaces. The corner.

And shadows don't have tails.

Close your eyes.

It was in my head, but it was also standing in the corner of the room, watching me.

Another flash of lightning, and I saw it.

The beast of the house. The demon.

In that split second of light.

A thing of pure nightmare. The face of hell. Of every hideous thing in the world, not just in aesthetics, but in spirit. Roadkill. Swarming bugs. Prey being caught in the jaws of a predator. Open wounds. Charred bones. Parts no longer connected to the body they once belonged to. War. Wreckage. Death. Every image you've ever seen that lingers behind your eyelids, that discomfort you cannot shake. The things that get inside and reassemble you. Make you uglier at your core.

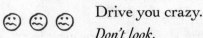

Drive you crazy.

Don't look.

Those big milky eyes staring back at me. Red slits for pupils. Gaping, drooling mouth open, crowded with sharp teeth glinting in the brief, bright flare . . .

I shut my eyes.

The thunder came.

Darkness. Not sleep.

When I finally opened my eyes, it was morning. My alarm clock squawking.

"Some storm last night," I said to the girls over toast.

They hadn't heard it.

When we left the house, the ground was dry—as if it hadn't rained. As if there'd been no storm at all.

PLAY NICE

IT'S raining now. It's been raining on and off for I don't know how long. I've lost track.

Lightning. Thunder.

I ordered a pizza that I have no appetite for. It goes cold on the coffee table in front of me.

I read. Turn the pages. Turn, turn, turn, turn, turn.

Mariella arrived Saturday morning, sweeping into the house dressed in a satin blouse with matching trousers, as if she were attending a glamorous luncheon, not a suburban paranormal investigation.

She didn't come alone.

There was Ruth, a woman about my age with blue hair and a tattoo of a butterfly on her chest. She was a self-described clairvoyant specializing in nonhuman contact.

Then there was Jed, who looked like a California surfer but was a paranormal technician—an expert in EMF (electromagnetic fields) and EVP (electronic voice phenomena). He carried with him a backpack full of funny-looking equipment. He wore a Tommy Bahama shirt barely buttoned, had an August tan in June, and shaggy blond hair.

And finally, Roy. The demonologist. Mariella's nephew. He was handsome, subdued. He seemed more focused than the rest of them. They were on an adventure; he was on a job.

I welcomed Mariella and her team with coffee and donuts.

They were all nice. Enthusiastic. Empathetic.

"Yep! Something's here for sure," Ruth said as soon as she walked in. "You're not wrong about that!"

They all laughed. Except Roy.

We sat down for coffee, and I told them everything that had happened, including the incident two nights prior when I saw the being in my room.

"I might have been dreaming," I said, dismissing myself out of habit.

"I don't think so," Roy said immediately. He seemed embarrassed, like he hadn't realized he'd spoken the words out loud. He blushed and shook his head.

All I felt was relief. It was different from the validation from Father Bernard because these people seemed to be on my side. Allies. More than just believers, they wanted to help me. They didn't appear to be in any rush to leave. There was no judgment. No fear.

When they looked at me, I could tell they didn't see a middle-aged single mother in distress on the verge of losing her mind, of losing everything. They saw me as a person.

My problem didn't intimidate them. And they took it seriously. Took me seriously. Took themselves seriously, but not too seriously.

"We're going to do separate walk-throughs and then compare notes," Ruth explained. "You don't need to worry about anything right now."

Jed laughed. "Nothing to worry about. Except for the fact you've got a bunch of weirdos roaming around your house."

Ruth elbowed him. "You know what I meant."

"We're here to help," he said, smiling. All his teeth were chipped.

Mariella escorted me to the back deck. The two of us smoked cigarettes—she used one of those old-fashioned Holly Golightly holders—and talked for hours. She told me about the spiritualist movement, about her upbringing, her beliefs.

"Does it bother you?" I asked. "That some people think . . ."

I stopped myself, not wanting to offend.

"Darling, what other people think of me is none of my business," she said.

We spoke until it was her turn to make a pass through the house.

When she left me, Roy joined me.

He didn't speak. He looked paler than he had when he arrived. I offered him a smoke, and he accepted.

After a while, I asked, "It's bad, isn't it?"

He reached out and put his hand on my hand. His way of both answering my question and comforting me.

By the time they were finished, the sun had set. They called me inside and we gathered around the dining table.

Jed spoke first. "The bad news is you have a demon living in your crawl space. The good news is we can help."

"How?" I asked.

"We will need to call in Father Bernard and have him perform an exorcism," Mariella said, pouring me a glass of bourbon from a bottle she must have brought—it wasn't mine. "Ruth and Roy have experience with demons and can assist."

"I'm glad you called us. With all our experience, I feel confident in our assessment," said Ruth. "We can help. But we shouldn't delay the exorcism. I believe the demon has taken an interest in your daughter, ~~Cici~~." CLIO

"What does that mean, 'taken an interest'?"

"Please know that it won't come to this. We won't let it," Roy said, standing. "But from what we can tell, the demon living in the house has attached itself to Cici. That attachment will be severed through this exorcism, but the sooner the better, before it progresses to codependency. Now, I don't think it will. If the demon had any intention of possessing Cici, I believe it would have done so already. Some demons want to possess bodies. Humans. Minds. Others are content to possess places. Some demons thrive by causing chaos. Others pain, and grief. What most people fail to understand is that demons, above all, are beings of attachment. On their own, they have no power. We give them power. We give them purpose. Now, some use their power to exert control. Others for fun. They're just bored."

IT'S maybe the most jarring thing I've come across in the entire book.

They're just bored.

I'm not sure why I find this particular detail so unsettling, why it's got me queasy.

I set the book down on the coffee table, stretch, check my phone. Austin sent me a novel-length text about having to cover a coworker's shift because their babysitter fell through and they have no one to watch their kid, so now he has to stay on until one a.m.

I type out a response. **Okay but who's gonna watch me??**

I delete it and say nothing instead.

I'm unjustifiably angry with him for not being around. I resort to scrolling to temporarily change my brain into placid mush.

Once I've had my fill of social media fluff and internet gossip, I get up to go to the bathroom.

It's pretty dark out now. Getting late. Still raining, so I can't open the windows even though it's hot and sticky and gross. I flick on every light switch I pass. Living room. Kitchen. Hallway.

Bathroom.

I go, flush, wash my hands. Splash some water on my face. I look tired. Am tired. I lean closer to the mirror, my hips pressing into the vanity. There are bags under my eyes, a few blackheads on my nose. I haven't been keeping up with my skincare routine, and it shows. While studying my pores, my breath fogs up the mirror. I take a step back.

As the fog dissipates, my surroundings arrive in my reflection. The bathroom. Tile. Shower. Shower curtain. Swaying. Moving. The squeal of rusty hooks traveling across the rod. There's something in the shower, behind the curtain. It's about to reveal itself. It's—

I spin around, reach out and grab the curtain, yank it back. I'm too rough with it, and the rod dislodges, almost smacking me in the head as it comes down. The shower is empty.

There's this heavy, animal panting. It fills the bathroom. It's . . . me. It's me. *I'm* the thing making these ugly sounds. Sounds I've never made before. Sounds of panic. Of fear.

I hold a palm flat to my chest and feel my heart thump against it. Again and again and again and again.

My phone rings in the living room.

I manage a long, deep inhale. Exhale. Another breath. I shake out my limbs, roll my shoulders back, and open the bathroom door.

It's dark.

The lights are off.

"Really?" I ask through a clenched jaw. I sound like Leda. Is this what it's like to be her? To walk around with all this tension and anxiety? Just a giant knot of dread.

Maybe Daphne's right. Maybe I am too tough on her.

I feel around for the switch and flip it back on. The hall illuminates.

My phone stops ringing. Whoever was calling, I missed it.

I shuffle over to the couch, turning on lights as I go. I search for my phone in the abyss between the cushions. When I eventually find it, I have a missed call and text from Daphne on our sister thread.

> **We need to sit down and talk about everything. I made us reservations. Saturday in Manhattan. Mandatory.**

Leda responds with **Okay**.

I give both messages a thumbs-up, the most passive-aggressive response I can think of.

But truth be told, this works out great for me. I want this sit-down. I need it.

Until then, it's just me in this house. Waiting.

With the book.

More paper cuts.

27

The exorcism was scheduled for the following weekend. I asked my ex if he was available to take the girls, and he said he was. He didn't ask any questions, and I was grateful I didn't have to lie. He still didn't know about the possession, and I thought I might be able to keep it that way.

Mariella returned to Connecticut, but Jed, Ruth, and Roy stuck around, renting a room in a local Super 8 hotel. I invited them over for dinner every night that week, as a thank-you and for the company. I told the girls they were friends.

Dee was fascinated with Ruth's blue hair and tattoos. Elle had a crush on Jed. I was enamored with Roy, who was very sweet and attentive to Cici, even when she was peppering him with rude questions.

Their presence in the house made me feel safe.

IMPATIENT, I skim ahead to the exorcism.

"I can't take them," he said. "I never said I would take them."

"What do you mean, you 'can't take them'? We talked about this."

"I didn't know you meant *this* weekend. I thought you meant next weekend."

"Why would it have been next weekend? That's already your weekend!"

"Alex. Don't raise your voice at me. It's *your* weekend. This is the temporary custody agreement. If you can't hold up your end of the agreement, we can discuss it in court," he said.

He'd set me up to fail. It was intentional. I should have known it was too easy when I asked.

"Please," I said, thinking about the exorcism, how it was too late to cancel and too dangerous to put off.

"Can't. We're going away this weekend," he said. "We've had it planned for months, per our original schedule."

"Oh, fuck you!" I said, finally breaking.

"Nice language, Alexandra. Do you speak that way in front of our daughters? Is that the example you want to set?"

I was so angry, I knew my only option was to hang up before I said anything worse.

I called Ruth. "Can they be here? Would it be all right for them to wait outside on the deck?"

"Um...yeah," she said, not sounding confident. "That should be fine."

On Friday night, I took my daughters to mass and to McDonald's, which I rarely did. I let them stay up late and watch TV. I let them sleep in on Saturday. I allowed them sugary cereal, with cut-up strawberries and bananas to alleviate some of my bad-mom guilt, and I told them we were having company. Ruth, Jed, Roy, and Father Bernard.

"That guy?" Cici asked. "Hmm. I don't know about that."

"Is this about the haunting?" Dee asked.

"Yes," I said. "They're going to help make it go away."

Cici burst into a fit of those wild, shrill giggles.

"Cici!" Elle said, plugging her ears, horrified by the sound. "Stop that!"

Dee reached out and shook Cici's arm.

"No one can make it go *away*," Cici wheezed through her giggles. "It *lives* here."

"*We* live here," I said. "This is our house. You, me, and your sisters."

That got Cici's attention. She went quiet and swiveled her head toward me. "It was here *first*!"

She jumped up from the table and ran downstairs. I followed her.

She'd shut herself in her room.

"Cici," I said, knocking. I realized I was still holding the knife I'd been using to cut fruit. "Cici, open up."

"It's never going to leave, and neither are we!" she shouted.

"Cici, stop this."

I tried the knob. Locked.

"Cici, unlock this door right now!"

She started her giggling again.

"This isn't funny! This isn't a joke. This is serious," I said, pounding on the door. "Please, Cici. Open up."

Her giggles got louder and louder, and I recognized something inside them or maybe hiding underneath—a distinction I couldn't make—that terrified me.

The demon was laughing with her. Harmonizing with her.

It set something off inside me. Fury. I'd been on edge all morning, with the coming exorcism, with my ex-husband's cruelty. Roy's words echoed in my head: *The demon living in the house has attached itself to Cici.*

I lost it.

I beat against the door.

"No! You will not take my daughter!" I screamed. "You will not take her! You will leave this house! This is my house! *My* house! It's mine! Cici is mine! You will not take her!"

The knife in my hand found its way into the door. I lifted it high and I stabbed into the wood. Over and over.

"I will bleed you out!" I heard myself say. "I will bleed you out!"

I wasn't sure when Cici stopped her giggling. When it went quiet in the house, save for my screaming.

Elle and Dee stood in the hall, wide-eyed. Trembling. Aghast.

When I turned to them, they screamed and ran upstairs.

I called after them, but that only made them scream louder, run faster. They were afraid of me. I took a step back, looked at the knife stuck in the door, and was afraid of myself. For myself. For all of us.

PLAY NICE

I pulled the knife from the door, fell to my knees, and prayed.

The door opened, and Cici stepped out. She was pale, her hair standing on end. She looked at me, reached out and touched my face. Her hands were cold.

"I would never hurt you," I said softly, setting the knife down on the carpet. She looked from it to me, back to it. "Never, ever, ever. You know that. Don't you?"

"I know," she said sweetly. "But what about you?"

"What about me?" I asked. I wanted to hug her, hold her tightly, but I couldn't move. She must have known, because at that moment she wrapped her arms around me. She leaned in close, petting my hair.

Then she whispered in my ear. "You're going to die here."

THE book smacks against the wall. The sound surprises me, even though I'm the one who threw it.

I sit and stare for a minute.

"Yeah. No."

My legs are restless, and I'm chewing on my nails because why not? My manicure is already ruined. I call Aunt Helen again, but this time she doesn't pick up. I'm upset. I'm upset and I have no one to talk about it with, which only makes me more upset.

I will bleed you out. I will bleed you out. I know it happened because I remember it happening, but the specifics of Mom's version reframe my recollection, leave this sticky residue of doubt.

You're going to die here. Absolutely not. I did not, would not ever say that. She's making it seem like I was possessed or like the demon was over my shoulder, constantly whispering in my ear. But I would remember that, wouldn't I?

I can't deny that there's something in this house. And she did die here.

Was she proving a point? Was it vindication? Was it her obsession? Was it inevitable?

Years of excessive drinking. Years of returning to this place, the stress of it. A self-fulfilling prophecy.

I get up and fish my vape out of my bag. I wish I had cigarettes. I've never in my life wished I had cigarettes.

My favorite vices are unavailable to me. I have no liquor and Austin is still at work.

I'm in the suburbs. There are no distractions here, no trouble to get into except for this.

So I walk over and pick up the book—its already fragile binding barely holding together, pages coming loose. I settle back on the couch, pull on my vape, and find where I left off.

I waited on the front steps, smoking a pack of cigarettes, drinking vodka out of a mug. I wasn't proud of myself, of the state I was in, but I could no longer pretend that I was okay when I wasn't.

Father Bernard gave me a passing glance as he went into the house, carrying a Bible and a briefcase. Ruth and Jed were uncharacteristically solemn.

Roy sat beside me on the step. He put his arm around me.

"Rough morning?" he asked.

"What gave it away?"

He smiled at me. "It's going to be all right. We know what we're doing. We've done this before."

"It's powerful," I said. "It doesn't want to leave. And I

don't think . . . I don't think it wants me to leave. You said it's attached to Cici . . . but I feel . . . I feel like it's attached to me, too. Like it wants something from me. My attention. My time. My energy. And I'm giving in. And the more I do, the more it wants."

What I didn't admit to Roy then was that part of me felt at home in this. That the pattern, the dynamic, was familiar to me. That I'd spent my whole life trying to prove myself. That I was used to being siphoned from. That destruction, invisible or unfathomable to outsiders, wasn't anything new or extraordinary to me. That as long as the demon remained in the house, in my life, I could point to it and say—*this*.

I still wanted it gone, but I didn't know who I'd be without it.

NEED ME

Roy put his hand on my knee. What he said next proved to me that I didn't need to admit anything to him, because he already knew.

"It's what I always say, and my aunt, Ruth, Jed . . . they all get sick of me, but it's true. Demons are beings of attachment. Ghosts, they haunt with their own purpose. Sometimes they have messages they're trying to deliver, but it's more about conveying that purpose or posing questions. Depending on why they linger, there can be peaceful coexistence. But not with demons. They're not content to coexist. They seek codependence. Demons will figure out a way in, the most effective way. You're right to suspect it wants your attention, time, energy. They love attention. They'll learn how to get it from you. They'll engage with you to find your triggers. It turns into a dance."

I put out my cigarette. "I seem to have a habit of picking the wrong dance partners."

He stood and reached out his hand to help me up. "Maybe the right one will find you."

I wonder if she incorporated this romantic subplot because she thought it would appeal to female readers, which I find pretty insulting, or if she did it for herself. Or if this actually happened and she found love in a hopeless place.

I think about the handsome grief-stricken man I met at her funeral. Why wasn't he here with her when she died? Were they still happy at the end?

If he was her hero, her soulmate, why did she still die alone?

Maybe he did care, but he didn't care enough. Maybe she thought she found someone who accepted her demons, but if he was really so good for her, wouldn't he have encouraged her to exorcise them? To get and stay sober? To reconnect with her daughters? To sell the fucking house?

I think of the version of the book with Mom's commentary, her notes to me, and in that version she probably clarified whether Roy said these words or if she embellished, and if she embellished, why? There were answers in that book. Not all of them but some. More than I have now. More than I will ever get.

Now I'm angry at Dad all over again.

This is the second time he's separated me from her. The second time he's driven someone close to him into a house possessed, into cohabitation with a demon.

I listen for the demon, but it's been quiet. Politely allowing me to read. I vacillate between fear and affection for it. For the book in my hands. For everything. My life.

Ruth gathered the girls and escorted them outside onto the deck, set them up with various activities—sketchpads and colored pencils, brand-new board games, a deck of cards, a stack of paperback books. She'd bought them a barrel of animal crackers and glass bottles of cream soda. I was so grateful, I started to cry.

Once the tears began to fall, they didn't stop. Wouldn't stop.

As if my body knew of the horrors to come.

-17-

The Exorcism

Father Bernard brought in silver crucifixes and began to place them around the house. Ruth sprinkled baby powder on the carpet downstairs and a line of salt at the top of the stairs in the living room, promising she'd clean up after. She hung a bell on the door to Cici's room and another on the door to the closet. Then she closed both doors.

Jed had a lot of equipment, including cameras.

"Don't worry," he assured me, "the footage is only for us."

We gathered at the dining table. I watched the girls through the sliding glass doors. Elle had picked up a paperback. Dee played solitaire. Cici drew—another picture of the house, her new favorite subject.

"All right," Roy said. "The demon is aware of our presence. However, it operates on its own time. It will decide when to make itself known to us. While we wait, I'd like to establish some ground rules. Do not engage. Ruth, Jed, Alexandra, do not speak to it. Do not acknowledge it. Do not listen to it. Do not look at it. We don't know how powerful it is yet. If it's violent."

I thought about what I'd said to Helen, how I'd told her that I didn't think the demon wanted to hurt me. That what it really wanted was for me to hurt myself.

I wondered, sitting there at the table, silent tears streaming down my face, if that was true.

Any illusions I'd had of safety were suddenly gone.

"We shouldn't underestimate it," Roy said, "but it hasn't shown itself to be aggressive thus far. Whatever happens, I'm here to walk you through it. Don't hesitate to speak to me or ask me questions. Let's join hands. And let's begin. Close your eyes."

I reached out for Roy. For Ruth.

Father Bernard began to pray.

"Lord heavenly Father . . ."

Roy held a rosary and muttered under his breath in Latin. *"Ecce crucis signum, fugiant phantasmata cuncta. Rogamus te ut hunc locum in pace relinquas. Apage! Apage!"*

This went on for what felt like hours. Until we were interrupted by the sliding door opening, to Cici stepping inside.

"Cici. No. Back out," I said.

"It's hot out there," she said.

"Cici," I repeated, my tone sharp.

"It doesn't matter if I'm in here or out there. It won't change what happens."

I looked to Roy, to Father Bernard.

PLAY NICE

Father Bernard took a deep breath, opened his mouth to speak.

He was interrupted by the chime of a bell.

The sound echoed throughout the house.

I turned back to Cici, who raised her eyebrows at me as if to say, *Told you so.*

"Cici," Roy said, giving up his chair. "Will you join us at the table."

"Whatever," she said, climbing onto the chair and smacking her sketchpad down on the glass. In her picture of the house, all the windows were blacked out.

The bell rang again.

Roy continued to mutter in Latin. Father Bernard continued to pray, his voice now booming.

Jed fiddled with his equipment.

And Ruth . . . Ruth started to sweat.

She was pale, pale like Cici had been earlier that day. Sickly looking.

"Ruth," I said, reaching out for her. We'd been holding hands. I couldn't remember when I'd let go. "Ruth, are you okay?"

She grunted. Retched, like she was about to vomit.

Cici didn't flinch. She was busy eyeing Roy.

"Ruth!" I said, standing.

"Okay there, Ruthie?" Jed asked, without taking off his massive earmuff headphones. A rhetorical question.

No one else seemed worried about her. But I had a feeling in my gut. A writhing dread.

I regretted ever calling them. Ever seeking help. I'd doomed them.

The thought was so clear.

I've doomed them.

Bells. The sound now incessant. Somehow louder than Father Bernard, than Roy.

Ruth shook. Her eyes rolled over white. "No, no, no, no, no, no, no, no, no . . ."

"Ruth!"

"She's fine. Leave it alone," Roy instructed me. "Close your eyes. Pray. Cici, what does it want?"

"Don't speak to her!" I snapped at him, panicked, completely terrified.

"Come out, come out, wherever you are . . ." Cici sang, finishing with a grim little laugh.

"Cici," Roy said.

"Stop!" I shouted at him. "Stop this! Stop all of this. This is ridiculous. Ruth needs help."

Ruth's head whipped from side to side, side to side, side to side. Gibberish poured from her lips. I worried she was having a seizure.

"This is normal," Roy said, calmly. "Ruth."

She came back to herself immediately.

I remembered the couple from Maine. The woman walking toward me, her tongue out. It was acting. It was all acting.

"I don't think this was a good idea," I said, doubting every decision I'd ever made in my life that brought me to that moment. I collapsed onto the floor in sobs, holding my knees to my chest. "What have I done?"

They all ignored me. Roy carried on in Latin, Father Bernard with his prayers. Jed with his equipment, Ruth with her head jerking in every direction. Even Cici with her drawing.

PLAY NICE

Even the demon. Ringing the bells.

My sobs turned to screams. I couldn't stand it.

I unleashed the words I'd been holding in for who knows how long. "Get out of my house! Leave me be! Leave me alone! Get the fuck out of my house!" I pounded my fists on the floor, on my chest. I pulled out my own hair.

Still no one looked at me. No one acknowledged me.

I crawled toward the stairs, feeling the grainy salt in the thick carpet. A mess.

"Alex," Roy said. Urgent. "Alex, come back!"

There was a distinct line of salt on the top step. My wrist slid right through it.

"Alex!"

The front door swung open. And shut. Open and shut.

The laughter came. The demonic laughter.

I didn't fall down the stairs. I was pulled.

I was being dragged out of my own house. MY HOUSE SKIN MINE

Or so I thought. Until I hit the landing and the door slammed shut. My head collided with the brick floor, and the world went black. And just as I came to, I saw it. Eyes watching me from the dark of the downstairs hall. Pale and cloudy with vertical red slits for pupils.

By the time everything came back into focus, it was gone.

The ringing in my ears wasn't the bells. The bells were quiet.

Everything was quiet.

Except for the laughing.

And then Jed.

There are no words to describe the sounds he made.

Sounds of absolute anguish. The chaos emanating from the worst pain imaginable. Sounds of hopelessness. Of the kind of harm that can never be undone.

As I ascended each step, my vision blurring, my body aching, I knew whatever waited for me at the top of the stairs wasn't as terrible as the thing lurking at the bottom.

My eyes found my daughters, the three of them standing out on the deck, the sliding glass doors wide open. Elle looked at me, her expression full of contempt rather than fear, and she pulled the door shut. She'd never open it again, not for me.

That's when I turned to Jed and saw what was happening to him. He was struggling to remove his headphones. Whenever he pulled them away from his ears, they would snap back onto his head, like magnets. Or maybe his fingers were slipping because of all the blood. It was pouring out of his ears.

Father Bernard stood rigid, clutching his Bible to his chest.

Ruth opened and closed her mouth like a goldfish. She was facing forward, but her gaze was all over the place, her eyes rolling around inside her head.

Roy crossed himself repeatedly.

Something compelled me to do the same.

Then I made toward Jed, readying myself to help him. But he'd done it. He'd finally gotten the headphones off.

His ears were charred and blistered, spewing crimson everywhere. His blond hair was soaked with blood.

He took a wobbling step back and then fell to the floor with a thud.

PLAY NICE

Elle and Dee screamed so loud, I thought they'd shatter the glass.

Cici, unaffected, gave me that same smug look she had when she first came in. The raised eyebrows. *Told you so.*

"I'm calling nine-one-one," I said, heading toward the kitchen for the phone.

Roy caught me by the arm. "Wait. This is what it wants."

"He's hurt!" I tasted blood in the air. I smelled sulfur. "This is a disaster."

"It's disrupting," he said.

I pulled free of Roy's grip. "Disrupting what?"

"It won't go," Ruth said, her voice raspy. Not her own.

"Don't let it in, Ruth," Roy said. "Don't listen to it!"

"Too . . ." Her eyes rolled to the front. She looked at us. Looked at me. "Too late."

Her head flew forward, bashing into the table. There was no time to react before it happened again. And again. And again.

Father Bernard held out his Bible, a crucifix. "In the name of our Lord and Savior, Jesus Christ, be gone! Leave us! You have no power here!"

Again. Again. I heard a crack that I thought was the table, but it wasn't. It was Ruth's nose. Her teeth. Her pretty face now gore, a Halloween mask.

"In the name of our Lord and Savior, Jesus Christ—"

"I don't want to see it anymore!" Ruth cried. Her hands shot to her face. Fingers climbing up her cheeks. Nails digging into her eyes. She was clawing out her eyes right in front of us. The violence of it was quick. The noise was terrible. Ripping. Wet.

I grabbed her forearms, and she struggled against me. She was strong.

"Help me!" I called to Roy.

He finally relented, coming to my aid. We pinned Ruth down on the floor. Roy held her while I called 911.

They sent two ambulances that arrived, mercifully, within five minutes.

Still, it was the longest five minutes of my life. Ruth and Jed bleeding on the salty carpet, their bodies eerily still, breath shallow.

Father Bernard continued to pray but without his former gusto.

We were defeated. Handily.

My daughters cried outside on the deck. Hugged each other.

At least, Elle and Dee cried. Cici allowed them to embrace her, but she didn't turn away from the violent scene. Didn't cry. She showed no emotion.

Father Bernard went to the hospital with Jed and Ruth. Roy refused to leave me and the girls alone in the house.

He cleaned blood and salt from the carpets. He escorted me downstairs to show me the hoofprints in the baby powder, more proof I didn't need.

Elle and Dee locked themselves in their bedroom. They refused to see me, and I didn't press.

Cici sat on the couch with her sketchpad and the big barrel of animal crackers.

"Are you okay?" I asked her.

"Yeah. Are you?"

I would later find out that I had a concussion and two bruised ribs from my fall. "No. I don't think I am."

"Play stupid games, win stupid prizes."

"What?" I asked.

She repeated herself, speaking slowly this time, enunciating each word. "Play stupid games, win stupid prizes."

"Where did you . . . who . . ."

"I don't remember where I heard it," she said, shrugging. "But I thought about it today. I'm sorry you're sad. But you should have left it alone."

"Cici. What's going on with you?" I asked. I hadn't yet exhausted my tears. "Why are you speaking to me like this? Why did you say that thing earlier. About me . . . me dying in the house."

She looked up at me. "It's okay, Mom. I'm going to die here, too."

MY phone rings. It's Helen.

"She made it up," I say. "The book is fucking bullshit."

"I'm doing well, thanks for asking," she says.

"That whole exorcism, that's not how it happened. We were outside for all of it. I didn't come in because I couldn't come in. She locked us out there. For hours. There were no ambulances. No one was bleeding out of their ears or clawing out their eyes. That didn't happen."

"I'm not going to argue with you, Clio."

"Why would she write this? Why would she lie?"

I hear her breathing. I hear her smoking. I don't hear an answer. I try another question. "How did she die?"

She sighs. "If I were the sentimental type, I'd say she died of a broken heart. But technically, she had a heart attack. Years of drinking. High blood pressure. Stress. She'd get sober and then—"

"Let me stop you there, because if she loved and missed us so fucking much, if she was so brokenhearted, she would have gotten sober. Stayed sober."

"It's not that simple, Clio. It's not that easy."

"She could have reached out. She could have apologized."

"She was ashamed. She thought you'd be better off without her. Your father convinced her of that."

"Yeah, see, this is why I can't talk to you. It's not all his fault. Everyone's so quick to point fingers and blame someone else. Dad blames Mom. You blame Dad. Mom blamed the demon. Why can't anyone just give me the truth?"

"Clio, I asked you. I told you I didn't want to damage your relationships or cause chaos. You said it wasn't my call."

"Why was she here? When she died, why was she here at Edgewood? And don't tell me it's because she wanted to feel close to us."

"I don't know. You'd have to ask Roy."

"Okay, yeah. For sure. I trust the demonologist will have some honest answers for me. I'm sure he's a real straight shooter. Where was Roy when she was here dying?"

"What do you want, Clio? I don't think it's the truth. I think it's a version of the truth you can live with. A version of it you can sell yourself. You're curious, you're open, but up until the point it's ugly. I'm sorry that you're struggling. I'm sorry that I can't give you whatever it is you seek. You're asking me why Alex was at the house. Why are *you* at the house?"

The lights flicker, and in the brief but total darkness there's hot breath on the back of my neck. An ugly truth.

"I'm sorry, too," I say.

I hang up, pull my knees to my chest, close my eyes and wait for morning.

28

HANNAH'S baby hates me, which is fine, because it's mutual. Morpheus cries whenever I go near him. He screams now as I push his stroller up a hill in Green-Wood Cemetery.

"Shh," Hannah tells him. "The dead are sleeping."

"Yeah, but they'll sleep through anything," I say.

"I envy them for that. I haven't had a good night's sleep in eighteen months. Here. I'll carry him for a while."

We pause, and Hannah gets Morpheus out of the stroller and attaches him to her chest with some kind of wrap thing. They're both in all black, a little skull adorning the kid's onesie. Hannah covers his head with a black bucket hat.

"Where does one buy goth baby clothes?" I ask.

"There are places," she says. "You'd be surprised."

We pause for a brief photo shoot near some mausoleums. Content creation among the bones. It's more her aesthetic than mine, but I participate because I need something to post, to make my life appear haunted in a glamorous, aspirational way instead of a depressing, tortured, terrifying way.

I've been staying with Hannah for the last two nights. Before that, Veronica. But her boyfriend and I used to hook up before they got together, and she doesn't know, and he's not subtle, so it's complicated. And they only have a pull-out couch, which is not ideal. Hannah has a guest room and a partner I've never touched. But she has this asshole baby.

He side-eyes me now from her chest, curling his tiny baby lips into a punk rock snarl.

"You're meeting your sisters tomorrow?" Hannah asks.

"Yeah," I say. "Then I'll be out of your hair."

"You're welcome to stay," she says, but I know she doesn't mean it.

After being freshly traumatized by the exorcism chapter of *Demon of Edgewood Drive* and my little chitchats with Aunt Helen, I redirected my energy to looking at apartments online and scheduling viewings. I've been back in the city working and checking out new places all week. My friends have been willing to put me up because they feel sorry for me, which I've reluctantly accepted. I decided to stay in New York through the weekend, for the big lunch with my sisters.

Avoidance has been an effective strategy for the house, the book, the demon. The same can't be said for Austin. I miss him. But I don't want to see him or talk to him because I'm afraid I'll open up, be honest with him about what's been happening, and if I do that, I can't undo it. There's no putting the toothpaste back in the tube.

"You all right, dollface?" Hannah asks me.

"I'm heartbroken. The boy I love doesn't love me." I lean in to kiss the baby's cheek and he squawks. "See?"

"He's just fussy," she says. "Don't take it personally."

"What if Morph grows up and decides he likes to dress in beige? What if he joins a fraternity. Listens to country music and wears boat shoes?"

PLAY NICE

"I'll love him just the same," she says, booping his nose. "But he won't, because he's mine."

THE restaurant Daphne picked is in Hell's Kitchen. I've never been before because I avoid Midtown, as a rule.

It's a sunny summer day, and I wear my Dolce & Gabbana strapless charmeuse dress with the bluebell print, my black Chanel sunglasses, label-less beaded gold clutch from a stoop sale, and patent leather platform heels with an open toe and ankle straps from some slutty discount store in the mall near Dad's house. Amy picked out these shoes, and I figured, why not? Touch of tacky never hurt anyone.

I got a blowout this morning, a manicure and pedicure. I feel like myself. Composed and confident. In my element.

But it's still there, under the surface. The nag of everything that's happened over these last few months. Mom's death, her funeral, her book, Dad's burning of that book. The new book. The happenings at Edgewood. Austin. My sisters. The fire at my apartment. Ugly truths. Ugly fiction. Ugly words. Ugly house. Ugly feelings.

There's no room in my beautiful life for all this ugliness.

And yet, here it is.

I push open the door to the restaurant. It's an upscale gastropub. Dark wood, polished concrete floors, exposed brick, dimly lit. It's busy.

Daphne and Leda wait for me in a corner booth. I'm not surprised they're already here—Leda is always early, Daphne on time, and I'm always late—but I am surprised to find them sitting on the same side of the booth. Usually, Daffy will sit next to me. It feels like a strategic move. Like I'm walking into an ambush.

"Hey," I say, sliding onto the empty bench. I pick up the cocktail menu. "Twenty dollars for a drink. Intriguing."

"Are you complaining?" Daphne asks.

"No. I love a craft cocktail. I was just expecting beer and burgers."

"You can get a beer," Daffy says. "And they're known for their burgers."

Leda sighs, impatient.

"Leeds," I say. "Let's enjoy ourselves now. While we can. Before the *talk*."

"I took the six a.m. Acela," she says.

"Then let's hope for all our sakes that the drinks are strong and the food is good," I say, kicking her restless leg under the table.

"Ow!"

"Please," Daphne says.

Our waiter arrives. Exquisite timing.

Everyone calms down after ordering drinks and starters—truffle fries and spicy shrimp. Then Daphne tells us about a date she went on earlier in the week with a pastry chef named Daisy.

"Daphne and Daisy," I say. "I don't see it going anywhere."

"Stop," Leda says. "I think it's sweet. Do you like her?"

"I do," Daphne says. "She has cats, though. She adopted them."

"'Them'? How many?" I ask.

"Two. Betty and Ophelia."

"Two is too many," I say, taking a sip of my twenty-dollar cocktail. It's not strong enough. I flag down the waiter and order a different one.

"Don't listen to Clio," Leda says. "It's good she has pets. Shows she's compassionate and responsible. Tom grew up with dogs. He wants one now, but we're too busy. Never home. Maybe down the road."

"I'm fine with her having cats, but I'm allergic. Remember?"

"Like I said, I don't see it going anywhere." I reach for another fry as Leda scowls at me.

"You hate love," she says, which makes both me and Daphne laugh.

"I don't hate love," I say. "Just seems like more trouble than it's worth. It's fun until it isn't, and once the fun part's over, why bother?"

"Companionship. Partnership," Leda says. "Tax benefits."

"How romantic!" I say, swooning.

"All right, all right," Daphne says. She sips her cocktail, a mezcal Paloma.

"I have companionship when I want," I say. "Austin."

"Who's that?" Daphne asks.

"The neighbor."

"That's still going on?"

"When I feel like it."

"That's not a relationship," Leda says.

"It could be."

She and Daphne both stare at me.

"What?"

"Do you want it to be?" Daffy asks.

I almost say yes, but I don't like how the word feels in my mouth, so I swallow it down.

Leda shakes her head. She turns to Daphne. "See?"

"What?" I ask again.

"You're not normal," Leda says. "This is not normal human behavior."

"Plenty of people choose to be single, Leeds."

"It's not that," she says. "It's—"

"Don't," Daphne says. She takes another sip of her drink.

The waiter drops off my second cocktail and takes our lunch order. I get a lobster roll, Daphne a burger, Leda a salad.

"If we're going to get into it, we might as well get into it," I say. The second cocktail is better. Worth what it costs.

"Look, I'm glad we're all sitting down. But let's not have it be . . ." Daffy trails off. "It's been tough since Alexandra . . ."

"Died," I say. "The audacity of that woman."

"Dude, come on," Daffy says. "Don't be difficult."

"She can't help herself," Leda says.

"You're upset that I read the book. You're upset that I went to Mom's funeral. You're upset that I'm taking care of the house. Those things have nothing to do with you. They're *my* decisions."

"They affect us. You must understand that on some level," Daphne says, chewing on her cocktail straw.

I shrug.

"She doesn't. You know what I think, Clio?" Leda asks, leaning forward. "I think you don't care about anyone but yourself. I think you're incapable of empathy. And either what happened in our childhood affected you so deeply that it made you this way, or it's something you can't help. Honestly, I think you might have antisocial personality disorder."

I've never taken an arrow to the chest, but I imagine it feels something like this.

Daphne closes her eyes and exhales.

"You think I'm a sociopath?"

"Tom has a minor in psychology," Leda says. "And I've done some reading."

"You've talked to Tommy about this?" I'm hurt, and I have nothing to disguise my hurt. Nothing to hide behind. I can't force a laugh or a smile. I have no wisecrack. No comeback. I'm empty.

"Leda," Daphne says. "Both of you. Just . . . stop. Take a breath. Clio, she didn't mean it."

"I do mean it. I know you want to be mediator, Daffy, but you don't get to make me bad cop. We've talked about this, too."

"You talked. I listened. I'm always listening. Always in the fucking middle."

"You two said you saw Mom burn me," I say. "Is that true?"

They look at each other.

"You really don't remember?" Daphne asks.

"No. There . . . it was a pink lighter, right?"

"Being in that house, in that environment, it was bad for you," Leda says. "You were acting out. And she was encouraging it. You did it because of her."

"Wait, what? What are you saying?"

"Leda," Daphne says.

"You were sleeping in our room. Mom and Roy wouldn't let you in yours after the exorcism. We weren't even allowed downstairs. Daffy and I woke up in the middle of the night and you were gone. We found you at the table talking to yourself. Giggling. Messing with the lighter. Burning yourself. You said it felt like nothing. Just like *it* said it would. *It* being an imaginary demon. *It* being Mom."

I look to Daphne, but she won't look back at me. "Daffy?"

"That's what I remember," she says. "You said you were playing with it. With the demon."

"It was her fault. You were clearly in distress. Confused. She was brainwashing you. And when we told Dad, he had to explain to us how important it was that we help him get you out of there. Get us all out of there and away from her," Leda says.

"So she didn't do it," I say. I sound the same, which is strange because everything is different. The world just changed color. "You knew, Dad knew—this whole time—that she didn't do it, and you just let me believe it? You lied."

"We didn't lie, Clio. She *was* responsible," Daphne says. "You don't remember this stuff because you were fucking traumatized. She convinced you, a seven-year-old girl, that there was a demon living in her house. She made us afraid all the time. It was the right thing, and you know it."

"Do I? I spent my whole life thinking my own mother burned me."

"Dad did what he had to do to keep us safe. We did what we had to do. We couldn't be there anymore," Leda says. "And I'm not sorry. I don't regret it. We saved you. It was only going to get worse. More dangerous. She was hosting exorcisms."

"What do you remember about the exorcism?" I ask. "Jed? Ruth?"

"Who?"

"Do you remember a guy with bleeding ears? A lady with blue hair clawing her eyes out? Ambulances?"

"What? No," Daphne says, shaking her head. "I remember a lady with blue hair, but the exorcism was just a bunch of yelling and Alexandra throwing herself down the stairs. She limped around after, but there was no ambulance."

"It was all dramatics," Leda says. "Whatever you read in the book, I promise you that is not how it happened. Would you please just trust us? The people who are here and love you."

"You just admitted you've both been lying to me. And you just called me a sociopath."

"Because you might be one! I'm trying to help you."

"Enough with the armchair diagnosing, Leeds," Daphne says. She downs the rest of her drink. "Maybe we should go to family therapy. With Dad and Amy. Get back to a healthy place."

"Were we ever in a healthy place?" I ask, twisting my napkin for something to do with my hands. "Or is everything just a big lie?"

I wait for them to say something, to argue with me. But they don't. Maybe that's my answer.

"I'll tell you something true. Something real," I say, tossing my napkin aside and grabbing my purse. I get out my wallet, finger for some twenties, drop the cash on the table anticipating what's coming next. "The house is haunted."

Daphne closes her eyes again. "Clio. Come on."

"You don't believe that," Leda says.

"I do. It is haunted. There's something there. It's always been there. The demon or whatever it is. It's real."

"What are you talking about?" Daphne asks, her face going pale.

"It communicates with me. I've heard it. And it draws. Leaves me messages. I have another copy of Mom's book. It's written inside it."

"Oh my God," Daphne says, holding her head in her hands. "Oh my fucking God. Not this again. Not this . . ."

"Ignore her. She's just saying this to spite us," Leda says. "To make us upset. To make us worry about her. She just wants the attention."

"I don't need it from you," I say, sliding out of the booth.

"She's just like her," Leda mutters to herself. "She's just like her."

"Where are you going?" Daphne calls after me.

"Home."

29

BEFORE leaving the city, I buy a new sketchpad, some Sharpies, a bottle of vodka, a pack of cigarettes, and a hot pink lighter. When I get to Edgewood, I spread them out on the dining table, a grim but oddly satisfying tableau. I'm compelled to capture the image, so I do.

Dad calls me while I'm editing the photo, adjusting the brightness, and before I think better of it, I hit answer.

"Clio, your sisters told me about today," he says. "What's going on?"

"You knew that Mom didn't burn me," I say, picking up my new lighter, turning it over in my hand. "They lied to me. You lied to me. Everyone's lying. That's the irony. The only one telling the truth in this family is me. And I'm the one no one believes."

"Clio, I'm coming over there to pick you up. Enough is enough."

"Don't. I have plans tonight."

"'Plans'?"

"With a guy. So don't show up here. You wouldn't want to interrupt, would you?" I hang up before he can respond. I'm confident that I've deterred him, considering the awkward note and condom wrapper incident from a few weeks ago nearly sent him into cardiac arrest.

I put my phone down and light a cigarette. Take a drag.

Cough.

The stale taste of tobacco, the sting of smoke in my throat—it's horrendous, and I hate it, so I take another drag. Another. Another before I stub it out on the table.

The rebellion doesn't feel good, not like I wanted it to. I stare at the pack of Marlboros, something ugly that I thought I could have control over, that I could wield in my hands and feel powerful again. But I don't feel powerful at all.

Dad and Daphne think I'm crazy. Leda and Tommy think I have a personality disorder. Mom is dead.

I open the bottle of vodka and take a swig. Unlike the cigarette, I like the way it burns.

I begin tearing out pages from the sketchpad. Slowly, methodically, careful not to rip them along the seam. I lay one out on the dining table, along with a Sharpie. One on the kitchen island. The coffee table. Daphne and Leda's room. Mom's room.

My room.

It's cold in here. I set the blank sheet of paper and Sharpie on the bed.

Staring at the blank sheet, I'm reminded of something in the book.

I drop to my knees, check under the bed for the plastic bin where I would keep my drawings.

It's still there.

I pull it out and open it up, releasing a cloud of thick, gray dust. Inside the bin are stacks of sketchpads and notebooks and loose sheets of paper. School art projects. Random drawings on napkins.

There's a manila folder and, inside it, my illustrations of the house. Must be twenty, at least.

I place them in neat rows on the carpet. I want to see them all.

I would do this a lot as a kid. Draw the same subject over and over in pursuit of perfection. I remember drawing these. I remember being frustrated, feeling like I could never get the house quite right.

I find my phone on the floor beside me. I take pictures of the drawings. I don't know why.

None of them have blacked-out windows.

I reach for the Sharpie on the bed, lean over the nearest drawing, and scribble in the windows.

There's movement at the corner of my eye.

I turn toward the closet, the door swinging wide.

In my head, a bell chimes.

Was that part real? What would Roy have to say if I called him and asked about the exorcism? How much did Mom make up?

What would Roy have to say if I asked him if he really loved my mother or if he just has a hard-on for demons?

The closet is shallow; I barely fit inside. Above me is the panel to the attic.

I've never been up there before.

I go upstairs to get the ladder, but before I can bring it down, there's a knock at the front door. The ladder gets abandoned.

I open the door figuring it might be Dad, but it's Austin.

"Hey," he says, leaning in to kiss me. "Been a minute."

"Yeah," I say, turning away from him. I'm still in my Dolce dress, but I'm barefoot, my makeup smudged, hair tangled, drenched in sweat and covered in dust. I don't want to be seen.

"Are you okay?" he asks. "Is this a bad time?"

I blink at him. "No."

"No?" He rests his arm against the doorframe. I haven't invited him in yet.

"You want to sit out here?" he asks, gesturing to the front steps.

"Yeah, okay," I say, thinking about all the paper scattered around that I don't want him to see, all the questions I don't want him to ask. "Let me go get something first. I'll meet you, just a sec."

I run upstairs and grab the vodka. There's less than I remember.

Austin sits with his hands on his knees. He accepts the bottle when I pass it to him, but he doesn't drink. He reaches over and pulls one of my curls straight.

I'm hyperaware of my appearance. I want to shrink. I want the sun to set faster. I want darkness. I want shadow. I want to black out the world. I should have held on to that Sharpie.

I don't want him to look at me the way he's looking at me. With what might be concern or pity or fear.

I reach for the vodka and take a gulp.

"I watched your stories," he says. "That's how I knew you were here."

"What?" I ask.

"Your stories. The pictures you posted."

"What pictures?"

"Are you . . ." He laughs. "I can't tell if you're fucking with me."

"Why would I ever do a thing like that?"

"Well," he says, and I recognize something sour in his tone.

"Well?"

He stands and steps down to the walkway. "I'm kind of worried about you."

"What do you mean?"

"You seem . . ."

"What? I seem what, Austin?" I say, suddenly on offense. He's judging me. I knew he would.

He looks down at his Vans, runs his hands through his hair.

"You don't need to worry about me," I tell him. "I don't need you to worry about me. That's not what this is."

"I thought . . ." He looks at me again. He expects something from me. He's waiting for me to intuit what he wants to hear, and then for me to say those words and to be pretty while I say them.

So I say nothing.

Because what I want, what I need, is for him to just be here and not want or need anything from me.

I take another swig from the bottle.

A minute passes. He sighs and says, "I can't tell if it's me or if you're dealing with . . ."

"Dealing with what? I'm sorry if it's inconvenient that I don't just exist to fuck you."

His mouth falls open. He laughs. "What?"

"Never mind."

"You can talk to me. About stuff. I'm not just here to hook up."

"You don't want to hear about my problems."

"That's . . . that's not true. At all."

"It is," I say. "You're here because I'm fun and because this isn't serious. I start crying to you about my feelings, then I'm not fun anymore. Then I'll be too much. And then you'll go find fun someplace else, and then I'll be alone and all fucked-up. So let's just quit while we're ahead. It's for the best. Because where was this really going, anyway? I work in the city. I live in the city. And you live out here. In your mother's basement."

He adjusts the thin chain around his neck, bites his lip, nods. "For what it's worth, you're already alone and fucked-up."

He starts to cross the lawn, walk away.

"For what it's worth," I say, "only douchebags wear chains like that."

"It was my dad's," he says without turning around.

I sit on the front steps until Austin is out of view. Until he is gone. I take another sip from the bottle. Another. When I finally manage to stand, I teeter on rubbery legs, stumbling as I turn to go into the house. I left the front door open, and a breeze comes through, pushing it all the way back against the wall. It's like the house is welcoming me in.

The door slams itself shut behind me.

I crawl up the stairs on all fours, my balance off from the alcohol. I haven't had anything to eat today except a few fries and a single shrimp. There's no food in the house.

The sheet of paper on the dining table remains blank. As does the one on the coffee table. In the kitchen. In Leda and Daphne's room. In Mom's room. In my room.

"What? Now you're shy?" I ask.

I eye the opening to the attic again, return upstairs for the ladder. But it's too heavy, and I'm not coordinated enough right now to maneuver it down to my room. Or to climb it.

I'm alone and fucked-up.

In the dark.

The sun has set, and I engage in my new routine, turning on every light in this house.

I sit on the couch and wait for something to happen.

When the nothing becomes intolerable, I get up for my phone. Austin said something about my Instagram stories, didn't he? I don't remember posting anything to my stories.

I swear I left my phone on the dining table, but maybe I didn't, because it isn't there.

The book is.

This stupid book. This funhouse mirror fiction.

But what's the harm in finishing it now?

What more damage can it do?

How badly do I want to find out?

"Why would you say that?" I asked her.

"Everyone dies, Mom," she said, rolling her eyes.

"We're not dying in this house," I told her. "Say it."

"Whatever." She returned to her drawing. She would no longer engage with me.

I asked her if she wanted a glass of water. She didn't respond.

I went into the kitchen, and Roy met me there.

"I'm sorry," he said. "The demon's hold on this house is strong."

"Why?" I asked. "Why this house?"

What I was really asking was: *Why me?*

Why had I, all my life, come up against such adversity? Would I never know peace? Was I cursed? What had I done to deserve my father? Or these cruel men I seemed to gravitate toward. The cruelty of my own body and the attention it garnered—so often unwanted. The restlessness of my mind. The ruthlessness of motherhood. What had I done to deserve these demons?

"It's been here for a very long time. Even before this house was built. It lived in the woods. This is its home.

Demons aren't eager for change. That may sound surprising, since often they're depicted in the media as entities keen to take possession of new bodies. Children, mostly. Corrupting innocence. An easy sell in Hollywood. For the Catholic Church, God forgive me."

"I'm telling Father Bernard," I said.

He smiled, and it was the first and only happiness I felt that day. "Tattletale."

I mimed zipping my lips. Locking. Throwing away the key.

"Most of the demons I've encountered, I compare them to channel surfers. They stay in one spot, watching. If they get bored, they might sleep, hibernate. If they aren't tired and they don't like what they see—or, depending on their personality, if they like what they see—they might intervene. Communicate. Engage. Attach. They've been around for so long that they don't understand or don't care about the degree to which they affect us. They don't have empathy."

"Is this your way of telling me it's hopeless? That it won't leave?"

"It's not hopeless. But it won't be easy. It likes your channel."

"That makes one of us," I said. "So, what's next? I move?"

"You could try. But you may not be able to sell the house. Not if it doesn't want you to leave."

I turn to the next page, and there's a word scribbled in giant letters, in red Sharpie, rendering the text beneath it unreadable.

HOME

My phone rings somewhere in the house, throwing me for a second.

I look up to see that it's right in front of me. It's on the coffee table. I set the book aside and reach for it. Veronica's calling me.

I hit ignore.

So many missed calls. Messages. Notifications.

Pressing my thumb down, unlocking, opening Instagram; I do it all with this calm detachment. When I watch my stories, one with the photo of the cigarettes and vodka and sketchpads on the dining table, a dozen others with the pictures I took of my childhood house drawings, I don't panic. Why panic when it's already too late? People have already seen them.

The last two stories feature photos I must have taken by accident. One of the closet, more specifically, the opening to the attic inside my closet. And finally, a blurry selfie of me smiling, my eyes bloodshot, mascara streaming down my dirty face, hair a mess, snake charm dangling toward the camera.

It takes so much to build an image. It takes next to nothing to destroy one.

There's a *thud*. The sound tears through my body like an electrocution.

Heat surges, sweat pours, and then I'm empty. I'm freezing.

It's terror and it's relief. And it's here. It's here. It's home.

"Hello," I say, keeping my gaze straight ahead.

Another *thud*.

A moment of quiet. And then the dragging. The floorboards squealing underneath a creeping, ambiguous weight.

There's a faint *clink*—contact with glass, followed by the abrupt arrival of pain.

Something just hit the back of my head.

The hot pink lighter. It's landed on my shoulder, slid down to my lap. It rests now at the heel of my right hand.

"Hello," says a voice. A disorienting, incomprehensibly foul voice.

My thoughts go sticky with fear, cling together, scream over each other. *What do I do? Turn around. Look. Don't look. Don't move. No. Run. I'm cold. I'm so cold. I'm sweating. I'm ruining this beautiful dress. It's ruined. You're ruining your beautiful life. It's ruined. It's been ruined. You ruined it. You want to feel something. You feel too much. You. You hate everything you feel. You need to feel something different. Something louder.*

You should light yourself on fire.

The lighter is already in my hand. The flame is yellow with a dark core. It drifts. Dances. I watch it. All the different shapes it makes.

Mom in my head. *It hurts right now, but by the time we get home, you won't feel it.*

I am home. And I don't feel it.

That foul voice at my back. *It will feel like nothing.*

The flame meets my skin, my scar, my old burn. And I feel *nothing*.

But the smell.

The smell.

My gasp echoes through the house as I understand what I'm doing, as my skin smokes. I turn around and pitch the lighter into the living room. The lights have gone out in the hall, which stretches back like an open throat. Laughter rumbles out from it.

The door to Leda and Daphne's room slowly closes itself, hinges singing at an earsplitting pitch.

As soon as it shuts, the pounding starts.

Whatever's behind it, it bangs against the door.

Mom in my head again. *I will bleed you out! I will bleed you out!*

"Stop!" I cover my ears. Close my eyes. "Stop!"

My hands only muffle the sound. The hinges. The dragging.

I think about Jed. His headphones. Bleeding out of his ears.

Made up. Not true. Not real.

I let my hands fall. Open my eyes just in time to see a flash of something vanish downstairs, a shadow in darkness.

Not real. Not true. Made up.

There's one person who could validate what actually happened. Who might be able to help me. Who will believe me. I don't know if I can trust him, if I can trust a single word that comes out of his mouth, but he's all I have.

I'm here for you, Clio. You and your sisters. If you ever need anything.

It's time I take Roy up on his offer.

30

I DON'T sleep. I chug water to sober up.

My burn has blistered yellow. It would be convenient if there were a nurse who lived down the street who didn't now hate me.

What did I do?

What have I done?

I gather up the blank sheets of paper and Sharpies, leave them on the dining table, sad remnants of a failed experiment. It did communicate with me, but not my way. Its way. On its terms. The way it wanted to communicate.

It doesn't need to play nice. I have nowhere else to go.

Nowhere I want to be, at least.

When Dad calls, I concede to him coming to get me.

I meet him outside.

"Jesus, Clio! What happened?"

I catch my reflection in the car window. I look psychotic. And I'm just now realizing, I forgot to put on shoes.

"Can you take me to get something to eat," I say, my voice hoarse.

"Clio, sweetie," Dad says, pulling me in for a hug. I lean my head against his shoulder. He smells like smoke. After what he did, burning the book, maybe he'll forever smell like smoke to me. I want to forgive him, to be at peace, to be happy in his embrace. I want it to feel like it used to. I want to be who I used to be. Before Mom died. Before ugly truths. Before any of this.

"What's this?" he says, noticing the burn.

I consider confronting him about how he manipulated my sisters into a lie that estranged us from our mother. That did irreparable damage. But I just don't have the energy right now. "I hurt myself."

"How?" he asks, the distress in his expression eliciting in me a strange mix of guilt and satisfaction. He still loves me.

"Working in the house," I say. "Dad. Please. Can we go? I'm starving."

"You need shoes," he says. He goes into the house and comes back out a second later with my heels.

He opens the car door for me, hands me my shoes, then goes around to the driver's side. He starts the car, we back out into the cul-de-sac, and then he says, "You smell like cigarettes. And alcohol."

I almost tell him that he smells like smoke, almost tell him that he smells like fascism, almost ask him if, after libraries, he plans on taking his flamethrower to the museums. I almost tell him how close I am to hating him. But my throat is sore, and I'm struggling to keep my eyes open.

"Clio. You're making me worry. You're making everyone worry."

What does he want me to say? Does he expect me to apologize? Everyone in my life wants me to behave in a very specific way that's beneficial to them, and as soon as I deviate from their expectations, it's an issue. As soon as I act out of whatever role they cast me in in their lives, it's somehow my fault.

"This pattern of behavior is concerning to me," he says sternly. "I've seen it before."

"What, with Mom? You and Leda like to throw that in my face. But I'm nothing like Mom," I say, playing with my snake charm. "The only thing I have in common with her is great hair and a haunted house."

"It's that book. And spending time there by yourself."

"Why can't you even entertain the idea that she was right? That I'm right? Why can't the house be haunted by a demon?"

"Because that's crazy. Don't you hear yourself?"

"Why is it crazy? If I was a son and not your daughter, would you assume I was crazy?"

"Not everything is misogyny, Clio," he says, taking a sharp turn. "What happened to your arm?"

Now I can't resist, can't hold my tongue lest it shred the inside of my mouth. "It was Mom. She did it. Right? Right, Dad? She hurt me."

"Clio Louise."

"Fuck it. Can we just get breakfast? Please? Please."

He sighs. "Okay."

We go to a diner—a different one than Austin took me to, though it still reminds me of him—and eat in silence.

Dad pays the check and then we go back to his house. Amy's not around.

"I'm going to sleep," I tell him.

"When you wake up, we're going to have a talk about what comes next."

"Ominous," I mumble. I climb the stairs to my room. I fall into bed, fall asleep in an instant.

WHEN I wake up, it's the middle of the night.

Yawning, I turn over and reach for my phone, wondering if Roy has gotten back to me.

I could have asked Helen for his number but wasn't keen on swallowing my pride after our last conversation, forcing my return to the tragically archaic website of the New England Occultist Collective. It was outside of business hours, but I called the contact number anyway, figuring there was a chance that Occultist Collectives might not maintain traditional business hours or whatever. I left a voicemail stating my name and requesting a callback from Roy. I said he'd know what it was about.

But even if he did call, I wouldn't know since apparently my phone is dead, RIP. Its absence aches like a phantom limb. I plug it into the charger and steep in my thoughts. I have to pee, which means I have to get out of bed—something that doesn't really appeal to me.

I groan and kick off the sheets, swing my legs over the side of the mattress. Shuffle out the door and down the hall to the bathroom.

The lights are too bright. I squint, still sleep drunk as I sit on the toilet, wipe, flush, wash my hands.

It's the hurt of my burn that pulls me into full consciousness. I turn off the faucet and lift my arm closer to my face, water dripping off my fingers.

The burn is pretty disgusting. Pink and yellow and shiny—the blister on the verge of eruption. Now would be a good time to have a charged phone, to Google how to treat a burn, something I should have done last night if I had been in my right mind.

I open the cabinets looking for a Band-Aid or ointment or whatever. There's a tub of Vaseline that might be as old as I am. I get it out and set it on the counter.

Before I make any poor attempt at delayed first aid, I think better of it and just leave the wound alone. I peel off my dress and take a cold shower, emerge shivering but clean.

I wrap myself in towels and go back to my room, find some clothes to change into. My dance team sweatshirt, some Soffe shorts. I look like a teenager, but I feel about a thousand years old, my bones weary.

The cold shower was a bad idea. I'm freezing. Dad and Amy always blast the AC. I go out into the hall to fetch a blanket from the linen closet.

There's a light on downstairs. They never leave lights on. Someone's awake.

I find the fuzziest blanket available, wrap myself inside it, wear it like a cloak, and head downstairs, careful not to trip over my blanket train.

"Dad? Amy?" I call out, keeping my voice low.

The light is coming from Dad's study.

What else is hidden in here?

Maybe the devil lives somewhere in the words "I know I shouldn't." Or maybe God does.

There's a stack of photo albums on his desk. I lower myself into his comfy rolling chair and start to flip through.

Pictures from childhood. Leda, Daphne, and me on the first day of school. At our dance recitals. At Six Flags, soaked from a log flume. Leda at the kitchen table doing her homework. Daphne outside in the yard dribbling a soccer ball. Me posing with my hands on my hips, wearing a tutu as a shirt over a pair of jeans, a heart on my cheek drawn with red lip liner.

The three of us with Dad and Amy on a beach in Maui—our big

family vacation before Leda left for Harvard. There's a magnificent sunset behind us. It's a beautiful photo.

I go through another album, where we're all younger. Leda and Daphne in matching dresses, having a tea party on the kitchen floor in our first house. Me in a bib and onesie sitting in a high chair, frowning, green mush smeared across my face. Somehow, Mom isn't in any of these pictures.

I slam the album closed, and Dad's computer screen illuminates.

His password is written on a Post-it in his top drawer. Amateur hour.

I type it in, and up comes Chrome. His email. I open Google and check his search history.

> Healthline. Symptoms of a nervous breakdown.
> Mental Health Services NJ.
> Behavioral Help northern New Jersey.
> Psychotic episode.
> Psychosis.
> Genetic psychosis.
> Delusions.
> Can grief cause delusions?
> Can grief trigger psychosis?
> How do you get someone mental help when they refuse?
> 5150. Psychiatric Hold.

I push away from the desk, and a sharp pain ignites my forearm. The blister. It's split open. My skin curls back, releasing iridescent ooze.

Footsteps. Upstairs. Coming downstairs.

Panicked, I stumble out of the study and into the kitchen, get a glass down.

"Clio?" It's Amy. She wears a matching pajama set patterned with berries. Her hair is pulled back in a French braid. She looks like she's coming from a sleepover.

"Oh, hey," I say, my voice high and squeaky, giving away my anxiety. I clear my throat. I fill the glass with water from the fridge. "Sorry, did I wake you?"

She shakes her head. "I've had trouble sleeping lately. Daphne thinks I should try these CBD gummies, but I don't know."

"What about melatonin?" I ask. I offer her the water.

"I tried. No luck," she says, accepting the glass. "Thank you, Cli."

We haven't spoken since Memorial Day. She doesn't know what to say to me, and I have nothing to say to her. Except maybe *Is my father about to try to have me committed?* But I know she wouldn't answer me. All she'd do is go right upstairs and tell him. Then he'd confront me. It would escalate. I'd try to defend myself and get frustrated and cause a scene that would then be cited as proof that I'm unhinged and need help. Crazy is quicksand.

I can't mention the demon or Mom or the house. I can't do anything but apologize. Play nice.

"I'm sorry about the barbecue," I say, hoping she can't detect the glaring insincerity. "I didn't mean to upset you."

Her eyes well up and she puts a hand to her heart. "Thank you, Clio. I know you didn't. I know."

"We're okay, then?"

"Of course," she says. "Are you okay? We're worried about you."

"So I've heard," I say. "But you know me, Amy. When have I ever not been okay?"

She opens her mouth to say something, then changes her mind. I fake a yawn. "I should get back to sleep."

"That sounds like a good idea," she says.

I give her a hug and go upstairs to my room, locking the door behind me. In the soft, warm light of the lamp on my bedside table, I examine my burn.

Skin puckers around where the blister burst. I reach out to touch it, graze it with my fingertips. There's a sheen to it. I'm still oozing. I stare as the ooze goes from watery clear to yellow to pink to viscous red. Blood.

I grab my towel off the floor and press it to the wound, which is difficult because my hand is shaking. A deep breath.

When have I ever not been okay?

I gently pat away the blood, the ooze, the color. Now the burn looks like a pale eye staring back at me. Watching.

Hello.

31

DAD sits at the kitchen table reading a newspaper. There's coffee, creamer, bagels, butter, cream cheese.

He sets the paper down. "Good morning."

"Morning." I give him a big, toothy smile. Resentment clanks against the prison of my teeth.

"You're rested?"

"Yeah, I'm rested. Fresh as a peppermint."

"Good." He takes a deep breath, and I brace myself. "I would like you to stay here, with me and Amy. Temporarily. If you need to work, I'll drive you into the city, and I'll drive you back here. I've scheduled an appointment with a family therapist for this Friday afternoon. Daphne and Leda have agreed to come. They're staying through the weekend, and I hope you will, too. I'm asking."

He looks at me, and he's my dad again. The captain of the ship, steady and reliable, who would do anything for me and my sisters. Who braided our hair for dance recitals, who came to every school function, who would take us to the mall and give us carte blanche, waiting patiently on a bench with a biography and a coffee while we shopped.

It could be that everything he's done has been motivated purely and genuinely by his love for us. It could be that he's a possessive, self-serving asshole who was a shitty husband to Mom, who held no compassion for her, who erased her from our lives, painted her as this unreliable violent monster to protect his own image. It could be all the above.

But who's to say that Mom wasn't motivated by love, too? Maybe good intentions don't actually fucking matter. Only the action. Or the perception of the action.

"Yeah, okay," I say. "I'll stay here. I'll go to therapy."

"Thank you," he says.

Normally, I wouldn't consent without negotiation. Without getting something I want in exchange for doing something he wants. But what would he do if I put up a fight?

An awkward silence descends like an invisible wall between us.

After a few minutes pass, he picks up his paper, hides behind it. "These are the good bagels. I got blueberry. Your favorite."

"How thoughtful," I say. It comes out more sarcastic than I intend it to.

He folds his paper, stands with another deep sigh. "I'm working from home this week. I'll be in my study if you need me."

"I always need you," I tell him. There's a noise in my head, a sound like the chime of a bell, ringing in a thought. *That's how he wants it. My need is by his design.*

He puts a hand on my shoulder. "I love you, Cli. You know that, don't you? You know how much I love you, and that I only want what's best for you?"

"I know," I say. "Promise, I do."

I cross my heart.

"Have a bagel. If you don't want a bagel, order in. Whatever you want."

"Thanks, Dad."

When he's out of the kitchen, I sip on the coffee he left and pick at a bagel and stare into space.

My phone vibrates. Someone's calling me. It's either Roy or spam. I pick up.

"Hello, this is Clio."

"Clio." I recognize his pretty voice.

The line crackles.

"It's Roy."

NOT wanting Dad or Amy to overhear, I go out back, sit on the swing set.

"Clio?" Roy says.

"You said if we ever need anything..."

"What is it?"

"What do you think?" I ask.

I hear him breathing. When he finally speaks, it's in a whisper. "The demon."

So dramatic. I wonder how good of a demonologist he is. How good of a demonologist can one really be?

"Yeah," I say. I try using lingo I think he'll understand. "It's made its presence known."

"It's communicating. How?"

"Writing. Drawing, mostly. It says hello," I say, digging my bare feet into the dry mulch.

"Don't engage with it."

"We're past that, Roy."

"Has it made physical contact?" he asks.

I stare at my burn. It's hideous. "I don't think it wants to hurt me. But it's okay to watch me hurt myself."

He's quiet.

"Roy? Are you still there?"

"I am. I'm . . . We were afraid of this."

"Then why didn't Mom just sell the fucking house?"

"It's complicated."

"Explain it to me, then, Roy. Because I'm starting to think it was you." I know I shouldn't alienate the one person who could potentially help me with the demon, the one person who I know believes me, but I can't stop myself. My anger is in control and I'm just a puppet on strings, a doll in a kid's tight, gummy grip.

"I'm sorry, Clio. I don't follow."

"I think she held on to the house because of you. Because you wanted access to the demon. That's your whole thing, right?"

"That is not true," he says, an edge to his pretty voice that gets my attention. "Alex knew as well as I did that the demon was attached not only to that house but to her and to you. The demon didn't want Alex to sell the house. Even if we could have successfully off-loaded it, there was a chance it would find her. Follow her. Or you. All these years, she tried to appease it for fear of that scenario. She did what she could to keep it happy. If it was content, it would sleep. Go dormant."

"Was that why she was there when she died? Trying to keep it happy? What does that even mean? And where were you, Roy? Why weren't you there?"

"We . . . we'd hit a rough patch. She wasn't in good health, wasn't taking care of herself. She was . . . she was drinking a lot. Another relapse. We'd agreed to take some time apart."

"Ah," I say. I remember what Mom wrote in the book, in one of her footnotes. *Alcohol was never my problem. It was a response to my problems.* Either she was in denial or she just had too many problems.

The birds squawk. A squirrel dashes across the yard. The neighbor's dog barks.

"What would you like to do?" Roy asks. "I can come down. Walk through. Call in my team."

"Your team," I say, wriggling my toes in the dirt. "Jed and Ruth and Father Bernard?"

He goes quiet again.

"Sorry," I say. "I just . . . I just read Mom's book. So . . ."

"They've all passed on."

The sun disappears behind a cloud, and the day goes gloomy. "To different professions?"

"To the afterlife," he says. "They're all dead."

"But . . . nothing in the book really happened. It's all bullshit, right? I don't remember any—"

"Father Bernard had cancer," he says. "Jed drowned in a swimming pool. Ruth fell prey to addiction. Working in this field, it takes a toll. What happened that day was not exactly as it was described in Alex's book. She had to embellish some of the horrors we endured to get publisher interest. But the demon is real, Clio. You know that now. And it's dangerous. It's attachment to you is profound."

Part of me is flattered, because I love attention. We have that in common, the demon and me. I like being the favorite. This part of me feels an allegiance to it. A kinship.

But then I look down at my burn and I remember it throwing the lighter at my head. I remember the deranged photos I posted to my stories the other night and the all-consuming savage fear I feel inside that house.

"Okay, yeah. Please come. But don't bring a whole team," I say. "I don't want this to be a big thing. You have to keep it between us. My family, my sisters, they can't know. No one can."

It'll be hard enough to save face after posting those stories.

I think of Laurie with her lipsticks, who right now at this moment is in Orlando, Florida, probably in some princess-themed hotel doing makeup for a bride who thinks she's Cinderella, listening to a soundtrack of Disney songs. Couldn't be me.

"Clio, you have my word," he says. "I'm in Chicago. I'm lecturing here Thursday night. As soon as it's over, I'll get in my car and I'll drive to the house."

"I'll text you the code to the door," I say, swatting a mosquito. "I have something on Friday afternoon. I'm not sure when I can meet you there."

"You're not there now?"

"No," I say. "I'm at my dad's."

"That's probably for the best," he says. "You did the right thing. Calling. I won't let you down."

"Did you say the same thing to her?"

His longest pause yet. So long, I almost consider apologizing. Almost. If only I could ignore the truth, what's clear to me now, that before this moment incarnated as a vague mistrust. My intuition alerting me to what I couldn't yet articulate.

"I regret that I wasn't there," he says eventually. "I'll regret it for the rest of my life."

"Yeah, for sure. But here's the thing. You gave me the key to the house."

"It's your house."

"Nah. You wanted me there. You wanted this. You were waiting for my call. For me to need you. You used me—used *us*—to get to it. Maybe Mom drank because, deep down, she knew. I'm not fucking dumb, Roy. Don't treat me like I am. See you Friday."

I hang up, drop my phone to the mulch at my feet, which are now caked in dirt.

"Clio," Dad calls from the patio. "What are you doing back there?"

PLAY NICE

"Inner child work," I shout back.

"What?"

"In preparation of Friday."

"What are you talking about?"

"You're woefully unprepared for therapy," I mutter, picking up my phone and walking toward him.

"Come inside," he says. "Forecast says rain."

32

THE sky cracks open, and it pours rain for three days straight.
 On Friday morning, Daphne arrives early with donuts.
 She lets herself into my room, sits at the foot of my bed, and says, "I'm here. I brought donuts."

"It's eight a.m., Daffy. What time did you leave Hudson?"

She clicks her tongue. "Couldn't sleep."

"Yeah. Wow."

"Daisy made them. The donuts."

"I'm sure they're amazing," I say, kicking her off the bed so I can pull up my covers. "I'm sure they taste like new love. And cat dandruff."

"You don't get to be mad at me. I'm mad at you," she says, crossing her arms over her chest, lording over my mattress.

"I'm not mad. I have no emotions. I'm a sociopath, remember?"

"That was Leda, not me."

"Leda and Thomas," I say. "I've never felt so betrayed."

"Dad says you haven't left your room. You've just been up here. Alone. Brooding."

"I don't brood," I say, which is true. But it's also true I've been locked in my room all week, sleeping. I almost put out a statement that my Instagram was hacked, but then I decided I'd just pretend like it never happened, proceed as usual. But I haven't posted anything since those stories. I haven't responded to any messages or emails either. The longer I put it off, the less I want anything to do with it, with my life. The more I sleep.

"He says you haven't eaten."

"Haven't been hungry." I emerge from under the covers. "Wait. Why are *you* mad at *me*?"

"Let's save it for therapy."

"No," I say, reaching for her. "Tell me now."

"Fine," she says. "You couldn't help yourself. You had to go and tear open an old wound. For all of us."

"Mom died," I say. "That's the wound."

"You insisted on going to her funeral. Going to the house. Reading her book. You couldn't let it all die with her."

"And I'm the one accused of being callous," I say, turning my back to her. "You can leave now. I don't want any of your girlfriend-of-the-month's donuts. You should go eat them all to spite Mom. And to save Leda the anguish of depriving herself."

"You know, Dad thinks you're having some sort of nervous breakdown. But I know better. I know *you* better. You're just a fucking bitch."

For some reason, this makes me laugh. Sets me off giggling.

Daphne doesn't say anything else. She storms out of the room, slamming the door behind her.

The sound of her crying in the next room interrupts my fit of laughter, sobers me to the ugly reality of what just happened.

I'm making everything worse. I know I am, but I can't stop. Daphne's right. I can't help myself. Watching the damage unfold feels startlingly familiar. It feels like *home*.

LEDA and Tommy arrive early afternoon. Their muffled voices temporarily stir me from my nap. Our appointment is at four p.m., and I don't intend to leave my room a minute sooner than necessary. I set my alarm for three fifteen and go back to sleep.

I snooze through my alarm and wake up to Dad pounding on my door.

"Clio? Clio, time to go."

"Coming," I groan. I put on a pair of old jeans and a T-shirt. The clothes hang off me.

I go downstairs expecting a full house, but it's just Dad.

"Where is everyone?" I ask.

"Daphne and Amy went with Leda and Tom. They left ten minutes ago. They'll be on time."

"Good for them," I say as he opens the door to the garage for me.

The drive over is uncomfortable. There's no glam rock singalong. No conversation. At some point, he says, "Tom and Amy are there for support. They won't be joining this initial session. It'll be me. Your sisters. Us."

"Okay. Whatever you say. You're in charge." I yawn and check my phone. I have a message from Roy saying he arrived at the house. I respond, telling him I'll be there in a few hours. "I have to go back to the city tonight. After therapy. I have an early job tomorrow."

"Then I'll drive you in early."

"I'll catch the train tonight. It's fine. I'm fine."

His knuckles go white as his grip tightens on the steering wheel.

We pull into a labyrinth of an office plaza. Every building looks the same. Brown. Two stories. I know exactly what it's going to smell like before we even step foot inside.

"Have you been here before?" I ask Dad.

He doesn't answer. His shoulders are tense. He's nervous.

He leads me inside and up the stairs, confident in his direction, which tells me that he has in fact been here before. If he's already met with this doctor, there's a chance that he's already convinced them I'm crazy.

This could be bad.

Leda, Tommy, Daphne, and Amy sit in the waiting room. Everything is taupe and there are too many ferns.

"Did you fill out the paperwork I sent you?" Dad asks me.

"No," I say. "What paperwork?"

The door to the waiting room opens, and a woman pokes her head out. She might be in her fifties; she has streaks of gray in her dark hair. She wears a single-breasted pinstripe blazer—I think Stella McCartney—over a long black satin skirt and mahogany leather boots. Swap out her chunky sterling earrings for a pair of diamond studs, add some layered chain necklaces for texture, and it'd be a perfect look. I trust her more because of her fashion sense. If she can put herself together, maybe she can put us back together.

"The Barnes family," she says with a warm smile. "I'm ready for you. Come on back."

"Clio didn't fill out her paperwork," Dad says.

"That's quite all right. She can get to it later."

Leda huffs behind me—incensed by my free pass—as we file through the door to another taupe room. This one has couches instead of chairs, dried flowers instead of ferns. There are Rothko-esque prints on the walls, all cool tones. Dad and I sit on one couch, Leda and Daphne on another, and the woman sits on the chaise in the corner, directly facing us. She kicks up her feet, grabs a pen and legal pad from an end table. She seems unpretentious for a therapist.

"Welcome. I'm Maya. I'm a licensed psychotherapist and have my master's in family therapy from the University of Maryland. I've been working as a family therapist for twenty years and have owned this practice for about twelve. During this initial session, I would like to get to know you all and hear about why you're here, from each of your perspectives. Everything that is shared in this room is confidential. My approach is to be a facilitator of discussion, to listen, and to ask questions. My goal is to make this a comfortable environment to have uncomfortable conversations."

I resist the urge to roll my eyes.

"Do I have your consent to proceed with the session? I would appreciate a verbal yes. Let's start with James."

"Yes," he says, his voice deeper than usual. He's trying to sound more masculine to offset how he feels.

"Great," Maya says. She turns to me.

"Sure," I say, smiling. "Yes."

Both Daphne and Leda give their verbal confirmations.

"Thank you. And it's Clio, Daphne, Leda?" she asks, pointing to each of us as she says our names.

We all nod.

"Perfect," she says, leaning back. "Usually this would be the point where I say I've heard it all before, but I know your situation is unique."

I laugh.

"Clio," Leda says, teeth clenched.

I wonder if Maya can prescribe sedatives.

"No, laughter is good," Maya says, and I think Leda might jump out the window. "Laughter can be the best medicine. I'd like to turn it over to you. One at a time. Tell me why you're here. James?"

Dad clears his throat. Twice. "My daughters' mother passed away in April. She wasn't in our lives, but it's been . . . difficult. For my youngest, Clio."

"Yeah, just me," I say.

Maya cocks her head to the side. "Why are you here?"

"That's a great question," I say. "Come back to me."

"I think you should answer," she says, scrubbing any goodwill I had for her.

Why am I here?

Mom. The house. *Demon of Edgewood Drive*. Roy.

My apartment building catching on fire.

Daphne. Leda. Dad. Amy.

Austin.

Fiction. Truth. Belief. Doubt.

There are things I could say that wouldn't cause chaos. But I don't want to say any of those things. I want to say the thing I shouldn't say. Because it's the only way I can be in control.

"I'm here because my own father wants to have me committed for grieving my mother."

Dad folds over, puts his head in his hands. Leda sighs. Daphne closes her eyes.

Maya, to her credit, doesn't flinch. "What makes you say that?"

"Because I found Google searches on his computer for psychiatric holds in New Jersey."

"She's talking about demons," Dad says. "This is exactly what happened with Alex. She saw things that weren't there. Her behavior got aggressive. And there was substance abuse."

Now seems as good a time as any to turn on my tears. "I'm just trying to understand her. What she went through. What she believed. The house holds so many memories . . ."

"Oh, give me a fucking break," Daphne says.

"She's faking," Leda says to Maya. "She's manipulating you."

"I show any emotion, and this is what they do. I'm not allowed to feel anything." I sniffle, reaching for a tissue. "They used to pin all their animosity on Mom, but she's not here anymore."

"Dude, that is so far from the truth," Daphne says.

"Okay," Maya says. "There's a lot of intensity here. Everything is very raw."

"Clio makes everything about her, just like Alexandra did,"

Leda says. "There's a reason why we cut her out of our lives. Beyond just the custody arrangement. We chose not to have any contact. We're just lucky that decision was mutual, the cut clean."

Leda mimes snipping scissors.

"Ah," Maya says. "I wonder if that shared history of severing a significant relationship has had residual effects and if Alexandra's passing exacerbated some sensitivity around that. Leda, what do you think?"

"I don't know what you mean," she says. "Daphne and I have already worked through our issues with Alexandra. We suffered more because we were older and could understand—"

"I think we should try to avoid comparing our suffering. It's impossible for us to know what others feel. Even those closest to us."

Leda's turning purple, she's so mad. She looks like she's about to levitate. Like her head is about to spin all the way around.

"Leda's right, though," Daphne says. "We witnessed more. And Clio . . . Clio was never bothered by anything . . . long term. She wasn't affected the same."

"We can grow up under the same roof and have radically different childhoods," Maya says. "And those experiences can manifest differently throughout our lives."

"Yeah, but . . ." Daphne starts.

My phone rings. Everyone looks at me.

Roy's calling. I silence it.

"Sorry," I say.

"That's okay. We'll just need to remember to silence our phones before entering this space," Maya says, smiling.

There's quiet in the wake of the disturbance.

"Daphne," Maya says. "Why are you here?"

"I don't know anymore," she says, breaking down in tears. Real tears. "I don't know."

Maya nods her head. "Leda?"

33

WE walk out of Maya's office to the hopeful faces of Tommy and Amy. We watch the hope drain from their expressions when they see us.

They join us in our silent march out to the parking lot.

"Why don't I take Clio?" Tommy says.

No one argues. Not even me.

"See you back at the house," he says, the only one of us attempting communication.

He opens the car door for me, then goes around to the driver's side.

He waits until we're pulling out of the parking lot to make another endeavor to chat.

"The first session can be rough," he says. "Better luck next time."

"So, do you and Leda just sit around talking about what might be wrong with me?"

"No. Clio. Of course not."

"Actually, I don't care," I say.

"Leda—"

"I said I don't care, *Tom*."

He backs off. He turns on some music. His nu metal playlist, unfortunately.

A few Limp Bizkit songs later, we pull into Dad's driveway. I unbuckle my seat belt and get out of the car without saying another word to Tommy. I'm going to go gather my stuff and call a car and meet Roy at the house.

I'm almost past the kitchen table when I notice that everyone's sitting around it. Staring at me. Daphne. Leda. Amy. Dad stands behind his chair at the head of the table, his head down.

I want no part of whatever this is, so I keep walking.

"Clio," Dad says.

"I have to go," I say. "I need to catch the train."

"You went onto my computer," he says. "This is the second time you've broken into my study—"

"I didn't break in. The door was open."

"You violated my privacy. My trust."

"Your trust? You were trying to commit me!"

"I am trying to *help* you."

"You're trying to control me," I say. "You all are. You want to control my feelings, my behavior. My grief."

"What grief? You didn't even know her!" Leda shouts.

"Because of you," I say, pointing at Dad. "Because you gaslit her about cheating until she fucking lost it! Because you lied about her burning me! Because you had to villainize her to make yourself the hero. The greatest dad in the world, who rose to the occasion when his crazzyyyyy bitch wife couldn't handle being a mother. Wow. What a gem! How lucky we are!"

"I did it all for you!" He's so loud. He's the loudest sound in the world. "And you're nothing but ungrateful."

"You did it for *you*. It's all about *you*. You *cheated* on Mom—"

"Fine! I did! I cheated on Alex. It was miserable being married to her. She was a terrible wife and an even worse mother. Did she burn you? Let's think about this for a second. Where'd you get the lighter, Clio? Why did you believe in demons? Because of her! She was out of her fucking mind! She got exactly what she deserved. And sometimes you remind me so much of her, I want to—" He reaches his hands out toward me, his fingers curling in. "And I hate it. So I try to be so good to you. But you make it so goddamn hard!"

He throws his chair against the wall.

Amy screams.

Leda winces.

Tommy gasps.

Daphne buries her face in her hands and cries.

Dad stands there enraged. Chest rising and falling, fists clenching and unclenching.

This is the truth of him. Of us. It's been here this whole time. Dormant. Hiding. Waiting.

"Yeah. Wow. I'm going to go upstairs and get my stuff and call an Uber. I'll wait for it outside," I say, eerily calm. "Okay."

I walk out of the kitchen and into the hall, up the stairs.

I leave.

No one stops me.

WHEN I get dropped off at the house, Roy's car is in the driveway.

It's humid, sweltering even now at twilight. I mop sweat from my forehead with my T-shirt. My jeans slide down my hips.

Being back at Edgewood, I'm reminded why I left. Why I called Roy in the first place.

I'm reminded of my fear.

Of the unblinking eyes observing me.

Of how I haven't eaten anything in days.

Of how I'm alone everywhere except here.

The front door is unlocked. I open it. Cross the threshold. I expect Roy to come and greet me, but he doesn't.

"Roy?"

No answer.

"Roy? It's Clio. I'm here."

The front door closes itself behind me. I hear the lock click.

"Roy?"

I put a foot on the first step up to the living room.

My heart thumps.

Another step.

Another step.

My legs shake beneath me, knees buckle.

I use my hands to help me climb to the top, clinging to the banister.

"Roy?"

He's not up here. He's not outside on the deck.

All that's here is Mom's book, the hot pink lighter resting on top.

I look up, and I see it there on the wall beside the fireplace. Exactly where it was. Where I'd patched and painted over it.

I call out for Roy again.

It's shy of eight p.m., and daylight lingers on the horizon. Still, I flip every switch I pass. Upstairs hall. Closets. Office. Leda and Daphne's room. The bathroom. The shower rod is on the floor; I left it there after I ripped it down, the curtain crumpled.

I step back out onto the deck and scan the surrounding woods.

"Roy!"

There's a soft squeak behind me that grabs my attention. The sliding door pulls itself closed. Through the glass, I see a figure. Someone there. I can't quite bring them into focus—they're lost among the trees, in the confusion of the reflection.

Whoever it is, whatever it is . . . it isn't Roy.

I rush forward and yank the door open. The living room is empty, save for the ambiguous sound of movement. A clunking somewhere inside the walls or beneath the floorboards. I hold still to listen, but it's already gone.

The demon is committed to being intangible. An invisible threat is infinitely more frustrating. An invisible threat is madness.

I take my phone out of my pocket and call Roy.

It rings. I hear it.

It's ringing. His phone is here. In the house somewhere.

He's not answering.

"You've reached Roy Johnston, demonologist. Please leave a detailed message and I will get back to you as soon as possible. Blessings."

I hang up and call again, following the sound of his ringtone downstairs.

The cold creeps up as I descend. I feel for the light switch with trembling hands.

"You've reached Roy Johnston . . ."

Every door down here is shut except for my bedroom door. Roy's cell phone is on the floor just outside on the carpet.

Slowly approaching, I brace myself to find him in my bedroom.

"Roy . . ."

I step through the doorway. My room's empty.

I turn around and pick up Roy's phone. I open the door to the garage, which is also empty of demonologists. And of dismembered mice. There's no relief in this.

I try the bathroom. It's occupied only by a few dead flies in the sunken tub.

Mom's room.

Her bed. Her dresser. I've already been through everything that's in here. Some musty clothes. Expired bottles of Advil. A receipt for a Dunkin' Donuts iced coffee—no cream, no sugar. A Bible.

It's possible that it smells like her in here. But I don't remember what she smelled like.

I wander back upstairs, back through the house, searching for him like he'll magically appear. Like it's a game of hide-and-go-seek. Like it's a big joke. Even though I know in the dark depths of my squirming guts that it isn't. There's no more laughter.

Only the sound of my footsteps and ragged breath and hammering heart.

WE'RE coming up on midnight. The sun has vanished.

"The house is dark because the lights won't stay on."

My phone is in my hands, in front of me, facing me. I whisper into it. I'm filming. For proof.

"He's somewhere in the house," I say, between giggles. "But I can't find him."

There was half a bottle of vodka in the freezer when I arrived earlier this evening. Still no Roy, but that, that I found. It's just about gone now.

It's the ladder that finally pulls me from my wandering spell.

"That ladder isn't where I left it." I reverse my camera. "That ladder."

The ladder that leads to the one place in the house I haven't checked.

"How did I not notice it before?"

It's downstairs, in my room, propped up against the wall in my closet.

I set my phone down, wrestle with the ladder, pry it open. The panel above me is shut. I climb toward it.

"Roy?"

One hand on the ladder, one hand above me, palm flat as I reach for the panel. I push.

It lifts, but barely. There's something on top of it, a weight that I disturbed, that gravity releases. *Thud.* The noise is dense.

"Hello?"

Carefully balancing on the ladder, I lift my other hand. Push harder.

The panel doesn't budge.

I step up higher on the ladder, lean over so I can put my back into the lift.

I hear Leda's voice inside my head. *She can't help herself.*

Now Daphne's. *You had to go and tear open an old wound.*

The wound is open. It's always been open, festering. It doesn't matter if I keep this panel shut. If I climb down this ladder, walk out of this house, and never come back. Whatever's here will always be here, even if no one else acknowledges it but me.

It's not at rest.

It's why she was here.

It's why I am here.

Knock knock knock.

The sound disorients me. I think it's coming from above me, and I lose my balance. I fall forward, and my face collides with the top rung of the ladder.

And most of the other rungs as I slide down.

There's the taste of blood in my mouth. Warm, wet agony

radiating from my nose. I land on my knees, crawling forward as blood spews from my nostrils.

I think I just broke my nose.

My perfect, beautiful nose.

Knock knock knock.

The lock whirs, and the front door opens.

"Clio?" It's Daphne.

"I can't believe we're back here." Leda.

"She's our sister," Daphne says. "And this is just a dumb fucking house."

"It's smaller than I remember."

I get to my feet and stumble down the hall, to the bottom of the stairs.

Leda and Daphne stand on the landing, looking up toward the ceiling.

"What are you doing here?" There's too much blood in my mouth, and I accidentally swallow some, start to cough.

Leda screams when she sees me.

"Fuck!" Daphne says, rushing down to me and helping me up the stairs. "What happened?"

"I fell off a ladder."

"There's so much blood," Leda says, covering her eyes.

Daphne leads me to the kitchen. She rips off a few paper towels, runs them under the faucet, and hands them to me. Then she opens the freezer.

"There's nothing in here except for an empty bottle of vodka," she says.

"It's not empty. There's a little bit left."

Now, now Leda uncovers her eyes, looks at me. It's not a good look.

"Does it hurt?" Daphne asks. "You're already bruising."

"I think it's broken."

Leda sighs. "Do you have health insurance?"

"Yes, I have health insurance."

"She's still on Dad's."

"If she apologizes, maybe," Leda says.

"Why are you two here?" I ask, leaning back against the counter, holding the paper towels under my nose to absorb the blood. "How did you know I was—"

"You're livestreaming," Daphne says. "You're on Insta Live. People are calling me, asking if it's a joke, if you're okay."

"I'm not on Live," I say. "I'm not. I didn't . . . I'm not . . ."

If I say it enough times, maybe it'll be true.

I move to go get my phone, which I'm pretty sure I left downstairs, but Daphne holds me back.

"Wait," she says. "I'll go get it."

She leaves, and in her absence there's just me and Leda and the tension between us.

Leda starts opening and closing the kitchen cabinets to have something to do.

After a minute, she says, "Dad saw. I've never seen him so upset."

"Dad saw what?"

"Your Live. Amy showed him," Leda says. "I mean, you're clearly inebriated. Stumbling around, muttering to yourself, looking for something that isn't there. Isn't here."

"Stop. Just stop," Daphne says, rushing up the stairs, setting my phone screen down on the counter. "This can't be what it is. We love each other. What are we doing? What are *you* doing, Clio? You're not okay."

"No, I'm not. And I'm not allowed to not be okay. I have to be okay. I have to be pretty and fun and together and nice to look at and good to be around. But I'm not any of those things anymore. Because I have this *problem*. Because I'm having some *trouble*. And no one believes me—they just think it *is* me."

Daphne pushes her hair out of her face, tucks it behind her ears. "I'm sorry."

"We're here, aren't we? Here for you." Leda says. It's obvious from her tone that Daffy talked her into this. She didn't come willingly, didn't volunteer.

"Please," Daphne says. "Come back to Dad's with us. We don't need to talk about any of this shit right now. Let's just be together. It can't all be for nothing."

"What do you mean?" I ask. I pull the paper towel from my nose. It's soaked through crimson. I nudge Daphne out of the way so I can throw it in the trash.

"We didn't suffer all this"—she gestures around—"as kids to grow up and, like, hate each other."

"Hate?" I ask.

"We should probably take you to urgent care," Leda says, wincing at the sight of my face.

"What's that?" Daphne says. She moves toward the saloon doors, pointing.

She sees it. The smiling face on the wall.

Leda turns around, and the two of them exchange a look.

"I didn't do that," I say. "The demon did."

If they stay in the house long enough, maybe it'll show up. Maybe it will say hello.

"Um, okay . . ." Daphne says.

"What's this?" Leda goes through the saloon doors. I think she's going for Mom's book, but she goes for the lighter. "Why do you have this?"

"I was smoking. Cigarettes, like a true degenerate."

Leda scoffs. "Do you realize how traumatizing it was for us to watch you hurt yourself? We were helpless then. And I resent that you're making us feel the same way now. You don't give any consideration to our feelings. You act out, and there's nothing we can do. And then you do the Mom thing. You point to something to blame, something that no one can see but you, and when we question it, you freak out."

"I can't see it. I can only hear it. In the house," I say. "And you said, 'Mom.'"

"What?"

"You didn't say 'Alexandra.' You said 'Mom.'"

She picks up *Demon of Edgewood Drive* and stares at the cover. She ignores what I said, starts flipping through the pages of the book.

"What do you mean, you hear it?" Daphne asks.

"It communicates," I say, going out through the saloon doors and pointing to the wall. "At first, without a voice. Then with a voice. One time."

"Do you recognize how that sounds to us? Do you—" A door slams somewhere in the house. "Wait. Fuck. Is someone else here? There was another car in the driveway."

"Connecticut plates," Leda says.

Right. Roy.

I reach up to my face, gingerly feel my nose. The pain is nuclear. A mushroom cloud erupts between my eyes.

"I called Roy," I say.

"*Roy* is here?" Leda asks.

"I can't find him. That's who I've been looking for. Not the demon."

Another door slams. Startled, Leda drops the book.

"What do you mean, you can't find him?" Daphne asks. "That

scumbag is somewhere in the house slamming fucking doors, trying to scare us."

"That's not him, Daffy."

"Meet me halfway. It's the middle of the night, and I came here—to this place I never wanted to be ever again in my life—to come get you. We've already been through hell. Don't drag us back through it."

"Wha . . . what?" Leda says, distracted by something. She steps to the side to look down the upstairs hall. She narrows her eyes. "He's in our room."

She storms forward. I follow her.

"He isn't," I say. "I looked. He's not in there."

"He is. He's opening and closing the door," she says, throwing her arms up as she makes her way to the end of the hall, to her childhood bedroom. I look behind me, and Daphne stands at the other end of the hall, her shoulders hiked up to her ears, arms crossed in front of her like a shield.

She's afraid.

Leda might have gone to Harvard, but Daphne's the smart one.

"Roy!" Leda goes for the knob, but she doesn't need to. The door flies open. The lights flicker off and on and off and on again.

The twin beds are stood up vertically, headboards on the floor, legs against the wall, with the mattresses perched precariously on top, stretching up toward the ceiling. They frame the word carved deep into the wall.

HOME

Leda grips the doorframe, leans forward.

Daphne comes up behind me. "What . . ."

"Roy!" Leda says, stomping into the room. She spins around to the closet. It's open, and it's empty. "He did this. He's the one drawing on the walls. Not the demon. He exploits vulnerable people. That's what he does."

"Fair point. He does exploit people. But he didn't do that," I say. "He didn't—"

I'm interrupted by banging.

Leda pushes past me and Daphne, barreling down the hall. She stops dead in her tracks.

"Leeds?" Daphne calls out, her voice tinny.

Leda, the most rigid person I know, collapses to the floor as if her bones have dissolved inside her skin. Just to witness it is so unnerving, I experience a sudden wave of nausea.

The banging continues, the pacing of the noise more and more chaotic.

Daphne grasps for my hand. I give it to her and allow her to drag me forward toward the puddle that is our sister.

We make it to her and see what she's seeing. The kitchen cabinets fly open and smash shut. There's no rhyme or reason, no cadence, no pattern.

"See?" I whisper, my chest swelling with gratitude, with affection. It's showing them. It's proving itself. "See?"

"This is . . ." Daphne says.

Leda gets up and staggers into the kitchen, closing each cabinet as soon as it opens, just for it to open again. Her face goes red. "It's a trick! This is . . . there's a machine somewhere. Roy. Roy put it in. He . . . Where is it?"

She goes on mumbling, attempting to rationalize the irrational. Now she's the one opening the cabinets, but they close before she can look inside.

"We should get out of here," Daphne says.

"Do you believe me now?" I ask her, more smugly than I intend.

"I . . ." She shakes her head. "I think . . . Leda? Come on. Stop that."

Daphne steps into the kitchen. She reaches for Leda, trying to pull her away. But Leda is obsessive, and now that she's intent on figuring out the mystery of the cabinets, she will not be dissuaded.

Her platinum bleached hair has come loose out of its tight bun. Her neck breaks out in red splotches that match the violent hue of her face.

"Leeds," Daphne says, gripping her arm.

Leda smacks her. Backhands her across the face. It might have been an accident, but it doesn't matter.

The cabinets slowly, simultaneously close themselves. The house is quiet. The demon quiet.

Daphne holds her face. "You hit me."

Leda should say something. She should apologize. She really should. But she doesn't. She just stands there breathing like she just ran a marathon.

"You fucking hit me!" Daphne pushes her.

"Hey!" Leda says, shoving her back.

Daphne's hip collides with the kitchen island. She groans in pain. "What's your problem?"

"I didn't even want to come here!" Leda shouts. "You made me."

"I *asked* you! And not because I wanted to. Because if I didn't, you'd bitch about how you were left out because you're so deeply insecure about being the least favorite sister. Because you are!"

Leda lunges forward, grabbing Daphne's hair. Daphne tries to wriggle free, untangle Leda's fingers from her curls, but Leda's relentless. Daphne kicks her shin, and still Leda doesn't let go.

It's shocking to watch. We've never gotten physical with each other like this before. Not even when we were little.

"Let go of me!" Now Daphne's got Leda's hair. Clumps are coming away in her hands. "Stop!"

I hear the laughter. It's so loud it shakes the house. But Daphne and Leda don't notice, and a sudden understanding cuts into me.

The demon isn't doing this for my benefit, isn't revealing its presence to my sisters to vindicate me and Mom. It hasn't been communicating with me because it likes me, wants to engage with me, get my attention and give it in return.

It's doing it because it wants to. Because it's bored. Because it enjoys watching us suffer.

Our suffering is entertainment.

I'm only its favorite because I'm game, down to play. Because I'm a good pawn. The easiest. The most fun.

"Okay, yeah. Enough," I say, hurrying into the kitchen to break them up. I wedge myself between them. "Enough."

I catch a stray elbow to the side of the head, and everything disappears.

34

AFTER the disastrous initial exorcism, more attempts were made to rid the house of the demon. Paranormal experts were brought in from overseas. Priests from Vatican City. The demon resisted.

Roy left satchels of lavender and thyme and cloves of garlic in Cici's closet. He sprinkled salt in the attic. We had a witch come and cast spells of protection. None of it made a difference. None of it mattered.

It fed off my energy. Feasted on my anguish. My pain kept it occupied. Kept it happy. I wanted to defeat it. I wanted it gone. It cost me my daughters. But I had nothing left in me then. I spent less and less time at the house, often visiting with Roy in Connecticut and eventually moving in with him there.

Days turned to weeks turned to months, and I crawled toward healing, wanting more than anything just a moment of peace, a moment to forget all the pain and terror of the past. I was no longer there physically, but mentally, it would not let me leave. It would not let me go. The demon found me in my dreams. My nightmares. It leached the colors from my world, from my view. I understood then that there was no escape.

When I finally returned to the house, I went slowly up the stairs and stood in the living room, perfectly still, listening. It was quiet, and in the quiet I allowed myself that moment of peace I so craved.

WHEN I come to, it's on the kitchen floor, on my side, in a pool of blood.

It's to Daphne's voice.

"'But then I heard it. The cruel, soul-curdling sound of its laughter, and I felt a chill, a brutal cold that I knew was of death itself. The evil was not gone. It would never be gone. But it could be kept at bay.'"

"Daffy . . ." I say, my voice barely a whisper. "Daphne . . ."

She sits on the floor, her back against the wall, knees to her chest. Book hiding her face. "'My daughters are no longer in the house, but they are out in the world. A world that's unforgiving, that's brimming with unspeakable evil. I've devoted the rest of my life to fighting that evil. I have seen the face of it. It has slept under my roof. It is real. Denial will not—'"

"Shut up," Leda whines. I can't see her. I don't know where she is. I can't lift my head.

"'Denial will not save you. Skepticism will only buy you time. My hope is that my story gives a voice to everyone who has been haunted by evil, both of this world and the supernatural. Who has been met with doubt and ridicule. Who has been called crazy. Who, despite the adversity, hasn't abandoned the truth, or their fight against what works in shadow. May it all come to the light.'" Daphne smacks the book shut. She's got a black eye and a bloody lip.

"What's going on?" I ask. The bulb in the kitchen is searingly bright.

"Tell her," Daphne says.

I turn. Leda's propped against the refrigerator. There's a welt on her forehead. "You're both insane."

"Leda knocked you out. We fought. And she confessed to reading the book."

"What?" I'm dizzy. I slap my hands down to steady myself.

"Apparently, I'm the only one who hasn't read it. Who kept my promise. So fuck it. I'm catching up on my reading," Daphne says.

"You read it?" I ask Leda.

"You two don't understand. I'm the oldest. The pressure on me . . . I had to know. I had to be aware of what was out there. I had to—"

"The pressure on *you*?" Daphne says, standing. "What pressure? It all falls on me. Do you get how, like, crushingly exhausting it is to have to navigate all your bullshit? Everyone's bullshit. What about *my* bullshit? What if I want to be the asshole for once? What if I want to throw a fucking tantrum."

I reach up to the counter and pull myself to my feet.

"What if I'm angry?" Daffy carries on. "What if I want it to be about me for fucking once!"

"It's never about me either. It's always about Clio," Leda says. "That's why we're here. Because of her."

"You showed up here," I say. "I didn't ask you to come."

Daphne's expression doesn't change. It's disturbingly blank. "Let's just say it all, then. Let's just have it out."

"What's happening?" Leda says, breaking down in tears. "What's happening?"

"Exactly what it wants," I say. "We're putting on a good show."

"I hate looking at you, Clio. I hate that you're so pretty," Daphne says. "And I hate your stupid fucking outfits. I hate that you're spoiled. I hate that everything just works out for you. I hate that I hate it. I hate that Leda found someone to love her, but I'm somehow still alone. I hate how badly Mom messed me up. I hate that the truth of who she was and what she was doing to us wasn't enough to get us out of this house. That a lie was what saved us from her. I hate that she never changed, never got better. That she fucking drank herself to death and no one's surprised. I hate that I know Dad cheated on Mom with Amy, that deep down I've always known it. I hate that Dad hates that I'm gay but will never admit it. I hate so much about our family. I hate that I need you all."

"Daffy . . ." I say.

She looks down, a sob escaping. She slumps over, slides back to the floor.

"I'm sorry. I'm sorry. I don't . . . I shouldn't have said those things."

"But you meant them," Leda says. She gathers up her hair and pulls it high over her head, like she's holding a noose, about to hang herself. "You meant every word. It was honest. And if we're going to be honest, fine. I have a healthy, happy relationship. My life is stable. My career is stable. That's why you don't like me. You're jealous. You'll never admit it to yourselves because you think you're too cool to want what I have. But you do. And you'll never have it. You're too dysfunctional. You'll both die alone, likely in debt, and no one will be around to mourn you."

"Jesus, Leeds," Daphne says. She tongues her busted lip.

Leda lets her head back and releases a wild laugh.

She turns and stumbles out into the hall, then down the stairs.

"Where are you going?" I call after her.

"What do you care?" she says, still laughing. "I'm the least favorite sister."

"What the *fuck* is going on?" Daphne asks, grabbing my arm. I flinch at her touch, and she retracts her hand. She stares at it as if she's surprised to see it there at the end of her wrist. "Sorry . . ."

"No one cares about Leda. She's no fun," Leda calls out from downstairs. "She doesn't do anything fun. You both have substance abuse issues and self-medicate with drugs and alcohol, you sleep around, slut it up, but Leda's the issue, the wet blanket. All she ever tries to do is the right thing. Color inside the lines. But somehow, no, that's not good enough. Nothing is ever good enough."

"Leeds!" Daphne shouts.

"Who cares about Leda? She's so *boring*!"

"Leda," I say, lurching toward the stairs. My head feels like a cement block, and my vision is blurred, and my mouth still tastes of blood. "Leda, what are you doing?"

"What if I told you I knew about the demon. What if I told you that sometimes, if it couldn't wake you, Clio, it would come into our room at night and watch us sleep. It would go up in the corner, and it looked like a shadow, only I could see its big white eyes staring out at me from the dark. And it had this long, thin red tongue with a slit like a snake's . . ."

Daphne follows me to the landing and down the second set of steps to the hall. All the lights are off. I don't see Leda. She's hiding.

"What if I told you I pulled the covers up over my head and promised myself that when I pulled them down, it wouldn't be there. And I counted one Mississippi, two Mississippi, with Daphne across the room snoring, none the wiser. What if I told you, when I pulled the covers down, it was right there, at the foot of my bed. I remembered what Dad told me about bullies. If you ignore them, they'll go away. And so I ignored it, and it stopped coming into our room. I was glad it was gone, but I missed it. I missed the attention. I missed how I felt with its eyes on me. I missed how it watched me. I knew we came second to you. I could hear you, sometimes, talking to it. Laughing with it."

I take a cautious step down the hall, approaching the bathroom. I push the door back. "Leda . . ."

"There were times when I wondered if it'd be worth it, to invite it back in. Acknowledge its presence. Give it the attention it wanted so I could get some back. Didn't matter what form the attention came in. If it made me afraid or sad or angry."

The bathroom's empty.

"Leda," Daffy says. "Leda, where are you?"

"But I chose to ignore it. To shut it out. And I've held that door closed ever since. It hasn't been easy. It requires such strength, such discipline."

I can't even tell which direction her voice is coming from.

"What if I told you I lied about the burn not because Dad asked or because Mom would drive us to school with vodka in the glove compartment, because she would get drunk and tell me how ugly I was. What if told you I lied because I wanted out of this house. *Needed* out of this house. Away from *it*."

"Leda?"

"Goddamn it. It's so cold down here," Daphne says, her voice hushed. She blows into her hands. "How is it so cold?"

Daphne opens the door to Mom's room and finds the light switch. "She's not in here."

That leaves my room.

The door is locked.

"Leda," I say, pounding with a closed fist. "Leda, open the door."

I will bleed you out! I will bleed you out!

"Leda, please," Daphne says.

Now I can hear her. I can hear her breathing through the door. I can see her shadow underneath.

"Leda!" I say, trying the knob again.

"Move," Daphne says to me. "Leda, I'm going to break down this fucking door."

Leda erupts into a fit of maniacal giggles. "And here I thought if it was me alone in this house instead of Clio, you wouldn't have come. You'd have just let me rot here. You . . ."

"One more chance," Daphne says.

"Can you break down a door?" I ask her.

Leda resumes her deranged snickering.

"Guess we're about to find out." Daphne charges, bangs her shoulder against the wood. There's a *clunk*—and Leda stops laughing.

"Shit," Daffy says. "Leeds?"

A pause, a few seconds that hold back forever like a sharp knife.

"It's . . . it's in here. With me," Leda whispers. "It says come in."

35

LEDA unlocks the door. She opens it just a crack, just enough so we can see her face. There's a new welt on her forehead. Above her bloodshot eyes is all swollen, black-and-blue. She must have been up against the door when Daphne rammed into it.

She takes a few steps back, her head lolling. Daphne and I cross into the room. It's arctic in here. I can see my breath.

The tulip lamp is on, emitting a dull pink glow. Shadows crawl up the walls. I check to make sure they don't have eyes.

"I'm sorry," Leda says, sitting on the bed. She scratches at her splotchy neck. She's digging her nails in too deep. "I'm sorry . . . I . . . I don't know what came over me."

"Leda," Daphne says, kneeling in front of her.

Leda raises a shaky hand, points to the closet. "Up there."

There's a sound. A muffled voice. A man's voice.

"Is that . . . Roy?" I ask.

Somehow I'd totally forgotten about Roy again. Wow.

From the look on Daphne's face, she did, too.

She stands and approaches the closet.

"Daffy," I say. "Hold on."

She peers inside. She touches the ladder, running her fingers along the rungs. Her back is to me, so I can't see her face as she angles it up toward the ceiling.

"Wait," I say, the word catching in my throat. My eyes frantically scan the room, heart pounding in my chest. "Don't go up there. It's up there. That's where it lives."

"It's just Roy," Daphne says, starting up the ladder.

"Leave him!" I say. "Don't go up there. Daffy. Stop! I'm begging you."

She pauses, turns to look at me.

"Please. After everything that's happened, how do you still not believe me?"

"Daphne," Leda says. "Don't."

"So, what?" Daphne asks, stepping down off the ladder and sitting next to Leda on the bed. "We just leave him up there?"

Before we get a chance to answer, a scraping noise infiltrates the space. Wood against wood. The panel moving aside.

I peek into the closet, look up. "Roy?"

The panel shifts, revealing the dangling head of what was once Roy. His eyes are gone. Scratched or gouged out, caked in gore.

I don't have the chance to scream. He falls, landing with a *thud* at my feet.

Leda and Daphne eject high-pitched, terrified wails. Leda jumps up on the bed, but Daphne runs toward me, toward Roy. She flips him over.

He lets out this horrendous yowl, then appears to pass out.

But he's alive. He's still alive.

"Help me get him out of here!" Daphne says.

I'm wedged in the corner of the closet, mouth open, eyes wide, body useless. He'd been so handsome.

"Fuck. Leda?" Daphne says, coming around and slipping her arms under Roy's pits. "Help me!"

PLAY NICE

"This isn't happening. This isn't happening. None of this is happening," Leda says, leaping off the bed and flailing toward us. She gets Roy's legs and, together, my sisters drag him out into the hall.

With the two of them gone, I stand alone in the closet, gazing up at the dark void.

I climb the ladder.

When I get to the crawl space, it's exactly as I pictured it, as Mom described it. There's insulation, white like snow. Cobwebs hanging from the rafters, dancing in a nonexistent breeze. It's dark and it's freezing. I can't feel my face.

Death is strewn everywhere. Motionless flies. Mouse parts. Tiny skulls. Dried-up wads of fur. Tails slithering through the insulation.

But it's not just carnage. There are photos. Pictures of Mom, of me and my sisters. Empty bottles of liquor. A jewelry box—it was Mom's; I remember admiring it as a kid, seeing it on her dresser. The cups, *our* cups. The pineapple cup, the strawberry, the apple. And there are copies of the book. I count two. One out of reach, but one just at my feet.

I pick it up. Flip open the front cover.

For my Daffy—

Your kind and gentle spirit inspires me. You may be my daughter, but I've always looked up to you.

    I hope this book finds its way to you, and I hope you can find it in your beautiful heart to forgive me.

Love forever,
Mom

A sudden creaking startles me. I drop the book, follow the sound. There's movement. A bulge, a bending where there shouldn't be. Where the angles of the house should meet clean.

A shape emerges. I watch as it births itself from the rafters, peels free from the wood—sheds its house skin. It hunches in the gable.

It edges closer, its movements graceful.

Don't look.

I have to look.

So much of my life I've been preoccupied with beauty, and this face in front of me erases it all.

Big milky eyes. Red slits for pupils. A gaping, drooling mouth crowded with sharp teeth. A long, slim crimson tongue split like a snake's.

I wonder if it loves me most because I can see it in all its hideousness, in all its glorious depravity, and I won't turn away.

"Hello," I say.

Hello, I said the first night it showed me its form, the first time it came down out of the attic, into my bedroom. The first time I saw it in my closet. I didn't scream or call for Mom. I just said hello.

The memory reveals itself to me in the demon's eyes, like two screens playing home movies. All that was lost to me, all that was forgotten. My memories. It kept them for me. Or from me. So I would come back.

Its claws are sharp against my neck. Its split tongue strangely dry as it grazes my cheek. As it licks a rogue falling tear. As it laps up my fear.

It starts to laugh.

I understand why some ears bleed at the sound of this laughter.

It's not evil. It's not joyous. It's a lonely sound.

This being in front of me is what it is, and it cannot change. It lives in this place amid the damage and the chaos it reaps just by existing, and it breaks my heart because it's so familiar to me. I love it and I hate it, and I admire it, aspire to be it, and I resent everything about it that I recognize within myself.

It's got my hair now. It pulls me deeper into the attic.

Gently, at first. Until I resist.

It wants to keep me here. And maybe I would let it if it weren't for the sound of my sisters calling my name.

I pull back, and it snarls.

Its pale eyes watch me. They narrow as I struggle.

"Let me go!" I tell it. But my resolve is waning, and it knows. It laughs and laughs and laughs and laughs and laughs and laughs, and it tightens its grip.

I look around at all the mouse parts, at all the *stuff*. The photographs, the jewelry box, the bottles. The books. The cups. Why is this shit in the attic?

Did Mom put it up here?

She tried to appease it . . . She did what she could to keep it happy. If it was content, it would sleep. Go dormant. That's what Roy said.

My pain kept it occupied. Kept it happy.

I understand now, as the demon drags me into shadow. Mom couldn't figure out how to beat it, how to exorcise it, so she tried to live with it. Give it everything it wanted. Everything it could possibly want. She played along. Played nice.

"Stop," I say. "Wait."

I reach up around my neck, unclasp my necklace, my snake charm.

"For you," I say, dropping the charm into its claw. "An offering. A gift."

It closes its fist around the necklace, then leans in close again, its tongue prodding my cheek.

Now is the time to turn on my tears.

It recoils. Spits. Growls.

It knows I'm faking. It can taste it.

My inner rebel is reluctant to give in, but what happens if I don't? Will it keep me here forever, its claws around my throat?

So when I do start to cry, to really, sincerely cry, I don't cry for it.

I cry for my mother. I cry for my sisters.

I cry for myself.

I cry for everything it's taken from me that lives here now. With it. In it.

It drinks until it's satisfied, laughing again as it retreats into the dark of the attic.

It allows me to climb down the ladder, to replace the panel.

It allows me to leave, but I'm not sure it will ever let me go.

"Clio? Clio! Where are you? Come on." Daphne.

I find her on the landing. She throws her arms around me and practically pushes me out through the front door, down the wooden stairs to the pathway, to the yard, where Roy is splayed on the weedy grass, arms out wide, legs together, very "Jesus on the cross."

Leda paces up and down driveway. When we get to her, the three of us embrace, hold each other, as the sirens approach, without saying a word.

THERE are two police cars and an ambulance.

There are neighbors in the street, necks craned.

"Clio?"

It's Austin. He stands in the middle of the cul-de-sac in his sweatpants and tank top and gold chain.

"Shit! Your face," he says as I walk toward him.

"You need to work on your sweet talk," I say.

He runs to me, takes a good look. "Fractured. What happened? I heard the sirens."

"That is what they're for. That's their whole thing."

He drops his gaze to his shoes. His Vans.

I reach out and pull one of his curls straight. His hair isn't as springy as mine, but there's still some satisfaction in it. In touching him again. "I'm sorry. For what I said the other night. You didn't deserve it. Any of it."

"No," he says, "I didn't."

"If it helps, I think karma is on your side," I say, pointing to my massacred face.

"It does, kind of," he says, laughing a little. A good laugh. A laugh that erases the memory of all other laughs. For a moment. "Hey. Listen . . ."

"Cli?" Leda calls. She stands next to Daphne and a somber police officer, looking extra tense.

"I should go. I don't want to keep law enforcement waiting. I know cops are known for their patience, but I pride myself on my manners."

"Right, right," he says. "Well . . ."

"Austin. Would you believe me if I told you the demon was real?" I ask, because I have nothing left to lose.

He takes a beat, runs his hands through his hair. "Um, yeah. I would. I never wanted to say anything, but it's creepy as shit in there."

Wow. I love him. I love him. "Maybe I can take you to the diner sometime. We can get disco fries and I can tell you all about it."

"You know how I feel about disco fries."

I give him a smile and a wink, even though it hurts.

AFTER hours of statements and medical attention, my sisters and I sit in profound silence at a corner table in a particularly grimy McDonald's.

I dip a fry into my McFlurry. All I taste is the stubborn lingering of blood.

Daphne opens a packet of honey for her McNuggets.

"That's honey. Not honey mustard," Leda says, stabbing at a salad.

"I know," Daphne says. "I like honey."

"You dip your chicken in honey?" Leda asks, horrified.

It's like nothing ever happened. It's like nothing's different, even though it is. The things that were said and done in that house cannot be unsaid or undone.

The words, the violence, the ugliness, the fear, the sadness, the hurt—all that will continue to make a home inside us, even if we relegate it to the attic, and it lives cramped among the cobwebs, emerging sometimes in our sleep or causing chaos in our waking lives, an invisible hand pulling the strings, a shadow at the corners of our eyes.

I look down at the scar on my forearm. It looks back at me.

I remember flirting with Ethan at Veronica's launch party. *Lucky to live with scars,* I said.

And he said, *Better to live without.*

I'm not totally sure. Who would I be without my scars? Who would my sisters be?

We sit here, our faces swollen, covered in scrapes and bruises, wounds that will heal but won't disappear. But I think we're beautiful now, wearing the evidence of our pain. No one can deny it exists.

My scars are my vindication. We shouldn't need them to prove anything, but that's the world we live in. The world Mom tried to prepare us for.

"What do you think Mom would say if she could see us now?" I ask.

"About us at McDonald's?" Daphne asks.

"No," I say. "Just . . . us. As we are."

"I don't know," Daffy says. "I don't know."

"Me either," Leda says.

"I think"—I hesitate—"I think it's that. Everything we'll never know because now she's gone. She's gone."

There's quiet as the unknowns swim in the oceans between us.

A few minutes pass; then Leda asks, "That guy you were talking to in the street. Is that the neighbor?"

"Yeah. Austin."

"He's cute!" she says. "You should date him."

"He's too good for me. Too pure of heart," I say. "What if I destroy him?"

"Why don't you just be nice," Leda says. "What if you tried that for a change?"

"I could try. Turn over a new leaf."

"Maybe this could be a new beginning. For all of us," Daphne says, tapping her soda cup with a plastic knife.

Leda reaches for my McFlurry. She spoons some into her mouth. "Fresh start."

"I love you two. With a cherry on top."

"Love you, Cli," Daphne says, and I know she means it, just like she meant it when she said she hated me.

I reach up to my neck to play with my charm, forgetting for a second it's no longer there. Forgetting that there's some piece of me back at the house and always will be.

Remembering is not always a light shone into darkness. Sometimes it's a claw reaching out and dragging you back.

THERE'S the promise of a pretty morning, the sun teasing its grand entrance with pink phosphorescence. The view from Daphne's balcony is really something, and I for sure should be sleeping, but I want to see it. The morning. The light coming through the trees, turning the Hudson to glitter.

"Here," Aunt Helen says, stepping outside and handing me a giant ceramic mug steaming with hot coffee, the smell of it lush and nutty.

"Thank you. Daffy still asleep?"

She nods, then takes a cigarette out from behind her ear and lights it. Her hair is big and frizzy, and she wears a white ribbed long-sleeve T-shirt, silk pajama pants, slippers, and a pair of thick dark-rimmed glasses. Even unkempt, there's a glamour about her I admire.

"I'm really glad you're here," I tell her, because I know now that my heart is a soft thing. What's the point in pretending it isn't?

She exhales smoke out of the side of her mouth. "I would prefer it if the next time we see each other, it not to be under such grim circumstances."

"I wholeheartedly agree."

She ashes her cigarette over the banister. "But we can talk about anything you want to talk about. Edgewood. Alex."

"So strange that sometimes you don't know how you feel about someone until they're gone. And even then . . ." I say, taking a sip of coffee. It burns my tongue, a tiny tragedy. A temporary one. "They should really warn you about that."

"Some lessons can only be taught by regret."

I say nothing because there's nothing to say to that. I sit in silence as the truth presses its elbows in.

"I suppose the demon does exist," Helen says.

"Yeah? What convinced you? What happened to Roy?"

She takes a drag. "You. Your sisters. I don't know how Lex would feel about that. I hope she can be exonerated for some of it."

I understand that the demon exploited my mother's vulnerabilities, weaponized them against her. Her sadness, her addiction. The same way it exploits my penchant for chaos. It is not alone in that behavior. It is not special. It is one of many. My father taught me that.

I will not fight against it or try to appease it. Those efforts are futile. My mother taught me that.

I accept that it exists. That there's a being out there that wants my attention, my energy, my best, my worst. My joy. My pain. That's taken from me and would continue to take should I allow it, should I continue to dance with it, and if I were to say anything about it, no one would listen. No one would believe me. Not really. Not without their doubts. Without questioning my honesty, my integrity, my sanity. Whether I deserved it.

There's a being out there that would fuck with me just because it can, with no consequences. Because it's bored. Just because.

Too bad for it, I know that game and play it better.

I know that the real way to win is to not play at all.

I'm done with the demon. I'm done with Edgewood Drive. Game over.

I look at Aunt Helen and the beautiful view beyond her, and I inhale the scent of coffee and tobacco and a new day. That magic morning smell.

It's hope, is what it is. Hope for whatever comes next.

AFTER

THE open bar was a mistake; everyone's drunk half an hour into the party.

"Congratulations," Veronica says, kissing my cheeks.

"Thank you, thank you," I say, faking a smile. "I'm so glad you could make it."

"Of course! Wouldn't miss it," she says. "Even if we weren't friends. Your line is *amazing*."

Turns out that fashion is more forgiving of insanity than I'd initially assumed. I actually gained followers from my unhinged Instagram activity, inadvertently created an aura of mystery for myself. Hannah hooked me up with one of her friends, a designer for a London-based luxury brand with a romantic, gothic aesthetic. They brought me on as creative director, and we worked together on a line that we're celebrating tonight, on Halloween Eve. Mischief Night.

"This party, Clio! I'm obsessed with the decor. And these flower arrangements. Stunning," Veronica says, fawning. "And, like, *everyone* is here."

As much as I'm grateful to have landed on my feet, things are different for me now. People whisper when I walk by. They stare.

There's a caution in how I'm approached, a certain tone used to address me. Even here at this party, my accomplishment, my art, it isn't met with respect. It's met with the phony, condescending enthusiasm of an elementary school award ceremony.

That brief public exposure of my vulnerability—of my pain, my confusion, my fear, my grief—will forever overshadow everything I do.

"Hey," Austin says, handing me a flute of champagne.

"Thanks, babe. Austin, this is Veronica. Veronica, Austin."

"Oh my God!" Veronica says. "The man who finally locked Clio down. I've been so intrigued."

Austin shakes Veronica's hand. "Nice to meet you."

"Is my family here yet?" I ask him.

"Yeah, just got here," he says.

"I'll be back," I tell Veronica. "And we should get drinks soon, yeah? Next time I'm on your side of the river."

"I'd love that. I miss you! Call me," she says, blowing me a kiss.

Austin takes my hand and leads me through the crowd.

"Do you hate this?" I ask him.

He laughs. "No. But it's not nearly as fun as my work parties."

"I'm sure. I can't compete with bingo night."

"Appreciate that no one here's asked me for cookies or drugs, though."

"Not yet."

We approach the corner, where Dad, Amy, Tommy, Leda, Daphne, and Daisy huddle around a cocktail table.

"There she is," Amy says.

"Why is it so dark in here?" Leda asks. "I can barely see anything."

"It's the vibe," I say.

"Congratulations, sweetie," Dad says, hugging me. We exchanged apologies almost a year ago, but we don't look at each other the same. He overcompensates. Last week, he offered to pay for my wedding. Austin and I aren't engaged, but even if we were, I wouldn't take Dad's money.

I meant it when I told him I was sorry. I'm sorry I didn't see him for who he was any sooner. I'm sorry for the part he played in Mom's destruction. I'm sorry for the part he would have played in mine had my sisters not been on my side. I will never know his motivation—if it was pure and he really thinks himself the hero, the white knight, saving us from someone battling demons. Or if he was intentionally antagonizing our mother because it benefited him, because with her gone he could get everything he wanted. Amy. Us. Or maybe he didn't want to hurt her, but he was just fine watching her hurt herself.

Yeah, I said I was sorry for the sake of my sisters, to preserve some of what was good about our family. And yeah, he said it, too. But forgiveness is a different beast.

It's fine. I don't need him anymore. He has no power over me.

"It's all so lovely," Daisy says. She's button cute, and the few times I've met her, she's been dressed like a milkmaid.

"We're proud of you, Cli," Tommy says, pushing his glasses up his nose. He's crying. He's been crying continuously since they found out Leda's pregnant. Such a softy.

"I don't know how long we'll stay," Leda says. "But thank you for inviting us. Everything's beautiful. From what I can see."

"I'll be right back," Daphne says to Daisy. She grabs me and Austin. "It's too crowded; it's stressing me out. Let's go smoke."

THE three of us go out to the balcony and pass around Daffy's weed pen.

"Sorry. Long day," she says. "This is really cool, Cli. Congrats."

"The buyers fell through, didn't they?" I ask her. She took over all things Edgewood after what happened that night with Roy.

He's retired now, I hear. Probably for the best.

Daffy stays quiet, which I take as confirmation.

"That house will never sell," I say.

"It'll sell," Austin says. "Just could take a while."

I'm grateful for his optimism, and I trust that he actually does believe me about the demon. I'm just not sure he understands.

How could he? How could anyone? Our demons are ours and ours alone. My mother's demons were hers. Even if she were still here, I couldn't ever really understand what it was like for her, why she did the things she did. I tried in the wake of her death. A fool's endeavor. But I have no regrets, because I know now that she wasn't crazy. I'm not sure anyone is. I think it's just easier to call someone crazy than it is to admit that they could be right. Easier to call someone crazy than to confront the nuance of their circumstance, than to accept the callous cruelty that exists in the world we live in, the evil out there that revels in our suffering.

They say ignorance is bliss, and, yeah, maybe, but it's still fucking ignorance.

So, no. No regrets. Not even on the restless nights when I'm trying to fall asleep and I hear it. That laughter. Sometimes it slithers through my dreams.

"Nothing fell through, Clio. It's a good offer. Everything seems solid," Daphne says. "The sale is moving forward."

"Oh," I say. "Wow."

I haven't been back to the house since that night, haven't offered any more of myself, my time, my attention, my energy, my life, to the demon. I had no intention of ever stepping foot in 6 Edgewood Drive again. I was aware that my refusal to engage might come back to haunt me someday. I realize now there was some small, repressed, devious, boredom-prone, chaos-addicted, diabolical part of me that was hoping it would.

I down my champagne.

"Hey, that's great," Austin says. "Weight off your shoulders."

"Dude. You have no idea," Daphne says.

"It's a couple, you said?" I ask her.

She takes a deep breath. "Clio. We talked about this."

"Yeah, I know. Not my circus..."

"Not my monkeys," she finishes. "It's time to let the place go. It's gonna be fine. They're gonna be fine. The house is... it's... it's over. It's behind us."

"Sure," I say. Austin reaches for my free hand, and with the other I bring the flute to my lips, tipping it back. There's no more champagne. My glass is empty. Tragic.

Daffy clicks her tongue. "All right. I'm going in. I should get back to Daisy."

"Godspeed," I say, saluting her.

"It's cold out," Austin says. "You want to go in? You want my jacket?"

"I'm good," I say. "You can go in. I'm going to take a minute out here. To myself."

"All right," he says. "See you inside?"

"Yeah. I'll find you."

"You sure you're okay?"

I cross my heart.

ACKNOWLEDGMENTS

To Lucy Carson, for your partnership, advocacy, and encouragement. You're such a superstar.

To Jessica Wade, for your brilliance, for your faith, and for helping these books reach their full potential. You're exceptional.

To Danielle Keir, Chelsea Pascoe, Jessica Plummer, Gabbie Pachon, Katie Anderson, and the entire team at Berkley. Editorial! Marketing! PR! Sales! Production! Legal! Accounting! Contracts! All of you! You work so hard to make my dreams possible, please please please know how much I appreciate every single one of you. You're all the greatest. Thank you for everything. There's nothing I could ever do to repay you for what you've done for me, but can I at least take you to coffee or something? Lunch? Shoot me an email. I'm serious! Also, you can really write whatever you want in this part of the book. I'm off the rails!

To the booksellers and librarians and podcasters and reviewers, thank you for the work you do. I see you and appreciate you!

To anyone who has picked up one of my books, shouted it out, come to an event . . . I'm just so grateful. Grateful times infinity to the trillionth power. I love you.

ACKNOWLEDGMENTS

To Mom, <3<3<3. To Dad, Joseph, Julia and the whole gang, you're the best.

To Courtney Preiss. Oh God, what would I do without you? And Max. And Barry. From Boylston to Brooklyn to the Asbury boardwalk. You know what, even that godforsaken Harvard Square IHOP. Anywhere with you. Just preferably not that IHOP.

Maria Oliver, Abby Rose, Heather Settles-Cultice . . . you're angels. It's the greatest fortune of my life that I get to have you as friends. Thank you, my loves.

Deanna and Chris Yates, let's hang out all the time, okay?

To Clay McLeod Chapman, for being the first reader of this book—thank you for being in my corner since day one; this isn't an easy road but it's so much easier to stay on because you're on it, too. Thank you to Agatha Andrews, for your inspiration, for your wisdom, for it all. To Nat Cassidy and Kelley Rae O'Donnell, I love you two so much; thank you for putting up with me. To Molly Pohlig, for the rooftop, for coffee, for your cleverness, for your work—gosh, I'm such a fan. To Eric LaRocca, for being so iconic. To Ali Shirazi, I adore you. To Konrad Stump, for your talent, style, and for lighting me up again. To Stephanie Gagnon, for giving me the space to be my true self, for your empathy, for all the chats. To Kristi DeMeester, my dark sister, let's go set the world on fire. To May Cobb, bestie, I ride for you, cheers to you. To Lorien Lawrence, for your friendship; you're so wonderful. To the queen, Emily C. Hughes, for the impeccable vibes. To Tiffany Gonzalez, you're such a rockstar; thank you for everything. To Marguerite, to Violet, to Lisa, to Terri, and to Ryan, you're all amazing and make the world a much better place just by being in it. To Katrina Carruth, my port in the storm. To Jonathan Lees, for the cigarette breaks. To CJ Leede and Liz Kerin, I'm so lucky to know you both. To Paul Trem-

ACKNOWLEDGMENTS

blay, thank you for always giving a hand up to the new kids. To Neil McRobert, thanks, buddy. Very grateful for this whole community.

While I have you, a few indie bookstores that are near and dear to my heart I want to thank: The Dog Eared Book in Palmyra, NY; Another Chapter in Fairport, NY; Lift Bridge Book Shop in Brockport, NY; Bookeater in Rochester, NY; Books Are Magic in Brooklyn, NY; Thunder Road Books in Spring Lake, NJ; Curious Iguana in Frederick, MD; The Novel Neighbor in Webster Groves, MO; Gibson's Bookstore in Concord, NH; An Unlikely Story in Plainville, MA; The Doylestown Bookshop in Doylestown, PA; and Exile in Bookville in Chicago, IL. To all the bookstores out there and again to the booksellers and to the libraries and librarians (so nice I had to thank you twice), when I think of you, Belinda Carlisle starts singing in my head, because you make heaven a place on earth. Sorry, that was corny. Corny but true!

And of course, always and forever, to Nic. I think you're a superhero. I think you're Batman. I think the world of you. Thank you for your support, for the adventures, for being so good at everything, and for being so funny I have to write it all down. I will love you till the day I die, and then my skeleton will love you. Just remember, bones equal dollars.

And to you, dear beautiful reader. It's often easier for someone to dismiss us or call us crazy than it is for them to admit that we're right. Remember that. Trust yourself.

And, and, and . . . to all those who continue to count me out, to not take me seriously, thank you for the motivation. XO, me & my demons.